by John Christopher

THE
LITTLE PEOPLE

John Christopher

SIMON AND SCHUSTER
NEW YORK

I

THE WAITER was a little old man with a bright red wrinkled face. He took Bridget's order and moved crabwise around the table to stand beside Daniel.

Daniel said, "Porridge, I think, and gammon and fried eggs to follow. Two eggs, please, turned."

His eye caught the faint smile on Bridget's face as the waiter ambled off. "Well?" he said.

"Well what?"

"Something funny?"

"I was only thinking . . ."

"Go on."

The smile deepened. "All this talk of yours about breakfasting off a black coffee and half a slice of toast—whenever we have breakfast together, you do yourself pretty well."

He put his elbows on the table and brought his hands together, fingertips judicially joined in front of his chin. He said seriously, "A very plain discrepancy. And there are two very obvious possibilities that would account for it."

She put her lovely broad face a little on one side, watching him and waiting.

"One is that I tell lies about what I usually eat in the morning."

Bridget nodded. "Possible. Why, though?"

"Dissimulating my basic weakness. I'm a frenetic phagic."

The big gray eyes widened. "What's that?"

"A compulsive eater. Like an alcoholic, but food."

"No," she said. "You would have more flesh on your ribs. I wouldn't be able to play a tune on them."

Daniel said, "And that indelicate reminder would seem to lead us automatically to the second obvious possibility."

"Would it?"

"Yes. A mere matter of output versus intake. In the normal course of events I sleep soundly at night. The calorific loss of the average male during sleep has been scientifically established as only a quarter of the loss when he is sitting in an armchair and reading a nice but unexciting book. Whereas . . ."

She said hastily, "Point taken." He leaned back. "Except . . ."

"Well?"

"*I'm* having roughly the same as I always have."

There was a pause. "Well . . ." he said, in a different tone. They both began laughing. Daniel said, "I did say average male. Different thing for the female. Quite different."

"I suppose so."

"Long live the difference."

She said, "Dublin appears to bring out a coarse streak in you. I wonder why that is?"

"So do I. Actually, they're both wrong."

"Both what?"

"Explanations. The fact is, I always have eaten a large breakfast in hotels. Just as I can never resist the call to the dining car when traveling by train. The real explanation probably lies buried in my deprived childhood."

"Deprived! Very funny."

"Ah," he said, "the coffee. Can I leave it to you? Not black, just dark. And the reason for that is that bad as the milk is in most hotels, the coffee is so much worse that a touch of milk is bound to make it slightly more drinkable."

"Darling," she said, reaching for the coffeepot, "you really must start being a little careful."

"Careful? About what?"

"About not letting prejudice degenerate into affectation."

Bridget smiled and poured. Daniel watched her. Their table

was a few feet from a mirrored wall; their left-handed duplicates went through identical motions behind the glass. He let his gaze go that way in idle contemplation. They made, he told himself with smugness, a good couple and a not unprepossessing one. Bridget was the key in that respect, of course. As she was seated, one saw nothing of the erectness and elasticity of her carriage that was, he thought, the first thing about her that had attracted him. He could remember being struck by a view of her disappearing through the door to the main office before he knew her name. But one saw very clearly the soft auburn hair, the candid gray eyes, the good nose, above all the flawless skin. It was not unpleasant to think of people wondering, as they must from time to time, who that chap was with that beautiful girl.

And he made, he told himself with a quick glance at his own profile, a not unreasonable foil. A fairly typical English face— somewhat pallid of complexion, the mouth thinner than he would have liked, the hair mouse-colored and wispy. Nothing exceptional, but he would pass. He looked back, with greater pleasure, at Bridget. Even when the present more or less continuous desire to touch, to press and caress, had ebbed to a quieter level of affection, there could be no doubt that she would still be a joy to contemplate and a pride to accompany. They were the kind of looks that would last well, too.

He still, from time to time, totted up the balance sheet of their relationship, not from any doubt of the figures and the result, but for the satisfaction of going over them. It had been something of a shock when he first found himself seriously attracted by Bridget. It had been a long established rule, formulated almost unconsciously when he had first joined the firm from Oxford, to steer well clear of the girls in the office. And he had managed this with no great difficulty for ten years, during which time there had been half a dozen liaisons of varying duration with young ladies whose charms included the fact that they were neither employed by nor clients of Perkins, Gillow and Gregg, Solicitors, of Lincoln's Inn. The emotional intensity had varied, as well as the duration, and the winding-up had been, in a couple of cases, quite

7

trying, but in none of them had the thought of marriage crossed his mind, except as a dubious and risky ploy toward a quite different end.

Yet despite all this he had allowed himself to be attracted by Bridget, within a fortnight had asked her out to dinner, and within two months had been examining all the reasons why he ought not ask her to marry him. He had found, with alarm first and then with growing pleasure, that the reasons did not stand up to scrutiny. For one thing, she had, as a secretary (not to him, but to Joe Grayson, one of the other partners), that rare intelligent competence which would enable her to tackle any situation with a probability of success. That operated in the social sphere, too, where she had successfully overcome an intrinsic (and charming) shyness to the point of being able to put other people very well at ease, whatever her own private reactions. There was one other advantage in that respect, which he would have thought it dishonest to pretend to ignore—she was entirely alone in the world. Her father had been killed in the Western Desert only a month or two after her birth. Her mother, according to Bridget a shy, withdrawn woman of few acquaintances and no friends (and one could trace the mother in Bridget's own core of reserve), had died three years ago, leaving her daughter the proceeds of the baby-wool shop of which she had been the proprietress. Bridget had sold it. She shared a flat off Baker Street with two other girls. There were a few distant relations on her mother's side. There had been none, as far as she knew, on her father's.

So he had seduced her, finding to his surprise that she was a virgin, and after only a few weeks' more pondering the matter, had asked her to marry him and been accepted. He had thought there might be some opposition from his own family, his mother especially. He had taken it for granted that when he eventually married, it would be someone whose mother she knew or could have known, and was very well aware that the assumption derived from her in the first place. But, having brought Bridget around to the house a couple of times beforehand, he found his mother's reaction to his intentions not at all what he had expected. She told him it was high time he thought about settling down, and expressed an apparently honest admiration of Bridget. She said one or two other things which made it plain that he had not covered his tracks in the past as well as he had thought. The reference to Jane McKennon was barely veiled and made him burn with embarrassment. Jane had been, and still was, married to an old friend of the family.

The only point his parents had raised had been a minor one—they had wanted her to leave the firm immediately and spend the projected eight months of their engagement in idleness. Daniel had put it to Bridget and she had said no, calmly but firmly. His parents had not pursued the issue, which Daniel himself did not regard as important. On the contrary, it was very pleasant to have her around during the day. It would, of course, be entirely different when they were married.

Bridget leaned toward him, her breasts heavy in the high-necked green jersey dress she was wearing.

"What are you brooding about?"

"Not brooding, contemplating."

"Yes?"

"The satisfactoriness of this weekend." She made a mocking nod of acknowledgment. "You ought to come into money more often."

Either O'Hanlon and O'Hanlon were personally devout, or else they derived a substantial part of their practice from the clergy. The waiting room into which Daniel and Bridget were shown had half a dozen garish oleographs of New Testament scenes on the walls, and the periodicals on the table, apart from *Punch* and *Blackwood's,* were overwhelmingly Catholic. It was a cold, depressing little room, smelling of must and shoe polish, and it was a relief when the inner door opened again only a few minutes after the girl had gone through it to announce them. A short, fat, cheerful-seeming man of about sixty came through and greeted them.

"Miss Chauncey," he said. "And this will be Mr. Gillow? I'm

Michael O'Hanlon. Will you come into the office and we can have a talk?"

His office was an untidy clutter and had the same prevailing smell, but was warmer at least by reason of a coal fire smoldering behind a heavy mesh screen. A picture on the wall behind his desk showed Christ baring his breast to display his Sacred Heart: a precisely heart-shaped object in crimson with a brighter red glow emanating from it. The picture was at least four feet tall. The desk, Daniel noted with disapproval, was strewn with papers in no discernible order. Central among them was a large china ashtray depicting the lakes of Killarney, well obscured by ground-down cigarette butts. The fingers of O'Hanlon's right hand were stained walnut brown. He ushered them into shabby, cracked black leather chairs, and offered them Sweet Afton from an inlaid mahogany cigarette box whose marquetry had largely flaked away. Bridget refused, but Daniel accepted. O'Hanlon produced a box of Swan Vesta matches, and lit Daniel's cigarette and his own.

He said, "I see from your card that you're a member of the profession, Mr. Gillow. You'll be acting for Miss Chauncey, I take it. I hope my letter didn't give any sort of wrong impression —that the estate was a large one."

"No," Daniel said, "not that. Miss Chauncey and I are engaged to be married. And although, as you know, her father's family was Irish, she has never visited Ireland. It seemed a good excuse for making the trip."

O'Hanlon's eyes were brown and surprisingly big; in a less podgy face they would have seemed enormous. Surveying them warmly, he said, "I must congratulate you both. And we'll hope that though it's Miss Chauncey's first visit, it will not be the last. Now, you'll be wanting to know what I can tell you about things. Where have I put that file? I had it yesterday, looking at it." He plucked irresolutely at the papers on his desk and then, more purposefully, walked over to a bookshelf and extracted a manila folder from the top of one of the rows of books. "Ah, I knew it wasn't far away." He returned to his desk, sat down, and opened the file. "Here we are. The estate of the late Seamus Chauncey. I believe I told you in my letter that you were named sole heiress, Miss Chauncey, and that the value of the estate was uncertain. Well, it's still uncertain, but I can tell you as far as actual money goes, it's no fortune. By the time the debts are settled, I doubt if there'll be more left than a thousand."

Bridget said, "That's a thousand pounds more than I expected."

O'Hanlon cocked his head and stared at her approvingly. "And that's the right attitude to have."

"Our branches of the family have been completely out of touch."

"I know of that. The late Mr. Chauncey spoke of it. There was an estrangement, I believe."

"Between my grandfather and his brother Sean. My grandfather was in the British Army in the First War, and went to live in England afterwards. Sean was an Irish patriot."

"Yes," O'Hanlon said, "but the Troubles are long over, thank God. The old stories are worth preserving, but not the old quarrels. Seamus Chauncey was your father's first cousin, and the last of his line. He had it in mind to write to you before—or to your grandfather, because he knew nothing of you, of course—but this is a terrible country for putting things off. At least he made his will, and it was simple enough. Everything to your grandfather, or failing him, to his eldest, and failing that, to the eldest of the eldest. Though as I say, there's little enough, aside from the castle."

Bridget asked, "The castle?"

"Well, it's not exactly a castle, though it's called Killabeg Castle and it has some of the old ruins still. It's where Mr. Chauncey lived. It's a biggish house, though."

Daniel said, "Do you know it?"

"No. Mr. Chauncey was not a man for visiting. He came to Dublin no more than once a year, the last few years not even that, and there was no occasion for me to go down to him. It lies in a wild part of Mayo. There's no town within twenty miles, and the nearest railway is more than thirty."

Bridget said, "Grandfather never spoke of Mayo when he talked about the family. I thought they were all from Cork."

"So they were, as I understand. He would not know about the property in Mayo, because we acted for Mr. Chauncey in the purchase of it, and that was not much more than twenty years ago. He came into this office one hot summer afternoon, and I didn't know him from Adam, and he told me he wanted a solicitor to handle the buying of a house in the west."

Daniel said, "You knew nothing of him before that?"

"I did not."

"Didn't that seem a little unusual?"

"It did. As I say, he came from Cork—you only had to listen to him talk to know it. I asked him if he didn't have a solicitor there, and he said no. I asked him then if he wouldn't prefer to use a local man, and he said what use was there in that, because he was leaving the south and going to live in the property he was buying. Well, it's sense enough that a man would have his affairs handled in Dublin sooner than Ballina."

"References?" Daniel asked.

"A bank reference. He was a warm man. He was paying six thousand pounds for the house—and that was some twenty years ago, mark you, when values were very low—and he had plenty to spend on it after. There must have been three or four thousand spent on it in the next few years."

"Six thousand, twenty years ago," Daniel said, "and three or four thousand on improvements? What would the place be worth now do you think?"

"Not as much as you might fancy, unfortunately. If he had put the money into property in Dublin, and bought wisely, then you could say twenty-five thousand, maybe thirty. And as much or more around Shannon, to the Germans and the Japanese. But the house is at the back of beyond. And what's more, he bought it at the first figure they named. He could have got it for half the price by waiting and bargaining a bit. But he had to have it right away, for reasons known to God and himself."

"So what sort of value would you put on it, Mr. O'Hanlon?" Bridget asked.

"Ah, now, I'm not in the property business. I have the feeling it's been let go in the last few years as well. Mr. Chauncey seemed to lose interest in the place, and I suppose the money was tighter. And you would need to find a buyer who liked a lonely spot."

Daniel said, "So it might not be easy to dispose of it."

"It might not." O'Hanlon paused and, drawing in a great sniffing breath, stared at them thoughtfully. "Do you know what I'm thinking, though? Why don't you go and take a look at the place, while you're over here? You'll have no idea without seeing it, and having come so far, you might as well go a bit farther."

Daniel said, "The trouble is we have bookings for the London flight tomorrrow evening. And I imagine it would not be easy to get there and back in a day."

"No, it would not. The train journey leaves you thirty miles short, and it must be a hundred and eighty miles by road. I suppose you couldn't manage to stay a day or two longer?"

He was on the point of declaring a regretful negative, when Bridget said, "I wonder . . ."

He looked at her. "What?"

"Perhaps I could stay on. Could you make excuses for me? It shouldn't be too difficult to change the plane booking."

"You want to?"

"I've never owned a castle before. It does seem silly, as Mr. O'Hanlon says, to come so far and go back without even looking at it."

"I don't know that they could spare you. Joe has a pretty heavy load of work coming up in the next few days. On the other hand, I don't. I suppose I could always lend him Janice—as long as I get her back again."

"You'll stay over?"

"After all, she's the best secretary we've got."

Bridget pulled a face at him. O'Hanlon had been watching them with partly comprehending sympathy. Turning to him,

13

Daniel asked, "What would you say is the best way of getting there?"

"By motor. No doubt of that. There are not the traffic jams you have in England, at this time of the year especially. You should do it in four hours, with no trouble at all."

"Can you recommend a car-hire firm?"

"Now leave that to me," O'Hanlon said. "I'll arrange all that. Tell me what time you'd like it sent round to the hotel."

"We could get an early start in the morning. Eight-thirty, say. Would that be possible?"

O'Hanlon made a note on a dog-eared scratch pad. "Eight-thirty it is."

"Can you suggest anywhere we could stay the night? Is there a hotel in the neighborhood?"

"Nothing nearer than Ballina. But you won't be needing a hotel. There's staff in the house still, and they can look after you. I'll telephone and let them know that you're coming."

Daniel said, "That's very kind of you."

"No trouble at all. I hope you have a pleasant trip. It's lovely country out there, though you really need to see it in the summer."

As they were leaving, he said to Daniel, "There was another thing about Mr. Chauncey. I'm not a talking man, you understand, particularly as far as clients are concerned, but he's dead now, God rest him, and you're in the profession yourself."

"What was that?"

"His bank manager here in Dublin was a man by the name of Doonan. He's dead himself these seven years, but I knew him well. He told me Mr. Chauncey's account was only opened the month before he came to me. And opened with a large sum of money, in cash."

"You didn't take it any further?"

"I did not. He seemed an entirely respectable man." O'Hanlon laughed. "Not a train robber or one of that sort. If there had been reason to look into things, I suppose I might have done. Reason more than vulgar curiosity, that is. But a man's entitled to keep his money in a sock the most of his life if he wants to, and then

14

put it all in the bank at one time, and then buy himself a house in the wilds of Mayo for two or three times what it's worth. Would you not agree with me, Mr. Gillow?"

"Yes," Daniel said, "I would."

They walked quickly back through the cold, grimy, decayed grandeur of the city. A raw February wind blew from the Liffey, bringing a mixture of urban smells but with them the smell of the sea. The hotel bar was warm and pleasant, a soft cocoon.

Bridget said, "I wonder how he did make it."

"The money? Who knows? Twenty years ago was the time after the war. There were all kinds of money about then."

"And to buy a house in Mayo. Why?" Daniel shrugged. "Can we rely on O'Hanlon to arrange for the car, do you think?"

"I should think so. He probably has a friend in the business. It will turn up sometime. I said eight-thirty to be sure we had a chance of getting off by ten."

They were still breakfasting the following morning when the waiter brought a message. Mr. O'Hanlon presented his compliments, and the car was waiting. Daniel looked at his watch. The time was twenty-five minutes past eight.

He said, "My God! I don't believe it, but I suppose we'd better get moving. Are you all ready?"

She nodded. "I packed before I came down."

"I'll go and deal with the desk, then. See you in the lobby."

There was a black Zephyr outside, some years old and, though clean, showing signs of wear and tear. A young man in his middle twenties was standing by it. He was tall and well built, with black curly hair—one of the handsome black Irish. At the same time, there was something familiar about him.

Daniel said, "Sorry we've kept you waiting."

"That's all right." He smiled. "You shouldn't have worried. We've time enough." He put his hand out. "I'm Mat O'Hanlon."

The familiarity resolved itself; one could trace the podgy features of the father in the son's good looks. Daniel said, "Of course. I'm Daniel Gillow, and this is Miss Chauncey. It was very good

15

of you to bring the car. Have you got the documents?" The young man looked blank. "For hiring."

"Ah, I see what you mean. It's not a hired car, though. We thought it would be easier altogether for me to drive you up there."

Daniel was taken aback. "That's too great an imposition, Mr. O'Hanlon. After all, it's nearly two hundred miles. I'm sure it would be best if we hired a car. The porter—"

"It's no trouble. I was looking for something to do this week-end. And I may get some fishing in. I believe there's a bit of a lake there." He grinned widely. "Anyway, I've put my rod in."

II

M AT STOPPED for final directions in a village made up of
two rows of whitewashed cottages facing one another
across a broadened stretch of road which held children and
chickens and a donkey. Bridget noticed one shop, and three doors
carrying boards that proclaimed the owner's possession of a seven-
day liquor license. The sky, which had been bright and open for
most of the morning while they were crossing the central plain,
had clouded since they came up into the hills. The Celtic gloom,
she thought. But there was nothing soft or hazy about it, only a
grim draining away of light from a poor land.

As they left the houses behind, she shivered. It was the desolation of the landscape that was unnerving. The earlier part of the
journey, in pale, windy sunshine, had been through flat green
country. The day's darkening was too apt a match for this
rougher, inhospitable territory. She supposed it could be more
attractive in summer, but surely somberness would still be its
most important feature.

Horizons were close, provided by the jagged outlines of the
hills along whose sides the road wound. Then without warning
there was an opening out—a valley, or small plain, rather, away
on their right. Mat took a hand off the wheel to point.

"That will be it."

"Where?"

"In the distance, there."

She saw it as he spoke. It looked like a church at first sight, a nave joined to a Saxon round tower with a broken top. But so isolated. A ribbon of road ran toward it and ended there. A glimpse of what might be water on the far side of it, but all about a black sullen featureless landscape with, as far as she could see, not even one small hump to challenge the monotony.

Mat said, "That's the bog of Killabeg. It would have been a lake at one time, I suppose. There's a patch of water left behind the house."

Daniel said, "Why would anyone want to build a house in the middle of a bog?"

"There was a rath there, in the first place. An earth fort, that is. Someone built it as an outpost, maybe, or as a place to take back plunder to. It would be hard to find a way through the bog before the road was there, which would make the place easier to defend. Later there was a castle, which Cromwell's men found useful when they wanted to keep a garrison here for subduing the country. And after that the castle fell down, or was pulled down, and someone built the house."

The road wound down and down, and they came to a place where a pair of impressive stone pillars, ten or twelve feet high, stood on the right. They may have carried a gate at one time, but there was no sign of it now, and no apparent reason why a gate, or the pillars for that matter, should have been there. The track that went between them was of hard-packed stone and earth; it meandered across the flat emptiness of the bog to the house, a mile or so away.

The car jolted forward onto the track. Mat said, "Hard on the springs. I think you'd need a Land Rover if you were living here."

Daniel shook his head. "Even with a Land Rover it doesn't bear thinking of."

She took in more details of the house as they approached. It was a very odd building. On the left there was the round tower with its broken and crumbling battlement. The structure joined to it, vaguely Georgian in appearance, was on two floors, with a roof level much below the tower's rim. The two parts, separately fairly ordinary, together made up a monstrosity, whose hybrid ugliness was accentuated by the featurelessness of the surroundings. It was a relief to see smoke rising from a couple of the chimneys; the place looked deserted.

There was a housekeeper in residence and a girl. Mrs. Malone was a small dumpy woman, about forty, wearing a black dress and showing something of the nervous brashness that in the Irish often serves as a cloak for timidity and sensitivity. The girl—of fifteen or sixteen, Bridget judged—was called Mary. She was a thin, shy, fearful creature, very much dominated by Mrs. Malone. The latter showed Bridget up to her room and stayed, talking and hovering.

"Will this be all right for you, then? The sheets have been fresh aired, and I'll warm them again before you go to bed. It gets raw cold at night. I'll have the fire lit for you, too, but we didn't light it before as we're running short of the coal, you understand. There's the bathroom next door, and I've put out towels, but there's no hot water except what Mary brings up. We haven't the electricity because the generator's not been used since Mr. Chauncey passed on. He used to see to it himself, and I don't know the running of it. I'm thinking we'd need to have fresh oil for it, anyway. So the lights won't be working, either, but she'll bring you up a lamp. We've enough of the paraffin, thank God. She brought up the flowers, thinking you'd like to have some in the room with you. She's a great one for the flowers. There aren't many, of course, at this time of the year."

An ugly green glass vase on a table beside the bed held a few sprays of jasmine and a couple of sprigs of berried holly. It was pretty, despite the vase. Bridget said, "They're very nice. And beautifully arranged."

"I'm glad you think so, ma'am. You're only staying the one night?"

"Yes."

"And then you'll be selling the place?"

"I should think so."

Mrs. Malone nodded, with melancholy resignation. "It's no

surprise. You won't want a house the like of this, and you living in London. Can I get you anything else?"

"No, thank you. Everything's fine."

"The lunch will be ready whenever you're down. It's only cold meat and potatoes and a bit of cabbage, I'm afraid. We've little in the house."

When she was left alone, Bridget examined the room. It was large and well proportioned, the ceiling covered with an elaborate crisscross pattern in ribbed plaster. There was a large patch of damp at the top of one wall, but otherwise it seemed to be in good order structurally. The paper, she thought, was unusual for this kind of house in this country: a latticework of gray rods, lightly splotched with red. There were four pictures, none of them with a religious provenance. Unless one counted a reproduction of Böcklin's *Island of the Dead* as religious. A couple of Alpine scenes —indifferently executed original oils—were also on the melancholy side, but pleasanter. She found a signature: V. Chauncey, '27. The other had the same name and was dated the following year. Some one of her unknown relations, she supposed, who had gone on holiday to Switzerland or Austria. She stared at them, frowning. There was something wrong about that. It didn't fit, any more than the notion of Seamus Chauncey buying this house fitted.

The fourth picture was a print in a high narrow frame. At the top it showed a white crane standing on one leg at the edge of a pool and staring with one eye closed at the viewer. The lower three quarters were taken up by a poem, in German and set in Gothic type face. Bridget had a quick recollection of the school-room, and sweating over a paperback edition of *Don Carlos* for G.C.E. German. She peered at the lines:

> *Es lebte einst in Afrika*
> *Ein' alte Maribu . . .*

She picked her way through a rough translation. This old crane, it seemed, always kept one eye closed. And when he got tired of

20

that, what did he do? Why, he opened that eye and closed up the other one. He was a great philosopher, so the poet said, that old Maribu.

> *Denn wer zufrieden leben willt*
> *Drückt stets ein' Auge zu.*

Because anyone who wants to stay happy has got to close one eye to what's going on around him. How very German, she thought, and, since it presumably dated from the visits that had produced the paintings, how unpleasantly prophetic.

The furniture was reasonably modern and, again, un-Irish. The single bed was broad, in a dull red wood and having a bookshelf integral with the bedhead. There was a large wardrobe which, on being opened, showed on one side a honeycomb of shelves and recesses and little drawers, on the other a sturdy horizontal pole fitted with metal hangers. No dressing table, but a capacious chest of drawers in the same red wood. A washbasin with a mirror fixed in the wall above it, and a small two-pin socket, presumably for an electric shaver, on one side. Gray rugs on the floor, matching the walls. There was a fairly ordinary upright chair and a low club chair in maroon leather.

Altogether a man's room. Cousin Seamus? Presumably. She shook her head. Obviously the pieces of the jigsaw must fit somehow. It was a pity she would not have the time to work out how. The resulting pattern might be interesting.

The meal was as depressing as the forecast had sounded. The potatoes, according to size, were hard or soggily broken up, and the cabbage was heavily waterlogged. The cold meat might have been tolerable if it had not been swimming in the same liquid. There were slices of home-baked bread, exposing yawning holes and twists of uncooked dough. This was followed by stewed plums laced with condensed milk, and a drink, served in the drawing room, which was described as coffee. Daniel smacked his lips over this incredulously.

21

"That sticky bottled stuff. I didn't know they made it still."

"Maybe you don't find it much in London," Mat said, "but it's a popular beverage yet in backward parts. We're not renowned for our culinary arts, especially in the west."

One or two of his remarks had displayed a cynicism about life in Ireland which, Bridget thought, was defensive. She felt she detected something of a brittle earnestness behind it. Was anything in Ireland what it seemed to be? She looked about the room they were in. It was very large, and the coal fire in the marble fireplace was far from adequate. The settee and chairs had been brought up close to it, but she was still cold. Slim central heating radiators were fixed beneath the windows and against the facing wall, but of course they were not in operation.

The furnishings were reasonably good, though understandably there was no trace of feminine influence. Two settees and four wing chairs were covered in a fairly stiff green-and-rust patterned fabric—one of the chairs showed some wear on the arms but the rest looked almost new. The floor had a fitted Wilton carpet, reddish brown, and the wallpaper was a subdued cream with red Regency stripes. The sideboard was antique—rosewood with painted panels of nymphs and shepherds. There was a gilt convex mirror over the fireplace, more than a yard across and surmounted by the usual eagle with the usual golden balls suspended from its beak. The walls carried three small oil paintings and two larger ones. The small ones looked like second-rate Dutch genre canvases: one of a kitchen interior with a shadowy female figure chopping something up, the remaining two still lives of a dead hare and a fish on a plate. The large frames held portraits of a man and a woman, who looked foreign, Bridget thought, though she was not quite sure why.

Viewed as assets, a depressing collection. They might fetch a little if sold in the right sector of the Home Counties Affluent Belt, but scarcely enough to make up the cost of packing and carting. Locally their value would probably be confined to their potential use for stopping up a hole in the hen-house.

Excluding the tower, the house was split longitudinally by the hall and main stairs, latitudinally by a corridor whose natural lighting came obscurely from fanlights above the doors of the rooms leading off and also from a long window at the south end. At the north end there was a massive door. There were four rooms at the front, two on either side of the hall, but only those in the southern half—the dining room and the room in which they had had coffee—were furnished. The rest were bare even of carpets and curtains, with faded flowered wallpaper and, in the farther one, large patches of damp.

Facing the dining room were the back stairs and the door leading to the kitchen and staff quarters. They left those, hearing the distant chink of washing up from behind the tattered green baize of the door, and examined the other rooms at the rear of the house. There were three, the two at the end, like their counterparts in front, completely bare, the third a library. It had glassed bookshelves on two walls, four club chairs, and a long couch covered in brown leather. There were paintings of sailing ships on the walls and a half-size billiard table at one end; at the other, a mahogany study table with three upright chairs that looked like Chippendale but were, Bridget decided, almost certainly worthless copies.

The main stairs, of dark oak with a roughly carved balustrade, turned on themselves at the half floor, and opened onto a landing with a stained glass window directly above the front door. The glass, at least, belonged to the Ascendancy: St. George, with the sun almost haloing his head, had his spear stuck into a small but ugly-looking dragon. The dragon was green and St. George flaunted a shield in which the red cross was very bright indeed.

The staff sleeping quarters were above the kitchen. There were eight other bedrooms, four at the front and four smaller ones at the back. Nevertheless, the visitors had put considerable strain on the resources available. Only two rooms—one at the front and one at the back—were adequately furnished. Another front room held a shaky-looking bed, a marble-topped washstand, a rickety table, and a broken-backed chair. Mat had taken this, leaving the smaller, more comfortable bedroom to Daniel.

There were two bathrooms. One of them clearly had a venerable history, but in recent years of disuse. It was very large and an ancient bath squatted on heavy claw feet at one end. There was a cracked pedestal washbasin with a rust-spotted mirror, and a cupboard with a vast copper cylinder and rows of empty shelves. Next door was the lavatory, the actual apparatus being mounted on a dais eighteen inches high and having a bowl patterned with red and blue flowers.

The second bathroom, next to Bridget's room, was entirely postwar. The bath was long, low, and tinted pink, and had a shower stall at one end. Wide, shallow washbasin with flaring taps, towel rail designed to be (but not at present) heated, and low-flush suite. It was quite a contrast.

Daniel's room was smaller than Bridget's and different in other ways also. The bed was taller and narrower, looking as though it dated from the days when brass knobs first began to give way to wood; in fact, the headboard was supported by heavy brass uprights. The rest of the furniture was in keeping, and the pictures on the walls either printed views of glens and mountains or family photographs. There was one group, taken in a studio, with the ladies seated on a high bench, the men standing behind and the children cross-legged on the floor or bunched at the sides, which could have been of the right age to feature her grandfather as a boy. Bridget hunted for a resemblance to the gaunt old pipe-smoking man, but without success. She turned from that to look out of the window.

As in all the views from the house, the bog predominated, stretching out to the distant hills, but nearer at hand were the gardens and the lake. "Gardens" was a euphemism; they might have been impressive once but were in poor shape now. Lawns directly behind the house had rioted into long grass, in which a couple of oaks and a twisted cypress were hunched. There was also a ramshackle summerhouse with a hole in the roof. Farther off, a brick wall enclosed half an acre or so of flower beds and scrub, and some ragged fruit trees clung to the inside of it. That stood level with the house seventy or eighty yards away, and there was a glimpse, farther still, of what looked like a kitchen garden enclosed by a hedge.

The lake lay at an angle to all this. It approached the northern wall of the flower garden, and there was what looked like the remains of a boathouse at that point. It was roughly ovoid in shape, swelling out to lie directly under the tower; leaning from the window, Bridget could see that the waters lapped against the stones at its base. There was a small island, more or less equidistant from the boathouse and the tower, a grassy hillock about thirty feet across, bearing a few stunted trees and a tumble-down shack. A few ducks paddled nearby. Altogether the lake was perhaps a hundred yards long and three-quarters of that distance across at its widest point.

She found Mat standing beside her. She said, "It must have been quite attractive when it was kept up."

He nodded. "And the grounds take in the lake and most of the bog. But six thousand was too much to pay for it."

"The walled garden," Daniel said, "quite English."

"Why not?" Mat asked. "They brought their religion and their clothes and their manners with them. Why not their gardens as well?"

"You can get your fishing in," Bridget said.

"If there's anything in there to fish."

The back stairs, narrow and covered with a threadbare red carpet, led down as well as up. There was a light switch which Bridget, forgetfully, flicked with her finger. Nothing happened, of course.

Mat said, "We could get a paraffin lamp from Mrs. Malone if you wanted to go down."

She stared into the black well. "I don't think so." Turning away, she encountered the heavy door at the end of the corridor. "We could have a look at the tower, though."

There was an iron ring in the door, which she grasped and turned. The door did not budge, even when she put her shoulder to it and pressed. Daniel said, "Let me have a go," and tried with the same result.

"Locked," he said.

"I'll get the key," Mat said, "from Mrs. Malone."

She came out from the kitchen with him. The key was a fairly massive one. She said, "I forgot you'd maybe want to go into the tower. It's a question of habit, you understand. Mr. Chauncey always kept the door locked when he was alive, and I've done the same since he died."

"Did he keep things in the tower?" Bridget asked.

"As to that, you'll see." She shook her head. "I was never inside it till he died. Ah, that was a terrible day."

"It was his heart, wasn't it?" Bridget asked.

"A stroke he had," Mrs. Malone said, "and him in there at the time. He was mostly in there of a morning. He was late for his lunch that day, but he sometimes was. Then Mary said she could hear noises from behind the door here—kind of bumping, banging noises. And there was no way for me to get in, with there only being the one key. I called to him through the door, but it's thick enough, and all I heard was a kind of groaning back to me. I was at my wits' end with it. I was thinking of taking an axe to it when I heard the key in the lock. Even then it was long enough before he managed to turn it. And when we got the door open, he collapsed in my arms. He'd had the stroke in the room up there and managed to crawl down the stairs. He could hardly speak, but he was mumbling about the key. I suppose he'd thought of being trapped in there, and no one able to get to him. I told him there was nothing to worry about now, that the key was in the lock and the door open, but he kept on about it. He died in my arms within the hour, God rest his soul."

"A grim experience for you," Daniel said.

"It was that, sir. I'm used to death, but I've always known it to come decent in the past. I went up there once, but I thought it best to leave his playthings, and so I locked the door again and hung the key up till Mr. O'Hanlon asked for it just now. Is there anything else that you might want?"

Daniel shook his head. "Thank you. Nothing else."

The door opened onto a spiral staircase which wound upwards

to the right, downwards to the left. Some light filtered down, but not much. Daniel said, "Perhaps we should have asked her for a lamp, after all."

"We can manage without," Bridget said. Daniel started to climb, and she followed with Mat bringing up the rear. "What did she mean by playthings, do you think?"

Daniel's voice echoed down to her. "I've no idea. Be interesting to find out."

The walls were massively thick. They reached and passed the source of light, an embrasure opening onto a lookout covered by a rusting iron crosspiece. The thickness was over three feet at that point. The stairs wound on, and there was a door on the right, something like the one below. It had a large brass lock, but stood ajar. Daniel pushed it open, and they went in.

The room was circular, and took up the whole of the inside of the tower—it was getting on for forty feet across. It was naturally lit by half a dozen slits spaced equidistantly around the walls; but in these cases, Bridget saw, the openings at the end had glass and some kind of metal screen covering them. There were also electric lights, and an electric power supply to a workbench. The place was a fantastic mixture of workroom and living room. She saw chairs, a divan bed, a small electric cooker, quite a large sink, a pile of metal cages a foot square stacked one above the other, and a conglomeration of tools on and around the workbench—a vise, power drill, grinding wheel, all sorts. Her eye took in these things briefly, drawn past them to the real oddity, which occupied about a third of the room on the far side: a village of dolls' houses.

Daniel said, "So that's what she meant by playthings."

Bridget went across to examine them. They were miniature chalets, some two feet high, and there were more than a dozen of them, some set flush with the wall, others on the tangent of the arc. They were painted in various colors—yellow, red, blue, different shades of green, and she saw that many had tiny boxes in front of them in which there was earth and at one time had been plants. All, apart from a couple of yellowish succulents, were withered and dead. Bending down, she looked through one of the windows in the nearest chalet. What she saw gave her a shock of surprise. She was looking into a bedroom, with bedroom furniture scaled down to fit. She called Daniel and showed him. He looked and nodded.

"He took his obsession pretty seriously."

"Obsession?"

"What else? Dolls' houses—like some old men play with toy soldiers."

"But how did the furniture get in there, and in place? That wardrobe—it's a foot high—that wouldn't go through the window."

"He had some fairies who assembled it inside." He was grinning. "Look."

There were hinges on one side, painted to blend with the wood. Daniel felt on the other side, under the eaves, and clicked a catch. He lifted and pulled, and the roof swung up and over. The rooms underneath lay open and exposed.

"Well made," Daniel said. "He was something of a carpenter."

Mat said, "He was that. He took a lot of trouble. You mostly get things varying with doll's furniture—a lot of it matching and then maybe a saucepan as big as a grand piano. But I don't see anything of that sort here."

Daniel said, "Consistency is a very usual feature of certain kinds of monomania. The scale's about one to five. That bed's about a foot long."

"How old was he?" Bridget said. "Forty-five? It's rather pathetic, isn't it? And not very pleasant."

She went to the sink, and turned the tap. Water flowed out. There were two taps, with red and blue tops. They must be connected to the main plumbing of the main house, like the power supply. The waste pipe, she saw, led to a hole below the sink, but stopped short an inch or so above it. Tiles had been laid on the floor here—elsewhere it was made up of large stone flags with a few rugs—and they sloped toward the waste hole. Some of the metal cages were stacked against the sink, but that was a part of the general untidiness. After all, Mrs. Malone and the girl had had nothing

28

to do with it. In fact, although untidy, it was cleaner than she would have expected the retreat of a middle-aged bachelor to be.

Daniel had put the roof back on the chalet and gone over to the workbench. He said, "Some funny tools amongst this lot."

Bridget said, "Let's go. I don't care for this place." Her words came out more emphatically than she had intended.

Daniel said, "There's always something upsetting about the recluse, isn't there? Though this one seems to have been mild enough. Dolls' houses. There could be a lot worse things than that to mess about with."

"I suppose so," she said. "Anyway, we've seen enough, haven't we? There isn't much here as far as selling the place is concerned."

"Soundproofed workshop with power and plumbing laid on?" Daniel suggested. "No, I can't see it making a great deal of difference." He stood aside to let her go down.

Mat said, "And it's a thin market for dolls' houses. In these parts, at any rate." He glanced up at the window slits. "I wonder why he put the screens across the windows?"

"To keep out mosquitoes in hot weather," Daniel said.

"The mesh isn't close enough for that."

"Bats, then," Daniel said. "He was afraid the bats might come in and colonize his village. Makes a lot of sense if you look at it the right way."

The evening meal was as dreadful as the other had been. The first course had the same components, but the cold meat was fatter and the boiled potatoes had been allowed to burn. Afterwards, Mrs. Malone produced an apple pie which, she told them, she had made that afternoon. The pastry was thick, board-hard on top and slimily soggy underneath, and the apple had been spiced with cloves to a point where it tasted of nothing else. They ate what they could of this, and refused the offer of coffee. Daniel fell with explosive relief on the bottle Mrs. Malone had also brought up. There was no brandy, she explained, but this was the whisky Mr. Chauncey kept. It was from the cask, and he bottled it himself. Daniel opened the bottle, and inhaled deeply.

"My God," he said, "this is all right, anyway. Bridget?"

"Just a drop."

"And you, Mat?"

He shook his head. "Not for me, thank you."

"It will take the taste of that food away."

"Thank you, but no."

Daniel said, "You're not much of an Irishman."

Bridget saw his face flush slightly. "Maybe you're right, at that," he said.

She was suddenly tired. She drank her glass, and refused another, bidding them good night. As she left, she heard Daniel extolling the Irish virtues as beacons of light in a dark century. Mat was listening, but seemingly without much interest.

There was a lamp in the hall, on a table outside the drawing room, and another at the foot of the main stairs. She had a moment or two of unease, walking alone along the shadowy passage, and again on the stairs. Another lamp had been set up on the landing. It was natural, of course. People were no longer accustomed to the shades, the partial revelations, of lamp and candlelight. But there was nothing to fear here, not even the ghost of Cousin Seamus. If that walked anywhere, it would be in the tower room among the tiny houses.

It was better in her bedroom. The fire that Mrs. Malone had promised had been lit and glowed warmly. A lamp was burning here, too, beside her bed, a pretty one with folds and convolutions of rose-colored glass. Her sheets had been folded back, and the curtains drawn against the night. There was a feeling of coziness and security. Suddenly and strangely she felt at home.

She slept well and woke refreshed. She started to reach for a light switch to check the time on her watch, but her hand found the body of the oil lamp which she had put out before going to sleep. Some light filtered past the curtains at the window. Not much; it must be early still. She got out of bed and pulled them back.

The house faced east. Her window looked across the patch of

30

rough grass that had been the front lawn, far across the desolate waste of the bog, with the track winding through it toward the distant hills. The sun was still behind them, but the morning was beginning to be bright. The sky was deep pearly blue, the line of hills rimmed with a luminous glow. The air that came through the open window was soft and fresh, smelling of earth after rain. Bridget pulled the curtains back farther, opened the window to its fullest extent. It was cold, but the coldness was exhilarating. She went to the washbasin and ran cold water, washed herself rapidly and toweled with vigor. Then she set about dressing.

It was much darker outside in the corridor. She thought about lighting a lamp, but decided it was not worth it. She could just about see her way. There was no sound of anyone else moving. She went downstairs and after a moment's hesitation headed for the garden.

She had no particular objective. She had thought vaguely of the walled garden, but the lake looked more interesting, and she went in that direction. Where the wall no longer barred her vision she saw the western hills and drew a quick breath of delight. The rays of the sun, risen now behind the other hills to the east, had struck there in points and crowns of gold. She walked on through the long wet grass, looking at it.

She had almost reached the lake before she realized that the morning was not, as she had thought, entirely and privately hers. Someone was there already. She was sure, not rationally but out of the joy of the moment, that it would be Daniel and then, with a disappointment close to anger, recognized Mat. She halted, watching him. He was standing by the edge of the lake fishing.

She was going to turn back, but at that instant he reeled in his line and in the same motion swung around and saw her. He waved, and she walked toward him.

"You're up early, Miss Chauncey." He made a clownish bow with his free hand. "The top of this splendid mornin' to you."

Bridget smiled. "Not as early as you. Caught anything?"

"Not a thing."

"Is there anything there, do you think?"

"There's trout. I've seen one rise. Pound and a half, at the very least."

"It would be nice if you could catch a few. A relief from cold meat and cabbage."

"You shall have the first one for breakfast. When do you want to be starting back, by the way?"

"We have to be at Dublin Airport by six-thirty."

"Four hours is plenty. But if we set out this morning we can miss the lunch Mrs. Malone would be providing. We can get something to eat at Ballina or Castlebar."

She nodded. "I'm in favor of that."

He flicked and cast. She knew nothing about angling, but it looked expert. There was silence except for a few birds somewhere. Away, far off, sunlight lay full on the hillsides and now gilded the dark waste of the bog and part of the waters of the lake. There was no awkwardness in the silence, and nothing left of the resentment she had felt a short time before. It was the morning that did it, the place and the morning. There was such calm here.

She glanced back toward the house. It stood black against the glow of the sunrise. Its fantastic outline—Georgian practicality linked with Gothic fantasy—had briefly acquired dignity and meaning. She said involuntarily, "Oh, look!"

Mat turned. After a pause, he said, "It was worth the journey, was it not?"

"Yes. Very much so."

"But you'll still sell it?"

"What else can I do? I can't live here."

She had meant, of course, We can't live here. The idea was nonsensical. Mat had turned back to the lake. The line of sunlight lay diagonally across it; on that side brightness, on this a dark gray, almost black. The surface was a glass with not the hint of a breeze to ruffle it.

She said, "It might have been better not to see it."

32

She did not expect him to understand. He said, "It would make a hotel."

"A hotel?" She laughed. "Who would come? You've said yourself it's at the back of beyond."

"Isn't that the best Ireland has to offer: the chance to get to the back of beyond? There are a few places like this, and more demand each year. If you advertised in the right way, you would get the guests all right."

"Are you serious?"

"Why not? And doesn't it make more sense than selling it as it is? If you are going to put it on the market, you'll do a lot better offering it as a going concern. There's small demand for private houses in these parts."

"You mean—run it myself?"

He looked at her briefly and critically. "I think you would be capable enough."

She shook her head. "It's quite ridiculous."

She expected him to make more effort at persuasion, but he did not. A few moments later his arm flexed as he took a strain on the line. The rod whipped over.

She said excitedly, "You've got something."

Mat grinned. "I said I'd find you your breakfast."

In the departure lounge at the airport, Mat said, "I hope we'll be seeing you again. Maybe you'll come over for the honeymoon."

Daniel smiled. "That's an idea."

Though, in fact, they were to go to Rome. Daniel had it all planned, down to the hotel. They were called for embarkation and waved goodbye. It was black and cloudy, threatening rain again.

During the flight she was mostly silent. Daniel made an effort to talk at the beginning, but her brief replies discouraged him and sent him to *The Times*. She sat back in her seat, eyes closed, listening to the enveloping throb of the engines, and tried to talk herself out of the idea which had progressively engrossed her during the day. She went over the arguments against it, trying not to think of the one irrational argument in favor. Sleep on it at least, she told herself. Say nothing now.

But while he was driving her home from Heathrow, she said, "Darling."

"Yes."

"I think I might leave the firm earlier than I planned. Right away, in fact."

He glanced at her. "Of course. Mum would be very much in favor." He said thoughtfully, "We could bring things forward altogether."

"I'm thinking of the house. I might not sell it."

"We couldn't afford to keep it up." He eased the Sceptre into the fast lane. "You've no idea the kind of drain it would be."

"I was thinking of running it as a commercial proposition."

Daniel laughed. "How, precisely?"

"As a country hotel. Well, guest house."

"That's a bit fantastic, isn't it? It's not as though you've ever done anything in that line."

"I think I might manage."

He paused before replying. "Are you serious?"

"I think so. Yes. I am."

"With Mrs. Malone's country cooking?"

"Well, no. I would handle the cooking myself. I like it, and I'm not bad at it."

"Isn't it situated a bit far out?"

"Mat says that would be an advantage. People who holiday in Ireland want to get out in the wilds."

"Was this his idea?"

"Yes. But it makes sense. I'd get little or nothing for the house as it stands. If I ran it for a season, there would be a much better chance of selling it reasonably. It would make no real difference as far as we're concerned. I would be clear by October."

He said flatly, "You would never do it in time. It would take ages to get into shape."

"A couple of months. If I tackled it right away, I could take guests from the beginning of May."

"And it would need money."

There was a warning note in his voice: "Don't expect me to back you in this kind of lunacy."

Bridget said, "I've got enough, even without what's coming from Cousin Seamus."

"Have I got this right?" he asked. "You're thinking of leaving me next week, say, and I shan't see you again until the wedding, or near enough?"

"It needn't be so long. You could come over for your holiday."

They drove the rest of the way to her flat in silence. She said, "Coming up for a coffee?"

"No, thanks. We're both tired." He helped her out, and kissed her but not warmly. He said, "We'll talk about things tomorrow."

She heard him drive off, revving fast, as she put her key in the door. He was quite angry with her, understandably she thought. He was also confident that when he brought pressure to bear she would come round. She felt a little angry with herself, knowing she would not.

III

THERE HAD BEEN a savage row—the worst for months—only two days before they sailed. They had been to a party at the Greenbergs', and something had started Helen off on her Arab kick. It was partly Manny Greenberg's fault for making such strong martinis and hovering around to freshen glasses before they were empty, but that explained rather than excused things. He watched her with a quiet, sick hatred as she stood there clutching her glass, her tinted blond hair escaping from its elaborate setting, and ranting on about the Bedu. She talked about the good times on the Gulf in the old days, the splendid Standard Oil life with Daddy, from which he had taken her away. Waring Selkirk tried to remember what she had been like, how she had looked and sounded eighteen years ago. She had looked better, certainly, with a good hard figure and a pretty enough face, but no prettier than a score of other girls he had known. And that voice had been the same: harsh and flat and inclined to get loud when she was excited. The voice should have been enough. But he had thought her *intellectual,* for God's sake. He had thought she had an interesting mind. She had talked about the Bedu then, in just the same way, and he had been fascinated by it.

But she was older now, and fatter, and drunker, and she was in the Greenbergs' house with the Cohns standing listening as well. He looked at her over Julie Bennit's shoulder, and tried to make some sense of what Julie was telling him about her miniature Yorkshire—it was a hysteric, or something—but her little drawl was lost in the surge of babble from across the room. He stuck it until she started on the Palestine refugees, and then broke loose from Julie with some kind of apology and went across and cut into her tirade with the announcement that it was time they went home. They needed to have an early night with everything to be got ready for the trip tomorrow.

Helen gave him a blank look. Despite its massive confusion her mind worked quickly on occasions like this; she was calculating, he knew, the relative advantages to her image of an open fight at the Greenbergs' or an acquiescence. She chose the latter. The fight started the moment he got the car out of the driveway. It continued with growing bitterness during the twenty minutes it took them to get home and reached screaming pitch during the next half hour. At its height he heard the front door open and said, "That's Cherry. Shut up, will you?" But Cherry, of course, did not matter the way the people at the Greenbergs' did; if anything, she screeched louder. Waring turned from her. The front door closed as he got out on the landing. He was going to go after her, to call her back, but Helen had come out of the bedroom and gripped his arm, her nails digging into him. She hung on to him until it was too late, and he accused her of not caring about Cherry, not giving a damn what happened to her, and that started the physical violence. She tried her best to choke him, and he had to straight-arm her to knock her off. She fell heavily, howled (like one of those goddam pi-dogs she used to talk about), and then, as though picking up the unspoken comparison, grabbed at him and bit him in the leg. He kicked himself free this time, looked at her sprawled and groaning on the floor, and thought, *Intellectual*.

She quietened in the end and locked herself in the bedroom. There was a bed made up in the guest room, but he had no pajamas in there, not that sleeping raw worried him. Waring poured himself a whisky and pulled up his trouser to examine his leg. It was quite painful, and there was going to be a lulu of a bruise, but at least she had not drawn blood. No need to cauterize, he thought, and tried to grin. After a while he went into the kitchen and fixed himself a sandwich from the remains of a cold chicken. Then he put some Haydn on the record player to soothe his nerves and waited for Cherry to come back.

He had a long wait; it was quarter after eleven before the door opened again. He did not ask her where she had been, and she did not volunteer any information. She was pale and beautiful, and after all the waiting he had nothing to say to her, nor she to him. She went upstairs, and he heard her footsteps stop by their bedroom door, but she did not knock and a moment later went on to her own room. He sat five or ten minutes more staring at nothing before he went up himself.

He was tired, physically and mentally exhausted, but he could not sleep. His mind revolved around old mistakes, old resolutions and their bankruptcy. Things had been fairly quiet for a long time, and might have gone on that way. If he had not intervened at the Greenbergs', what would have happened? She would have gone on exhibiting herself as a stupid, callous, drunken bitch, and Manny and Lucy and the Cohns would have been hurt. But did her showing herself up matter, except to his vanity, and weren't Jews used to being hurt? Anything he had saved them had been at Cherry's expense, and nothing could make those scales balance out.

He thought of the idea behind this vacation trip: a chance to get away not just from the university but from the whole tangle and snarl and mess into which they had gotten. A place where life ran quietly, without fuss. It might do something for her. And for him. And Cherry. It seemed laughable right now. Peace was not something you took like spa waters. And the mess you had made of your life was not a piece of baggage you could mark "Not Wanted on Voyage."

He wondered if Cherry was sleeping. He would have liked to call in on her, but he knew that wouldn't do. He lit a cigarette, but it tasted of nothing.

The following day Waring was placatory and Helen, though she snarled at him from time to time, was for the most part merely

38

sullen. The improvement continued. She was excited by the embarkation. Susie Goring came along to see them off, which provided an audience before which she could preen herself, and the lift that gave her lasted past the departure time. She was exhilarated at dinner, and he ordered champagne, which increased the effect. The thing was that Cherry seemed happy, too, in her quiet, silently smiling way. She looked wonderful, Waring thought. There was a young man at their table, early twenties, who seemed to think so, also. Times like these, Waring had the conviction that life was not an inevitable progression from ruin to disaster, that there were points on the road where you could call a halt, find a way back. For the young, at any rate.

Things stayed pretty good for the duration of the voyage. There was one day of rough weather, which knocked Waring out and gave Helen a chance to patronize him—she had traveled a lot by sea as a child, accompanying her parents to far parts of the world, and boasted that she had never been seasick. Apart from that, she found a couple of buddies who were prepared to listen to the carousel as she whirled about on her hobbyhorses. They were going on to France, and before the ship docked at Cobh there was a great to-do of exchanging addresses and promises to keep in touch. Waring knew what that would lead to: long intimate letters from Helen which would surprise and flatter the recipients into fairly quick replies, provoking, by return mail, even longer letters. Which this time seemed too much of a good thing; the recollection of the hours sitting in deck chairs or around the bar was fading, and Helen's letters, it must be faced, were not only long but dull. There might be a short noncommittal note, some weeks or months later, but long before that Helen had suffered one more disillusionment. To be taken out, Waring thought, in the usual quarter.

In fact, the euphoria suffered an early and severe shock by what happened on landing. There was no sign of the car he had ordered, and he had to make a telephone call to the rental agency in Cork. This at the outset produced a girl with a lovely accent and, it seemed, a skull of solid bone. He eventually managed to get through to someone else, a man this time, the voice equally charming, the mind behind it seemingly intelligent and capable. Yes, he was told, there had been a slight hitch, but everything was under control. The car was on its way, and would be there in ten minutes.

It did, in fact, arrive half an hour later, though Waring failed to recognize it. He had specified a large car, with plenty of luggage space. The vehicle before him was a four-seater Morris, several years old, with a tiny trunk and a roof rack.

To his protests the driver, a cheerful tubby man with a wild head of red hair, insisted that there was plenty of room for them and their suitcases. He would strap the big stuff on the roof for them, and there was a plastic cover to go over and keep the rain off, though the forecast was for sunshine, and he hoped it would stay that way for the time of their holiday, God willing. He was already hauling cases up and onto the rack.

Waring made an ineffectual effort to call a halt to this. He said, "I think we ought to try to get hold of a bigger car."

"Sure, we've had three breakdowns and a smash in the last two days. There's not a car to be had that will get you as far as Killarney but this."

He could dismiss the man and try another rental agency, but remembering stories he had heard of travelers in Ireland, he realized there was no assurance that another firm would be any better. Helen might be furious, but so she would be if they were delayed while he hunted around for a replacement. And it was not much of a journey, by American standards. A hundred and fifty miles? Not as far as Chicago to Detroit. He handed a suitcase to the driver.

Helen, in fact, was amused to begin with. The tiny battered black car and the fat, redheaded driver would provide copy for her letters, and a good starting point for a far-ranging dissertation on Ireland and the Irish. She sat in the front and chattered away to the driver as they drove out of Cork. There was a good deal of cloud in the sky, but at this stage the sun was shining, the countryside fresh and gleaming green.

She still thought it amusing when, coming around a blind corner, the man was forced to slam on his brakes because of a donkey sleeping in the middle of the road. She went quieter, though, after an incident some ten minutes later when the car, traveling at about fifty on a straight and empty road, hit a bump which sent them all bouncing against the roof. The driver laughed and said there were some bad patches on the roads, here and there, and it was hard on the springs, so it was, but Helen did not laugh back. Cloud covered the sun now; the day was being swallowed by a gray murk, draining color as well as light from the landscape. Shortly afterwards it began to rain, a light drizzle which thickened soupily into a steady downpour. It was both stuffy and drafty inside the car, and the driver dabbed at the windshield with a grubby handkerchief to keep it from steaming up too badly. Then the car broke down.

They were lucky, the driver explained, that it happened in a town. Waring looked about him. There was a row of shops and houses on either side of the main road, and a minor road with a few buildings meandering away to the east. One of the buildings was a garage, though, and at least three were taverns. Reconnoitering, he was driven back from the doors of two of them by the revealed squalor and the overpowering stench of urine. The third was a little better, and he went for his womenfolk. Helen took a look inside and turned away in disgust. Three doors down there was a dry-goods shop with a small porch. She stationed herself there, sheltered from the rain, and began a low-pitched but penetrating harangue. He had done everything wrong that could be done wrong. She would have insisted on getting a proper car at Cobh, but for not wanting to show him up in public. But the more she showed consideration for him, the less trouble he took. It was marvelous how often she could say the same thing without exactly repeating herself. He looked at Cherry. She was staring through the glass at the terrible clothes ineptly laid out in the shop window. Keep quiet, he told himself. It was like the rain which, because of the smallness of the porch, was dripping down his neck: a nuisance, but no more than that.

They got going again. The long Irish miles crawled by, dragging the minutes and hours with them. Helen had gone quiet, perhaps intimidated by the unflagging cheeriness of the driver, and Waring told himself that this particular nightmare, at least, was almost over—they must be almost at their destination. He was framing a question about that when one of the wheels found another irregularity in the road, this time a pothole. There was a lurch which threw them all together, and a crack of metal overhead. The car seemed to be breaking up, but it was only, he realized, suitcases cascading from the roof rack into the road. When the car stopped, they were strewn at intervals over twenty-five yards of tarmac. One of the large pieces had burst open, and items of Helen's vacation wardrobe were scattered in the mud. The rain, which had seemed to be easing, pelted down more heavily.

Waring went with the driver to retrieve the bags. Helen waited till they had got back, and then cut loose. She savaged both men indiscriminately, but Waring got most of the lashing. He endured this once again in silence. The driver made a few attempts at mollifying remarks, but she was shouting, not listening. The driver gave her a look of horror mixed with reluctant admiration.

Between them they managed to get some of the luggage back on the roof, precariously balanced and roped, but two of the bags had to go inside. When they had done that, a momentary lull in the barrage allowed the driver to get a few words in. He said, "At any rate, we're almost there, thank God. That will be the Castle, down below."

Waring asked him where, and he pointed. They had come through the hills, and on the right lay exposed a saucer of barren land. The low clouds which covered the hilltops trailed rain over it; a dark sky pressed down on a black sodden country. Following the direction of the driver's arm, Waring could just make out a tiny regular shape in the middle of it all.

Helen had seen it as well. She said, "Good Christ, I don't believe it! Even you couldn't have picked a spot like that for a holiday. Well, by God, you can stay here yourself. Cherry and I are moving out tomorrow. We'll go to Morocco, like I wanted to do. At least we'll get some sun."

She had, in fact, said something about Morocco when they were planning things the previous winter. The Tuylbersons were going there, and she had thought of suggesting they might join up. Waring had not wanted the embarrassment of having to watch the Tuylbersons backing out of that, nor the prospect of her Arab mania being further stimulated. And, of course, there had been the notion of getting away from things, of seeing if they could make it work out in some quiet isolated place. He had talked up the idea of the unspoiled peace of Ireland, and it had impressed her. And she herself had said it was better for Cherry—safer.

They had put the two bags on the back seat, and he and Cherry had to perch uncomfortably on them, their heads hard up against the roof. Waring was soaked through by now, and he sat well over to keep his wet arm from her. He could see her quarter profile as the car started up again; she was looking out over the plain toward the house.

"First thing tomorrow, we leave," Helen said. "You can do what the hell you like."

She was sullen and angry after they got to the house, looking for things to pick on and finding them in small details: their room was cold, she didn't like the drapes or the soap provided, and the bed wasn't soft enough. But he saw her interest caught by their fellow guests. There was the young Irishman, Mat O'Hanlon, who was Bridget Chauncey's attorney from Dublin, and who seemed to be helping her get things running, and there was a German couple called Morwitz. The husband, Stefan, was large-framed, very blond, with a basically good physique which, although he was certainly no older than Waring himself, was running to seed. The wife, Hanni, was a small, still pretty dark woman. When they went up to bed, Helen said, "What do you think of them—the Morwitzes?"

"They seem O.K."

"It's a surprising combination."

"Do you think so?"

43

"You don't expect a big handsome German Aryan, which he must have been, to marry a Jewess."

"Is she Jewish?"

"Of course she is. It stands out a mile."

She might be right. All that mattered, anyway, was that the couple had intrigued her. Nothing had been said, for the past hour or two, about moving on. And she was entirely capable of clearing off with Cherry, which would mean he had to go, too— a humiliating defeat and one likely to lead to more, apart from being in itself exhausting. He made some noncommittal remark, and she went on, about the Morwitzes, about their hostess, about the Irishman. Bridget wore an engagement ring. Helen speculated about that, and about her being younger than she had expected— very young for this kind of thing.

Her conversation was mild and friendly, the virulent abuse of earlier in the day forgotten as though it had been spoken twenty years ago. Gradually, something else crept into it, which Waring reluctantly recognized. He had been undressing—she was already in bed—and she said, "Stand still." He looked at her in inquiry. "You've got a good body, honey," she said. "You look after yourself well. Not like that German." She propped herself on an elbow. "You know, you're quite something for a man of your years. I have to give you credit for that, if nothing else."

The summons was unmistakable. It was, he supposed, possible to refuse, at the expense of another outburst of fishwife's vituperation, and the probability of her carrying out her expressed intention of taking Cherry away. He went, mechanically smiling, toward her bed. You become an old man in the mind, he thought, however much you do toward keeping the body in trim.

He wanted peace, he told himself; he had to have it. It was for that reason he was committing this obscene act. The rain slashed heavily against the windows.

Waring awoke later with a need to go to the bathroom. He usually kept a flashlight beside his bed because Helen objected to lights being switched on when she was asleep. This time he had omitted to put it out, but it did not matter, because the room was full of moonlight. He found his slippers and dressing gown and went out quietly.

When he returned, he could see she was still sleeping, her face childlike and defenseless against the pillow. He went to the window. Their bedroom was at the back of the house; there was the garden and the lake, farther off the level plain and distant hills, and a moon nearly full standing above them. He had not bothered to put on his glasses, and his myopia turned the scene into a soft wash of gray and silver haze, differing shades of lawn and lake and bogland swimming into one another, with a few dim indeterminate trees and bushes. A Chinese painting? He stared at it. Normally his eyes strained for clarity and resolution, but these bright shapeless shadows contented him. He was alone and at ease in the night. He felt a faint tug of memory, a half recollection of a happiness long ago and far away. From his childhood: no one scene, but he could remember the sense of an amorphous, magic world whose edges trembled with implications. Before he was nine, then—before they found out why he was doing badly at school and took him to an oculist.

What he could remember very well was his feeling when he put the glasses on. Everything at once clearer, harsher, uglier. Faces that lost their gentleness, their pleasant vagueness, and became clear and distorted—with the marks of anger, discontent, cruelty. Was that the way it had seemed to him then, or was it his later interpretation of a child's confusion at a world suddenly leaping into reality? There had been an awareness of loss, though, he remembered that. He could even remember working hard at school in an attempt, surprisingly adult he saw now, to forget it, to put the dim dear world behind him.

It was an odd thing that he had never thought of trying to go back, of mislaying the glasses or breaking them. He had known that it was not possible, that happiness came by chance and by default. In fact, his adult life had been a continual battle with

45

opticians and their unrelenting determination to underprescribe for myopia. If he had to see the world as it was, he wanted to see it sharply, warts and all.

Something moved out there by the walled garden. An animal. A fox? He thought not. Something that raised itself up. Did badgers do that? Was this badger country? He strained his weak unaided eyes, peering at it. Not as big as a grown badger, either. A squirrel? Too big for that. It moved across the field of moonlight in a way both strange and familiar. Waring stared for another long moment then walked quickly to the bedside table for his glasses. Curiosity was stronger than enchantment.

The world took on hard shape again. The room first—a small stain on the carpet, a stubbed and twisted cigarette in the ashtray, the lines, harsh even when smoothed out by sleep, in Helen's face. And outside—the cypress tree black and malignant, the surface of the lake bearing shadows beneath the lucent silver, the stark desolation of the bog. He looked where he had seen the moving shape, but there was nothing. It would have gone on, of course; he had been away for a second or two. He looked for it beneath the oaks, by the lake. Nothing. And then a flicker at the corner of his vision. Over toward the tower. He caught it for one small instant, before it was lost behind the garages. He went on staring in shock and excitement. It was nonsense, of course, a hallucination. The whole country was hallucinated, and had been for centuries.

He realized he must have cried out when he heard the movement from the bed behind him. Helen sat up, brushing the hair out of her eyes. She said, "What's the matter with you, for God's sake?"

IV

A<small>T HOME</small>, Stefan arose punctually at six-thirty, the moment
Hanni's little alarm clock went off. He showered, shaved,
had a large breakfast, and drove the ten kilometers to Munich in
time to be at the store a few minutes before it opened at eight. It
was a routine which he maintained scrupulously and loathed
wholeheartedly. On holiday, he could be his true self, the idler, the
master of the clock without hands. He had explained this to the
English girl when he arrived, and she had been understanding.
Breakfast could be kept for him, an egg fried fresh and new
coffee made when he was ready for it. Though in fact there had
been no need to take advantage of that offer. For all his luxurious
rollings over in bed, protracted wallowing in the bath, the delib-
erate delays, he found himself hungry and waiting in the dining
room at just about the time the shutters would be going up at the
Stefan Morwitz stores in Munich and Frankfurt and Bonn.

But after that there was a difference, a day happily empty of
people, of buyers and sellers in whose faces, as in mirrors, he saw
his own lines of cupidity and anxiety deepen day by day. There
were the people in the hotel, of course, the staff, his fellow guests,
but one could walk away from them into a quiet open country.
This he did, relishing, even in the almost continuous rain, the wild
bare land of bog and hills. He had been disappointed at first to
find that there was only one passable route from the house, that
the first two and the last two kilometers must always be the same,
but he had quickly grown used to this, and even enjoyed it. One

walked by the side of the rough road through gusts of blinding rain and between the gusts there was the landscape, always the same and yet infinitely variable: the waste of bog, the subtly changing hills. He studied the bog, its hillocks and hollows, the ponds, the stretches of black mud, the patches of heath where a few plants and flowers grew. He had been warned about that— one could go for a short way into the bog in places but it was all deceptive, all treacherous. The only safety lay on the road that wound through it, narrow and stony, surrounded by the morass with its pools and islands, its immensity. By that slender way a man came through to the open hillsides and so again to house and home.

Beyond lay a wild bare moorland, rock and scrub and heather rising to the wet gray sky. The ground, where it was not stony, was soft underfoot; where grass grew, it was of an emerald brightness scarcely to be believed. He liked this country, more than Norway the previous year, more than the Dolomites, the Pyrenees, the Abruzzi. He had turned to the north, he told himself, because so many of his countrymen went south—on a brown hillside in Catalonia, thinking himself alone, he had crossed a spur and found a whole family basking in the sun, mother shapeless, daughter blond pigtailed, father and two sons in *lederhosen*. But he thought now there was something else. He had felt it in Norway: not an answer, but the stirring in himself of a kind of questioning, a sense of something to be found. He was aware of it here still more strongly. A land of age, he thought, and innocence.

Always at the start of a holiday his body, forced to exertion after a year's indolence and pampering, protested, punishing him with the ache of unused muscle. It was not necessary, he realized, nor sensible, to do things this way. A man could keep fit. There was a good gymnasium, used by several he knew of his own age, and it would have been possible to find time. Alternatively, there was a logic in letting go, in settling for ease on holiday as at home, with no more physical effort than was required to pull a chambermaid onto the bed while one's wife was out shopping. Either course would have its correctness.

48

Again, he thought, it was not just in defiance that he refused to conform with either. There was something here, too, that was almost to be understood, the fulfilling of a need. He walked more briskly over a patch of springy turf. The aches were much less, nearly gone. The rain beat against his waterproofs, cooling the sweating body beneath. He sniffed the damp air. Each day he could smell the country more clearly: the scent of peat and grass and heather, and the far-off smell of the sea.

He walked for a couple of hours among the hills before coming down again to the plain and the road to the house. There were gaps, one as much as half an hour, when it did not rain, but there was never a feeling that it would stop for long and as the day advanced, the sky grew, if anything, more dark and gray. The tops of his socks were wet, but his boots kept his feet dry. He felt well, and hungry.

He heard the sound of a motor car engine behind, but did not look around. It came up, inevitably traveling fairly slowly over this rough surface, passed him and stopped. It was an English car, dark blue, moderately luxurious. The window was wound down, and a typical Englishman's face looked out—thin, blond, colorless. The voice matched it.

"Can I give you a lift?"

Stefan shook his head. "Thank you, no."

"Quite sure? You're heading for Killabeg, I take it?"

"Yes, but I prefer to walk, thank you."

"Fair enough."

The head disappeared inside, and the car started off. That would be, Stefan thought, the fiancé of Bridget Chauncey, who was to arrive that day. He liked her, and was a little disappointed on her account. But it was too small an impression to mean anything.

The house was still more than a kilometer off, and refusing the lift had made the hunger pangs more acute. He stepped out resolutely, and found himself humming a tune. It was a melody that came from his boyhood, from walking with companions through strong, harsh sunlight—long cloudless days, ending in a dusk

49

of campfire smoke and tiredness, singing, the unquestioned, unquestioning assurance of comradeship. But that was Germany, he thought, and the boy who walked there so long ago was very young.

In the evening Bridget contrived to be with her guests during the hour preceding dinner; Stefan admired her for it as for other ways in which she concealed the hard work which went into looking after things. The arrival of Daniel had made no difference to this. She chatted with them over a glass of sherry. She said, "Did you have a good walk today, Herr Morwitz?"

He nodded. "Excellent."

"But so wet, I'm afraid. You couldn't have had worse weather for getting out. It isn't always like this."

"I do not mind it."

She smiled. "You're very polite. There's something I've been meaning to ask you about."

"I will be happy to answer, if I can."

"It's this notebook. I found it when we were clearing things up a couple of months ago and put it on one side. It turned up again today. My German is very weak, and the handwriting defeats me utterly."

It had a limp green leather cover, and the pages inside were blue ruled and of good quality paper. The entries, in black ink, were in a small, spiky, elegant hand. At the top of the first page it said "Juli 5," but there was no year.

"It is a journal," Stefan said.

Bridget nodded. "Yes, a diary. I've no idea whose. I don't suppose it matters reading it when one has no idea who wrote it. Do you?"

It was, he realized, part of the technique for keeping guests happy and at ease. She could, of course, have shown it to Hanni while he was out, but she would see Hanni as a person essentially contented, him as the restless one to be kept interested and amused. Once again he admired her application.

50

He said, "One needs privacy only from one's friends. It was in this house when you came here, you say? And you have no idea of the origin?"

"None. The house belonged to a cousin of mine; as far as I knew he had no German connections. There were a few other German things in the house, though—pictures and such."

Stefan had been glancing over the first page, and a sentence caught his eye. "There is no excuse for failure, no extenuation, no justification in remorse." He felt an automatic sympathy for the man who had written that, a quickening of interest. He looked up at Bridget.

"You would like me to translate?"

"I thought it would be interesting to have some idea of what it's all about."

"A moment, please."

The handwriting, difficult on first sight, was less formidable when examined more closely. Stefan found he could read it fairly easily.

The good weather continues, and has lasted for several days now. S. complains of the heat, but I find it no hotter than a spring day in Munich. The dampness remains in the air, and a breeze springs up from time to time and makes it almost cold in the shade. I am grateful for what warmth there is. I remember such a day as this, long ago, during the Maifest, when I was a young man, when V. was in Germany for the first time and we swam in love. It is strange. Up to a point, life widens out, prospect opening up prospect, seemingly limitless. And then, with no warning, comes contraction. The horizons draw in, one is hedged about by the bitterness of one's errors and defeats. This emotion must be resisted, of course. There is no excuse for failure, no extenuation, no justification in remorse. But self-discipline cannot restore the clear eye of youth. It is lost, with the leaping blood, the tensed and ready sinew. Thank God there remains work, to give a purpose and meaning to existence. Without that, what? The destiny of S.—a continual seeking of oblivion in a bottle, a succession of

drunken nights and hideous retching mornings? I despise him
utterly, but I recognize that he has chosen his fate less than it
has chosen him.

Stefan translated it as well as he could. He paused and said,
"I cannot express it very well in English, you understand. That
is where the page ends. Do you wish . . . ?"

"Don't bother now." She put her hand out for the book. "It
seems very ordinary. Rather sentimental and melodramatic."

"That is probably my bad translating. I find it interesting. You
know nothing of him? An elderly German living here, and from
my own city of Munich. And working? What sort of work would
that be? A writer, perhaps?"

She smiled. "Enjoying better weather than you've been having,
too. Would you like to keep the diary, and read it at your leisure?"

"If that is permitted."

"Please do. You can tell me what it's all about some time."

Stefan had formed no opinion about the Americans, except that
the girl was pretty in a pale, cold way, and the mother talked a
lot. She was less polite than other American women he had met
—though it was true that he had not met many, might even be
said to have avoided meeting them—and openly curious, asking
him questions which he found embarrassing both in the way they
were put, and in the hint they gave of even more demanding ones
to come. He dodged conversation with her as best he could and
during dinner concentrated on talking to Waring, who faced him
across the table. He learned that the American was a professor
in social sciences at a Midwest university, and found that he could
talk well and comprehensively on his subject. Stefan did not like
the social sciences, with their implication that men and women
could be broken down into graphs and statistics by the means of
a quantitative analysis, but Waring argued lucidly and reasonably,
and he found that stimulating. He became aware by degrees that
the wife, Helen, was getting restless; she interjected one or two

observations which Stefan thought silly, and which Waring acknowledged and ignored. Stefan was glad when she turned her attention from them. But he found he had been deceived in that. When she had made sure of an audience among the others, she said in quite a loud voice, "You'll none of you ever believe what happened to Waring last night!"

Stefan saw the muscles in the other man's cheek tense as his jaw clenched. He continued with his argument, ignoring the remark.

Elsewhere at the table there was a silence, which Bridget broke at last. She asked politely, "What was that?"

Waring said, "For God's sake, Helen."

She grinned at him. "Waring thought he saw a fairy out in the moonlight."

His embarrassment made him speak quickly, almost stuttering. "I guess it was a trick of the light. I was looking from my bedroom window, and I saw something moving. I caught just a glimpse after I'd put on my glasses. It must have been an animal of some kind."

"He woke me," Helen said in a general address, "to tell me all about it."

Bridget said, "Actually, he's not the only person to have seen something."

Her fiancé Daniel was grinning. "Don't tell me you have!"

"Mary, the maid, says she's seen the little people near the house."

Hanni said, "The little people? I do not understand that."

"It's an old legend in Ireland," Bridget said. "About this race of tiny men and women who can do magic. Mostly they're invisible, but occasionally people can catch a glimpse of them. Some people."

"In Germany, also," Stefan said. Hanni still looked puzzled, and he turned to her, explaining. *"Die Kobolde. Verstehst du?"*

"Ah, yes." She nodded. "They do wicked things."

It was a simple nod, but he saw in the tilt of her dark head the

53

pride and humility, the desperate suffering acceptance, of her race. It could still move him to anger and disgust. He said harshly, "Not wicked. After all, they are not human."

Bridget said, "The Irish fairies are reckoned to be a fairly mild lot, I believe. But Mat can tell us."

The Irishman said, "I'm not an expert on the national superstitions, by any means. But it's true that where the country people believed in them, they didn't fear them in the way, for instance, the Scots feared the ones they had. Or the English, for that matter."

Daniel asked, "Do you Irish fear anything, except God and themselves?"

"We fear reality."

"Isn't that another way of saying the same thing?"

Helen said, "If you catch one, and hold on, isn't he supposed to pay you a ransom to get free? A pot of gold? Waring should have gone looking for him. We could certainly use a pot of gold."

Bridget said, "That's the leprechaun. Though I can't pronounce it. Say 'leprechaun' for us, Mat."

He pronounced the word obediently. "Leprechaun. It's a different creature altogether. And then there's the banshee. This is a great country for inventions, except practical inventions."

Waring seemed glad that it had developed into a general discussion. He said, "Are they supposed to be found all over, or in some particular place?"

Mat said, "I don't think many have been reported in Dublin. Which is to say that, like nearly all rural superstitions, it can't survive urbanization. The deeper into the country you get, the more tales you hear. Though now we have television, you're more likely to be told the plot of the latest 'Dangerman.' "

Stefan asked, "Where do they live, the Irish fairies? In holes in the ground?"

"Some of them, maybe. But the raths were more popular as suggested residences."

"The raths?"

Mat smiled. "You are on one. Or right beside it. They were the old earth forts. Later, in many cases, castles were built on them. As happened here. There's a ridge of land just beyond the tower that's characteristic."

Daniel said, "So it's reasonable to expect this spot to be haunted?"

"Not haunted. They're not like ghosts. But it's a place that in the old days the country people round about might have expected to be inhabited by them."

"And might still? Mary's a local girl, isn't she?"

"It's over three hundred years since the castle was destroyed, nearer six hundred since it was built. I doubt if any would be hanging about yet."

Bridget said, "They've probably put a curse on me, if they are. I took all their furniture out, and had it shipped to a children's home."

It was Stefan's turn to be puzzled. Obliquities in English sometimes confused him, but he did not see how this one could make any sense at all. He echoed, "Furniture?"

Bridget smiled. "It's a joke, Herr Morwitz. There were a lot of dolls' houses in a room in the tower. The houses themselves are still there, but I sent off the dolls' beds, cupboards, and so on."

Waring said, "Dolls' houses, plural? Someone had several children here once?"

She shook her head. "It was just a hobby of my cousin's."

"Strange hobby."

"I suppose. Hobbies often are, aren't they?"

Daniel said, "Mr. Selkirk's fairy had probably been on an extended visit. He must have been terribly fed up when he got to the tower and found nothing but bare boards on which to lay his head. I'm sure you're right about the curse, Bridget. You'll get no sleep tonight for a certainty."

Waring said, "It looked . . ." He hesitated, and broke off.

Daniel said, "Looked what?"

Helen said, "Tell us how he looked, darling. You were a bit confused last night."

She was smiling, challenging him. He accepted that with a

55

glance and turned to Daniel. He said, "I guess I might as well look a complete fool. It was this impression I had in the moonlight. It was an impression of something female rather than male."

Helen said, "Pretty? Was that why you took your time about calling me?"

Waring ignored that.

Daniel said, "So you did see something—well, strange?"

It was a serious inquiry, and it unsettled him. He said, "I've told you—it must have been a trick of the moonlight—some kind of animal moving out there. There's no such thing as pure vision, is there? The mind always adds something and at night, when you're only half awake—what I mean is, it can add something strange. Isn't that what ghost stories are about?"

Mat asked, "What sort of animal, would you say?"

"I don't know. Does it matter?"

"I was wondering what kind of animal can give an impression of being female."

Helen laughed. "To Waring, any kind."

He said, with sudden biting anger, "That's not true, and not funny."

They stared at each other across the table. Bridget said, "It's not likely to be a cat, at any rate. Our cats have all died on us. Some mysterious epidemic finished them off."

The remark was plainly designed to lower the temperature, but Stefan doubted the likelihood of it being effective. Helen, however, looked away after a moment, her expression consciously martyred. The door opened, and the girl came in with the trolley. Bridget said with evident relief, "Ah, the pudding at last."

They both read books in bed, but after half an hour Hanni switched off her light and settled down. Stefan went on reading. It was a novel of Kirst's he had brought, and he read it with fascination, contempt, unwilling respect. A splendid exorcism. If you had the right approach, the right temperament, it was so easy to cope with the past. Profitable, also—this would sell its hundred

56

thousand, not forgetting the paperbacks. Not only the temperament, though. There was talent as well, very great talent.

He looked across at Hanni. She had fallen asleep with one hand up by her face touching her cheek. He studied her in the light from his bedside lamp. As in that moment during supper, he was very conscious of her Jewishness. In reality, half Jewishness. If she had been fully Jewish, nothing could have saved her from the murderous attentions of his own, of her father's race. It was lucky for her that her mother had died before the war. He thought of the list she kept, in her father's Christian Bible, of the cousins and uncles and aunts, their full names written out as a mnemonic of frightfulness. The Bible was in the back of her bureau at home; he had come across it by accident one day and had never spoken to her of it. All their names, and their relationship, the places where they had lived and the places where they died. Auschwitz and Belsen, Buchenwald and Theresienstadt.

Stefan put out the light. He lay in bed, aware of his body's rigidity, in the cool embrace of the sheets. He heard rain slashing heavily against the window, and his mind moved in strange paths, almost like the remote, distorted paths of fever. He thought of what the American had thought he had seen. The small slim figure in the moonlight, in a silver world of innocence. To know that, even for a moment, even as a delusion, was something which he envied, without bitterness.

He grasped at sleep, oblivion, but could not reach it.

V

M AT KNEW VERY WELL that he should have gone back before
Daniel arrived. It had been his intention to do so, but he
had put the departure off from day to day—a typically Irish pro-
cedure, he thought gloomily—and at the end had been overtaken
by a strange combination of failure of nerve and obstinacy. He
could not go and would not go. He telephoned the office, and his
father said of course he could stay a few days longer if he wanted
to, there was nothing much doing at the moment. He was being
sympathetic, which Mat found scarcely tolerable, and he answered
brusquely and ended the call as soon as he could. It must be
obvious, he saw, to everyone—to his father and mother in Dublin,
to Bridget, inevitably, to Daniel, to Mrs. Malone and Mary and
the bloody guests. He was looking a fool, and it was the thing he
could bear least.

On the other hand, he had to have the negative reassurance of
seeing how she behaved with Daniel. There had been moments
when they had seemed close, when he had thought her response
was something more than gratitude for what help he had been
able to give with getting things started. She had been quite happy
about leaving Daniel to come here, and an engagement ring was
nothing like a wedding ring. Hadn't his sister been engaged four
times before she married Mick Stacey? He would be ten times
more miserable than need be if he went away with doubts like
that in his head. Seeing them together would resolve it, one way
or the other.

He could not remember a day more excruciating, more wildly fluctuating in its effects on him. There was the morning's waiting, testing the temperature of Bridget's anticipation and finding it gratifyingly cool. She went about the day's routine as cheerfully, as casually as ever, gave instructions to Mrs. Malone for Daniel's bed to be made up with as much indifference as for one of the guests. Mat hung about listening for the sound of his car. When it came at last, he watched for her to go out to greet him, but she did not. Daniel brought his bag in, and Mat left his post at the upstairs window. He was on the point of charging down the stairs, fearful of missing the encounter, when he saw Bridget in the hall and realized it was going to happen now, any second. Daniel came in. She smiled at him, with nothing special in the smile, and opened her arms for him to kiss her. A light, casual kiss, the sort you gave a brother or an old friend of the family. Mat came downstairs, his heart thumping with relief, and she said, "You remember Mat, of course, darling. He's been a tower of strength."

And the cold, thin English face, probably not meaning to look contemptuous but conditioned into the look as they nearly all were, briefly smiling.

"I'm sure he has. You look very well, Mat. How's the fishing?"

For three hours after that, Mat had made plans. She must have been tired of him already in February—that was why she had been so willing to come out and start the hotel. He might not feel the same way—it was impossible to imagine any man wanting to relinquish a girl like Bridget—but the English had no depth of emotional feeling, the English men, that was, and in any case he would have to put up with it, as better men had done before him. He was wondering whether it was better to say something to Bridget quite soon, or to wait, when he saw them together again.

He was sitting in the library with the door open, and looked up when he heard Bridget's footsteps in the passage outside. He heard other footsteps following, and Daniel's voice saying something. Bridget gave a quick look into the room but did not see him. His chair was in the shadow and there was a vase full of flowers in the way. She had stopped, and now Daniel embraced her, and she was in his arms with all the passion that had been absent in the morning. He wondered if, not seeming to look, she had seen him then at the top of the stairs and been casual because of that. There was nothing casual in this kiss; her face worked against Daniel's and her hands gripped his neck, pulling his head down to hers. Mat did not want to see it, but could not look away. The two figures strained together. Then, as he watched in horror and fascination, Daniel's hand moved down from her back, rubbed along the curve of her thigh, tightened and gripped with assurance and proprietorial familiarity.

Mat still stared at the door after they had broken apart and gone. His legs and arms were quivering with tension. Part of his mind tried to tell him that at least he had been saved from making an absolute fool of himself, but the consolation was swamped by bitter wretchedness.

He kept away from them until dinner, when their company could not be avoided without conspicuousness. During the meal he concentrated, calmly and analytically, on other people. He thought with detachment of the incalculabilities of human coupling. The German pair, for instance—what series of accidents, desires, frustrations had brought them together? And even more so, the Americans. He found time to pity their daughter, the pale, dark Cherry. It was little enough fun for a kid of that age to be in a lonely place like this, with rain all the time and no amusements, without having to endure this bickering that went on between her parents. She was subdued, as well she might be. Dull, too, he thought, but she would need to be that.

He kept his attention away from Bridget and Daniel, but could not help observing that they were behaving in the coolly amiable way toward each other which had led him astray earlier. They would, of course. This silly topic of the little people was brought up, and Bridget turned to him, smiling prettily, for information. He was pleased by the naturalness of his own response, by his behavior throughout the meal. There was the coldness of sweat down his back and on his legs, but they could not know it. He forced himself to put questions, make comments. "What kind of an animal can give the impression of being female?" What kind of female, he thought, can give an impression of being virginal?

Part of his resolve went a little later. They all had coffee together in the library; from behind the cup and saucer he watched her covertly. She was still the same—gray, direct eyes under the glory of that golden brown mass of hair, red lips just parted in a smile. There was a discipline, a kind of honesty, even in the way she sat in the chair there. He tried desperately, for his peace of mind, to merge that figure with the one glimpsed in the passage, and could not. There was a mistake, an explanation; there had to be. He came to it suddenly, in a burst of illumination. It was the action of that hand which had so shockingly colored it all with its gross implications of intimacy. But that had been Daniel's act, not hers. It was what you would expect of an Englishman. She had tolerated it, but she had not wanted or welcomed it—could not have. Maybe she was not ready yet to send him off, but she was a pure girl. One corner of her mouth lifted, the cheek dimpled, as she smiled at something Stefan said. There could be no doubt of it, no doubt at all.

The sense of well-being, of release, lasted until he went to bed. He joined in conversation heartily, made jokes, laughed uproariously at the small jokes of others. When he said good night to Bridget it was with shame for the thoughts he had had. It did not matter, he told himself in a spirit of exaltation, whether she felt anything for him or not; it mattered only that she was what she was.

His room was next to the one Daniel had been given; he heard the other man come up only a few minutes after he had done, heard the door open and close, the creak of boards as he moved about the room, the running of a tap. Mat tried to think charitable thoughts about him, with moderate success. One had to be realistic; a lot of men were like that, in Ireland, too. He remembered with disgust some of the grubby ones you might see in the Bailey, writers they called themselves, and the talk overheard of this

61

fornication and that adultery. He had an automatic impulse to pray to Mary for them all. At times like this, on the edge of sleep, old habits of thought came back, and he was not a man who looked at the universe with cold appraising intelligence, but a boy again.

The creak of a board snapped him back into consciousness and alertness. He heard another—in Daniel's room—and after that, he thought, the quiet opening of the door. Someone passing his own door, the sound almost lost in a new surge of wind and rain outside. He sat up, staring into the dark.

Had he been asleep? He was not sure. Looking at his watch, he saw that it was half an hour since he had come to bed. Daniel had left his room. Why? Well, probably to go to the lavatory; he would need to pass Mat's room to do that. Pay no attention, he thought, settle down and go to sleep. But he stayed rigidly sitting up and staring into nothing. His heart was pounding again. Time passed. He looked at the luminous dial again. Ten minutes. More, a quarter of an hour. Loathing himself as he had done the time he had stolen chocolate from the village shop as a boy, but equally powerless to stop himself, he eased himself out of bed and felt for his slippers and dressing gown.

Outside he hesitated. The dim lights were on at either end of the corridor. He was no longer sure what he had heard or failed to hear. Daniel might have gone to the bathroom, and equally might have quietly come back. The wind had got up and was gusting heavily and noisily about the house. He went to the door of Daniel's room and listened. No sound, but why should there be? There was no reason to think the man snored. He ought to go back to bed, but he would go along to the bathroom first himself.

It was unoccupied, dark, the door ajar. Which meant, probably, that that was what had happened—the man had gone there and come back, and he had not heard him. But doubts and fancies were tearing at his heart again. Bridget's room was the last at the far end of the corridor. The one next door was at present unoccupied. There would be nothing wrong in going into it. He could sit for a minute, reassure himself with the silence and the thought of her lying on the other side of the wall, then go back to bed and sleep in peace.

He went quietly, opening and closing the door of the room with delicate care. A board creaked, but only a little, as he went toward the wall. He had to feel his way. It had seemed risky to put a light on, and the room was pitch black. But before his outstretched fingers touched the wall, he stopped. There was no doubt now. Distant voices murmured together in the darkness, a man's and a woman's.

They were not distinct enough for him to be able to make anything out of what they were saying. He found another rationalization; maybe they were just talking things over, about the hotel, their engagement, anything. They would not have had much chance to talk privately during the day. It could be that. He reached the wall and pressed himself against it. Louder, but still not clear. But he had to know—could not go back without knowing after all this. There was a trick someone had told him of once —a glass pressed against the wall, and your ear to it. There was a tooth glass, he remembered, above the washbasin. He groped his way to the corner and found it. Then back to the wall, to the point where the sounds seemed loudest. Louder, but still indistinguishable, distorted. He shifted the glass, and again.

A kind of sigh, and her voice, all too clear, all too explicit. He stood for a petrified moment, and then stumbled away. Even in his incredulity and confusion and disgust, he was careful not to make a noise. The one possible thing worse would be for them to know of him being here.

He went not to his room, but downstairs. This was at first aimless, a realization that he could not hope to sleep, a desire to get as far as possible from his listening post and the room where . . . The thought of a drink only came to him when he was in the hall. It had been—how long? Three years? Two and a half, anyway. He could remember the self-loathing, the physical and mental nausea, and the time, to the hour almost, when he had seen what

63

was happening to him and what would happen, and had made his resolution, relying on no saints or the strong arm of God but his own determination that he would not be dragged down by it the way his grandfather had been, and Uncle Tom, and old Donovan. He had kept it that long. At times it had been far from easy, but he had held on. Bitterly he remembered congratulating himself about it only a few days ago. Not being a drunkard was something —not much maybe but something—to offer a woman when you loved her.

He found an unopened bottle of Old Bushmill and a glass. Best take a bottle, so he could settle the account squarely. A good full drink, and another. In the glow of whisky, things seemed better. He still could not bear to think of her, but it was easier to avoid doing so.

He sat drinking in one of the chairs in the library and dozed off there. He woke from a dream in which the thin pure voices of angels called to him in mysterious tongues, and found himself shouting, "What's that?"

There was a scurrying noise not far away. A rat he guessed, and a big one by the sound of it. He walked unsteadily to the door and looked out. There was no sign of anything. By his watch it was three o'clock. He was glad he had awoken. It would have been terrible to be found down here in the morning. He could face bed now, but he picked up the remains of the whisky to take with him. He climbed the stairs steadily and did not look in the direction of Bridget's room when he got to the landing.

The next morning Mat felt tired, but he had no hangover. He had drunk about half the bottle of whisky. He stared at himself in the glass, bleary but not much more so than usual at this time; nothing would show after a douse in cold water and a hard rub with a towel. He had the constitution for it, as his grandfather had had, and, according to him, his father before that. He poured himself a slug of whisky and drank it. That was better already. He could start thinking of what to do.

There was nothing to keep him here. He would be glad to be away, glad to be back in Dublin. But he had said, both to his father and to Bridget, that he would probably be staying a couple of days more, and he was not going to give anyone the impression that he might be running away. What in any case was there to run away from? She meant nothing to him now, and he had always known there were loose, lascivious women in the world. He plunged his face into the refreshing coldness of the water, snorting into it the way he remembered his grandfather doing when he was a boy.

He found no difficulty in facing Bridget. He told her there was a bottle of whisky to go on his bill.

"What bill?" she said. "You should be charging me for all the work you've done."

"I invited myself here," he said, "and I'll pay my bill."

He had spoken more strongly then he intended. Bridget said, "We won't talk about it now, anyway. Did you say a bottle of whisky? I thought you never touched liquor."

"It was medicinal entirely," he said. "I feel I've got a cold coming on, and I find as often as not a drop of whisky knocks it out before it can settle."

"Would you like some Contac? Or codeine?"

"No," he said. "The whisky will be enough."

That day he motored to the village and bought a couple more bottles. He stored them in his room, underneath his socks. The rain, which had stopped for an hour or two, was beating in again from the bog. Looking from his window, he saw that there were more pools, and larger. If it went on long enough, he thought, the great lake would be here again, and the house and all of them deep beneath it. He had another drink, against the time.

He did not drink with the others, and he felt that he was holding his liquor well enough for them not to notice. They might have smelled his breath, but he sucked a few peppermints and in any case he was not one for allowing his face to get close to the faces of the people about him. In the evening the subject of the little people was brought up again, and he listened to their chattering

65

and said a few things as silly himself. There had been a good deal of drink taken by some of them, maybe because of the weather, and the talk was sometimes wild. The needling contest between the Americans started up again and showed signs of becoming more serious.

Bridget, intervening, said, "Do you realize something? The rain's stopped. Listen."

Daniel went to the window and drew the curtain a little to one side. He said, "More than that, the moon's out." He drew the curtain right across. "Isn't that better?"

The night was clear: lawn and trees silver and black, farther off the speckle of the lake, even the distant hills faintly visible. It was amazing how much detail could be seen—branches of the trees, a bush starkly outlined, the small island with the tumble-down shack on it. They were real and not-real at the same time, a dream still-photographed and preserved for the wakeful mind to gape at.

They looked in silence for a moment or two before Helen said, "On such a night as this . . . did Waring see his iddle-bitty fairy lady. What do you say we organize a posse to go look for her? A little-people hunt."

Bridget said, "We'd frighten them away, I should think, stamping about out there."

"The answer, surely," Daniel said, "is to sit here and watch. I'll put the light out, so the fairies will think we've gone to bed." His voice was slurred, too, Mat noticed. "Does anybody object?" He went across and switched off the light. "Look at that, now. Better than television."

Mat watched him come back to stand behind Bridget's chair. He rested his arms there, his hands not quite touching her hair. Her profile was visible against the light outside. It was funny how things changed in one's mind, he thought. She had been everything, and was nothing. They all chattered away, and he stared at the world of moonlight. He had been thinking he could do with another drink and planning to slip upstairs, but for the moment the need had gone. He was melancholy and contented. It was a passing show, all of it, and a man of sense could amuse himself in watching. With just a little aid, a small tincture to warm the gelid blood.

Something moved.

It was over toward the walled garden, in the shadow. He did not say anything, but waited for it to happen again. It did, and this time he was not the only one who saw it.

Hanni said, "Look, out there . . . by the wall."

There was a buzz of comment and question, a new concentration of looking. He could feel their tension, the half-belief that here and now there might be wonders. It touched him, too. His fingers tightened on the arm of the chair.

The third time the movement was better defined: a comic and identifying hop. Bridget laughed, her voice as silver as the moonlight.

Helen said, "Good Christ, a rabbit!"

"A hare," Daniel said.

"Hare, shmare, what an anticlimax. That's what you saw the other night, honey, a crummy bunny."

"No," he said, "it wasn't that."

"O.K. It was a fairy with a fur coat. And tonight she's practicing for a sack race."

Mat wanted the drink now, and he wanted to be away from them all. He stood up.

"I'm a bit tired. It's the cold I've got coming. Will you excuse me if I go to bed?"

Someone was in the room. He came out of sleep knowing this, his skin prickling with fear. He forced himself back and up against the headboard, pushing the sheets away so that he would be free to leap out. Making his voice hard, he said, "Who's that?"

For answer, the light was switched on. She stood by the door, the door closed, in something fluffy and red with white trimmings. She looked strangely concentrated. As though she had been sleepwalking? But could someone sleepwalking switch on a light?

He said, "Cherry."

"I'm sorry if I woke you." Her voice was low and level. "I couldn't sleep myself. I meant to go along to my parents' room, but I must have got the wrong door. I'm pretty bad at remembering directions and things."

He said, "They're right opposite. Number Four."

He pulled the sheets up again, but still felt embarrassed.

She said, "I get nervous when I can't sleep. In a strange place especially. And with all that talk of banshees and leprechauns and little people . . . I guess I'm pretty stupid."

Mat shook his head. "It's a different world at night. Different altogether."

"Now that I have woken you . . ." She hesitated. "Could I stay and talk with you awhile?" She smiled nervously. "Seems silly, waking two lots of people up. Am I being a terrible nuisance? Kick me out if you want to go right back to sleep."

"Stay, of course. I'm wide awake."

"You sure?"

"Quite sure."

She walked toward him. It was a silky translucent thing she was wearing, a kind of robe, with something silky and translucent underneath that again, of a deeper red. Her nightdress. It was terribly short, because he could see the line where it ended and it was high up on her thighs. Through the two materials the white of her skin was glimpsed and lost again. He was conscious of alarm and fear, mixed with a sickening overpowering sweetness.

She sat down, not, as he had expected, in the chair, but on the edge of his bed. He felt the mattress give under her slight weight. He stared at her and saw her smile in return. He had been thinking of her as a child, but she was not a child. Seventeen, and they grew up earlier in other countries. And she had come to him. It was the kind of fantasy he had had as a schoolboy, the occasion for sin and confession and disgust.

"What shall we talk about?"

She leaned forward slightly, and the V of her robe widened.

The white trimmings, he saw, were on the neck of the nightdress beneath it . . . and other white. Of her breasts beneath the diaphanous red.

"We could talk about you."

She shook her small dark head. "I'm dull."

"I don't think so."

The young purity of her face—but that was what he had seen in Bridget, and a fine fool it had made of him. They were all alike, and being young made no difference. It was a mask they put on, and it was their delight to exchange it for the grimacing mask of lust. As for himself . . . there was no confession any more, no belief in sin. Only disgust remained, and disgust was not always at war with desire; it could add spice to it.

He stretched out and took her hand. It was warm and small and soft, and he felt the delicate ridges of her knuckles.

"I know," he said. "We'll have a little drink together first."

He put his other hand down beside the bed and fished up the bottle. She shook her head very slightly.

"No. I don't drink at all. I don't like the taste of it." She looked at him, the concentration in her face making her seem almost to frown. "You have a drink, though, if you want one."

"No." He put the bottle back slowly. "It's a bit late for it, really, or a bit early." Her refusal shamed him, and he was confused again. He said harshly, "Why did you come here?"

"I told you. I was nervous. And lonely."

"Yes." He gazed at her in wonder. That trust and innocence, and he had mistaken it for brazenness. A movement showed the sweet curve of her breast again but this time provoked not desire but protectiveness. She was like a lovely daughter. "It can get lonely in the night."

The dark eyes stayed on his. "Could I lie down beside you on the bed? Would you mind that?"

He eased her down with his arm. She lay beside him. He said, "I'll give you a blanket. You'll be cold."

She lay silent while he tucked a blanket over and around her. She only spoke when he made as though to sit in the chair.

69

"No. Please lie with me."

He got into bed again. He had put his pillow under her head. She patted it with her hand, and he put his head down there. He said, "Are you warm enough, Cherry?"

"Almost."

"Tell me about yourself," he said. "Tell me what you do at school."

"That's dull, too. Tell me what it's like being an attorney."

"Even duller."

They looked at each other from opposite ends of the pillow. She said, "I like your eyes."

"I like yours. You're a very pretty girl."

"I'm glad—that you think so, that is."

They talked like old friends, without strain or awkwardness. In time her eyelids dropped and she fell asleep. Mat waited until he was sure she was off and then eased himself out of bed. It wouldn't do for them both to go to sleep, the world and people being as they were.

In the dawn, he woke her and packed her off to her room. She stood on tiptoe at the door, and he kissed her briefly on the lips. He felt tired, but happy and at ease.

VI

Daniel was wakened by Bridget's alarm going off; it was not a bell but an exceptionally irritating high-pitched buzz. She put her hand out and switched it off but did not immediately get up. He contemplated her hair, a silent riot on the pillow, and her shoulder exposed above it. No baby he recalled seeing had had so flawless, so white a skin. Happily brooding on this, he eased forward until her warm, rounded body was touching all along the length of his own and, putting an arm about her under the sheets, seized one perfect breast. She continued to lie motionless, and he made a further, still more intimate movement.

"No!"

As though electrified, she wrenched herself free, pushed back the sheets, and jumped out of bed. Her body against the morning light was a triumph, but he objected strongly to the way she was taking it toward her slippers and dressing gown.

"Brid," he said, "for God's sake!"

She slipped the dressing gown on and turned to look at him while she tied the sash.

"No," she said, more quietly but equally firmly. "No, no, no, no, no. Do you realize it's twenty-five to seven? And Mrs. Malone is quite capable of sleeping through her own alarm—she's done it a couple of times already. And Mat will probably be looking for his breakfast by half past seven, and the Morwitzes not long after. In fact, I *am* responsible for this place."

71

"Damn it to hell," he said, "and them with it. I've a good mind to get up and manhandle you."

"Just you see what happens if you try. And that's another thing. This is all very well, but it cannot go on. I reckon I've had about two and a half hours' sleep one way and another."

"The bed is too small," he agreed. "I woke once sneezing because your hair was tickling my nose. Haven't you got a double bed to move in here?"

"If I had, I wouldn't. I've risked my reputation harboring you, as it is. There must be no more of these nocturnal excursions."

"You mean incursions." He sat up in bed. "Are you going to bolt your door against me? Then I shall have to set about noisily battering it down. Or sit outside and howl like a dog."

She said pleadingly, "Darling, do please see. I have a fairly rigorous day of it. I'll be run ragged unless I get some proper sleep at night."

"The solution's simple. Give them their money back and pack them off. They can probably get in somewhere at Ballina. Now come back to bed."

The pleading expression changed to a mulish one.

"If anyone is going to be packed off, it will be you, my fine feathery friend. Once and for all, I am going through with this for the season. Later, we'll see."

She was moving toward the door. He called after her, "What do you mean—we'll see? See what?"

She turned, with her hand on the doorknob. "Just see. Now you get up. You can sleep all day if you want to, but not in my bed. I'll send Mary up to your room with tea in half an hour, and you'd better be there."

"You bring it."

"I shall be too busy. Remember to open the door a crack to see if anyone's about before you come out." She blew him a kiss. " 'Bye."

Daniel slumped back into bed as the door closed, but almost at once sat up again. As tired as he was, there was a very good chance of going back to sleep if he stayed horizontal, and this

72

present Bridget was tricky enough without asking for trouble. Cursing to himself, he collected his things, made the necessary check at the door, and padded along the corridor to his own room. Once there, he stared at his scarcely disturbed bed, a striking contrast to the one he had just left. He supposed he could get into it, but a short nap would leave him feeling much worse, and lying in would mean a superior smile from Bridget when he did come down. Wearily he rumpled the bed with his hand, sat on the edge of it, and lit a cigarette.

We'll see, he thought. Had she meant anything by it, or was it just a threat to keep him in line? Even that was disturbing enough, underlining the difference between this Bridget and the one who used to trot into Joe Grayson's office every morning clasping her shorthand pad and pencil. Could it have been serious, though? Could she possibly be contemplating carrying on with the place after September? No, he told himself, that was absurd.

He decided a wash would freshen him up and went over and filled the basin. Plainly absurd. Except, a nagging thought reminded him, that what he meant was absurd on the basis of the Bridget he thought he knew, not this one. Of course, there was really no discrepancy. The authority and responsibility—the discovery that she could do this sort of thing fairly successfully—had gone to her head. It was a thing not uncommon in newly promoted executives in the City of London. They settled down after a time and got over it, and so would she. It was not, he thought with a flicker of pleasant recollection, as though there was any sign of her having gone off him in the important sense.

Daniel dressed and shaved, taking his time. Mary brought him his tea while he was shining his shoes. He thanked her, smiling, and she bobbed her head and scurried away. He hated timidity in women, but reflected that he was not too fond of the reverse, either.

When he had finished his preparations, he found himself with time to kill before breakfast. He would not, he knew, be kindly received in the kitchen. He looked out of his window. It had rained again in the night, but now the sky was clear and blue

73

except for a few thin high bars of cloud in the south. Half an hour in the fresh air would do him no harm. He could go down to the garden or the lake. Or—the idea struck him—do as he had been meaning to do since Mat spoke about earth forts and go and have a look at that characteristic ridge on the far side of the tower. There were two routes he could follow to get there, that by way of the front of the house being shorter. He decided he would take the other, which would mean walking most of the way around the lake.

He studied the lake as he skirted it. It was not a very pre-possessing stretch of water. It seemed to him to have a stale, stagnant smell, but that might be coming in from the bog on his other side. An unlovely bit of country altogether. He could see the argument for the place as a stronghold, providing the bog were as impenetrable as it was said to be, but that anyone should choose to build a dwelling house here was a mystery that was probably rationally insoluble. And the same went for Cousin Seamus buying it. He reminded himself that this was Ireland, where the rational was not held in the same high esteem as on the other side of St. George's Channel, but was not entirely satisfied by that.

The ridge was parallel with the base of the tower and some ten feet away from it. It ran for sixty or seventy feet, at the near end broken abruptly by the margin of the lake and at the other crumbling away to the ordinary level of the ground. In places rock showed, which could be either the projecting faces of large boul-ders incorporated in it as a strengthening factor or outcrops of a basic structure on which, perhaps, the tower had been built. The whole was covered with stubbly grass with a few flowers like thrift and saxifrage, and a few small tenacious bushes.

The height of the ridge varied between four and six feet, and the elevation was steep but fairly easily climbable. Childishly, Daniel took a run and scaled it, using his hands to help him up. It was amazing, he reflected, what latent strength the old king of the castle complex had.

Daniel stood by the foot of the tower and looked around. As

74

far as he could see in any direction, there was no sign of habitation, no artifact except this massive crumbling pile whose stones might have been untouched for centuries. There were those who would find such a prospect entrancing, but he was not among them. He enjoyed Nature in its place, and the place was that of strict subjection to humanity. Nor was he under any illusion about the history evoked by these slabs of stone—a wretched, diseased, uncomfortable life, lit by the passing flames of drunkenness and orgy. There was nothing in it that spoke to him. He kicked a loose stone. With lives so drab, it was not surprising that they dreamed up beliefs in fairies and leprechauns and the rest.

It was time to go back for breakfast; he could carry on around the tower and so get to the front of the house. The turf was springy underfoot, a bright cropped green except for one small patch where the brown earth showed through. He glanced at it idly and had walked past before the smaller detail registered on his mind and brought him back. It was not loose soil but clay, capable of taking an impression, and the impression, though blurred, was unmistakable. The print of a foot in a sandal.

Daniel knelt down to look at it more closely. A footprint, yes. But no more than two inches in length.

Bridget said, "Darling, I just haven't *time* for jokes at this time of day. It will have to keep till later."

"The point is," he said, "whose joke is it? What devious mind thought of planting it? Not you. I'll concede you are too busy for little pranks of this kind. And I don't quite see Morwitz doing it. It's a bit too frothy for the German sense of humor. Waring? Or Mat, maybe?"

"Look," she said, "don't get in my way. I have a tendency to spray hot fat when I'm rushed with the eggs and bacon."

"The *how* is fairly easy," Daniel said. "You just need a doll's sandal, which you press gently into the mud. You could probably make one quite simply. Cherry, possibly? Sometimes these quiet ones have a weird idea of fun."

75

"Breakfast is ready. Go and sit down."

"Come and join me."

"You know I can't." She flashed a harassed smile. "I'll have coffee with you."

"It's very odd."

"I know. We'll talk about it over coffee."

They all went out with him after breakfast except Cherry, who was sleeping late. Daniel took opportunities to study their faces as they trooped around the house in the direction of the tower. If one of them had planned it, he or she was playing it well. Their expressions were those of people puzzled, mildly interested, rather more incredulous. Helen was talking a lot, but no more and in no way differently from usual. Waring seemed preoccupied with something, but it looked like something personal from the way his brow creased. Mat had a dazed look on his face, which could be part of a hangover; they were not supposed to know he had taken to the bottle, but one would have to be very unobservant not to see it—nor, Daniel thought with a complacent look at Bridget, to work out the reason. The two Germans walked side by side a little behind the others. Hanni seemed completely uncomprehending, Stefan doggedly determined to see something pointless through to the end. Bridget, it occurred to him, was glad to have something, however crazy, to interest the guests. His hand tightened on hers, and she squeezed back.

"Here it is," Daniel said. "Up here."

The approach to the ridge this side formed an easy gradient. Bridget dropped back, and Daniel led the way. He had a momentary apprehension as he did so that there would be nothing there—that he had not seen the footprint at all or that it had been removed. The thought of the idiot he would look if that were so sent a hot flush down his neck. But it was there, of course, as it had to be. Fairy footprints might fade with the dew, but this was real, a physical impression in the earth.

They crowded around, examining it. Helen said, "It's cute, isn't it? How'd it get there?"

76

Daniel said, "That's what I would like to know. The only thing that makes any sense is that some one of us came out early and made it. Or did it yesterday afternoon, perhaps, though that's less likely. It was raining pretty heavily then."

Bridget stared at it, wide-eyed. "It can't be real, can it? I mean . . ."

Waring said, "Made by a real foot, you mean? If so, and the proportions are anything like normal, the foot must have been attached to someone around a foot high, give or take the odd inch."

Stefan said, "It is a joke, you think? Because of our talk about the little people, someone came out here and made this mark." He shook his head. "I do not understand that."

Hanni asked him a question in German, and he rattled off an answer in the same language.

Helen said, "I don't think it's a joke at all. We're all too goddam disbelieving because we've seen everything explained on television."

Her voice had a dogmatic braying note to it which made one disinclined to take what she said seriously. Waring's voice, in reply, had an edge. "Let's try and remain rational. Even a pygmy would leave a mark twice or three times the size of that one. Physiologically, it's lunacy."

"Is it?" Helen said. "Are you so sure? The horse bred up from Eohippus. Maybe there was a race of really tiny men at one time. Maybe a few could survive in a wild and deserted part of the world like this. What about the coelacanth? Ten years ago they believed it had been extinct for a couple of million years."

"It's not the same," Waring said. "Nothing like. We've got fossil imprints of Eohippus and the coelacanth. There's nothing in the record that points to tiny primitive men."

She said triumphantly, "So the record may not be complete. Look at all the stuff Leakey dredged up in Africa only a few years back. That was all new—there'd been nothing like it before."

She looked pleased with herself in a different way from usual.

77

It occurred to Daniel that it might be because she had got Waring into an intellectual rather than a personal argument—that she could not feel herself recognized as a woman without first being recognized as someone capable of matching his thought. While for Waring, probably, the specification was reversed; the emotional discord vitiated harmony on every level.

Waring said, "Sure. It could be that we just haven't found the right fossils yet. Little people with wings. After we've got them, we can go and look for fossils of men with heads growing out of their armpits, and women with a fish skeleton from the waist down. They're just as well documented as fairies."

"Who said anything about wings? You can reduce any argument to nonsense. But you can't get over that footprint. You remember what T. H. Huxley said? A scientist should sit down before truth like a little child."

"That wasn't what he said when they tried to get him interested in spirit mediums. Another quality you've got to have is knowing where to draw the line."

Their points of reference were just about meaningless to Daniel, but plainly understood by each of them. T. H. Huxley? Some relation of the novelist? It came from a common ground shared some time in the past, in the days when they could talk to each other. The look in Helen's face showed that she might be recognizing that and remembering. As though slamming the door on a cupboard that had unexpectedly fallen open, Waring went on quickly: "The point is, I'm not going to assume that this is anything but a fake before I have to. Why should I? It almost certainly is a fake, as Daniel says. Someone amusing himself by trying out our gullibility. Well, whoever he is, my reaction is that I'm not interested."

In a quiet voice Helen said, "Why here?" Waring had turned to go, but now turned back. "What's that supposed to mean?"

"O.K., assume that someone in the party thought it might be fun to fudge up a footprint because of all that talk—about you seeing one of them in the moonlight and the rest. There are plenty of places nearer the house where you could make a mark like that. As far as I know, Daniel's the first person to come around here, and that was by accident. There couldn't be any reason to think anyone would find it, and the first heavy rain shower would destroy it. So what's the point?"

Waring stared at her, his mouth twisted in concentration. What she said, Daniel saw, was incontrovertible. The odds must have been fantastically against himself or anyone else making the discovery. He felt a shiver of unease, contemplating that. There was a sensible explanation, there must be, but . . .

Mat said, "As to that, there's one very easy way to account for it." Daniel looked up and found himself being watched with cold anger. "That's if he had faked it himself. Personally, I don't think it's the sort of thing an American or a German or an Irishman would find funny. The English always pride themselves on having a very special sense of humor. He could have made the mark and then fetched us out to look at it."

Daniel said, "I suppose I could. Except that I don't regard it as funny, either."

Bridget said, "And doesn't the same argument apply, really? I mean, it would be much more effective if someone else found it, surely. The obvious place to leave the mark would be out in the garden, where there was a reasonable chance of it being noticed."

Mat said, "And him noticed while making it, maybe."

The hostility extended toward Bridget, as well. The disgruntled obverse of infatuation; there was nothing one could do about that. They were at something of an impasse, altogether. He was trying to think of something to say when Stefan called to them. He had left the group and was standing about fifteen feet away. He squatted down on his haunches.

"Have you seen this?"

There was a hole near the base of the tower wall where, at some time in the past, one of the big stones had fallen out. It led downwards and inwards, a twisting funnel of blackness.

Mat said heavily, "And is that where the little man is supposed to have come out from? Well, there's confirmation for you, and

79

Daniel didn't find that. Though maybe he'd have drawn our attention to it if we'd looked like missing it."

Daniel said, "Confirmation of what? You expect to find holes in old walls."

Stefan said, "But this one has been used. The stone is shiny—there, see—where it has been rubbed. And there are scuff marks outside."

"There's a straightforward explanation for that," Daniel said. "Rats. It's a rathole."

"Well, now," Mat said, "do you want us to argue you into it? Maybe we aren't taking the joke in the right spirit?"

"You can take it in any spirit you like," Daniel said. "Whisky will do."

He regretted the stupid pun as soon as it was out, but was not displeased to see the Irishman flush in response. Waring had got down beside Stefan and was examining the hole closely. He said, "It doesn't look like a rat run to me. I don't see any droppings. No grease marks, either, and no trace of hairs. And the earth isn't loose enough."

Bending down and peering still more closely, Waring picked delicately with finger and thumb. Then he held his hand up to the light.

Helen asked, "What is it?"

"Cotton thread. It was snagged on a sharp edge."

It was green in color, not more than half an inch long.

Daniel said, "Does that mean anything? Bits of thread blow about and catch on things."

Helen said loudly, "That was snagged, not just caught. It couldn't just have blown there."

Waring stood up, stretching his back. He flicked the thread away. He said, "It could have blown there. More likely than one of the little men tearing his shirt on his way out. Or someone might have stuck an arm down there, seeing how far he could reach, and left it that way."

"And the footprint?" Helen demanded.

"A lousy joke. I don't care who made it."

80

Stefan said to Bridget, "At the bottom of the tower—there are rooms?"

"A warren of them. Cells rather than rooms."

"Is anything kept there?"

"There are various piles of junk that I haven't got around to sorting out. I've only been down with a torch. There's no light down there, and the air's stale."

Mat said, "They would have been the dungeons, store cellars, and so on. There used to be a ditch around the base, but it's earthed up long since, and blocked up the air and light vents."

"Could one look at the rooms?" Stefan asked. "Is it permitted?"

Bridget said, "Of course, if you would like to." She gave a slightly nervous laugh and glanced around the assembled faces. "How serious are we being about all this?"

Helen said, "I'm serious. I'd like to have a look down there as well. Didn't you say the other night that the girl Mary said she'd seen things?"

"Yes. But she's not very bright, and she's full of superstition. She's nothing to go by."

"And there has been nothing else strange that has happened?" Stefan asked.

"No. That is . . ."

"Yes?"

She said reluctantly, "Things missing."

"What things?"

"Food, chiefly. Oh, just odd things. A bar of chocolate, fruit, a packet of raisins. The sort of thing a child might steal."

Daniel said, "Mary, you mean?"

"Well, I thought so. And it seemed best not to bother. I would have given her them if she'd asked me. Even if she's not bright, she works hard. She earns more than I pay her."

Mat said, "And the candles. And the string and the penknife."

"They were probably just mislaid—the penknife certainly." She turned to Daniel, explaining. "It belongs to Mrs. Malone—one of those very tiny penknives. Not much more than an inch long. She was always putting it down somewhere and thinking she'd lost it. Eventually she did lose it. It will turn up eventually. She's a great mislayer of articles. That's another reason I wasn't surprised to find things missing."

Stefan said, "Food. And string and candles. And a very small knife. They are all useful objects."

He spoke with an earnest excitement. His Teutonic soul, Daniel thought, had scented a wonder and was nose down and baying on the track. His own feeling was that they were being led into absurdity, as much as anything else by their isolation from the world. No daily newspapers, no television, a barren landscape stretching away to the distant hills. It sounded marvelous, a wonderful corrective to the stresses and irritants of modern life. But people needed things to believe, and, losing one complexity, might well set about inventing another, even to the extent of dreaming up a race of Lilliputians inhabiting the dungeons at the bottom of an old tower. Stefan, clearly, was on the way to having it all worked out, with the potential uses of all the missing articles neatly docketed. And there was, in fact, no justification at all; as Bridget had said, it was not surprising that things should be missing, with Mrs. Malone and Mary in charge of them. A framework of speculation based on nothing.

Except, he was forced to remind himself, the footprint. Which, if it had been made as part of some peculiar hoax, could only reasonably have been planted by himself. But he had seen it for the first time and by accident not much more than an hour ago. There had to be an explanation of that, but he could not begin to get a glimmering of one.

Helen said to her husband, "Maybe I ought to apologize to you, darling." She was excited, too. But more than that she was trying hard, groping perhaps for that common ground, long covered by the floodwaters of marriage. "What you saw in the moonlight—what did it look like? Tell us some more about it."

Waring said in a hard voice, "I saw nothing. There was nothing to see. Talking about it inspired someone to pull this thing with the footprint. O.K., then—enjoy yourselves." He turned away and walked rapidly back toward the house.

VII

STEFAN HAD READ the journal late at night, with the rain beating hard outside and Hanni peacefully sleeping in the next bed. It was a strange, exhilarating experience, this contact with the mind of a man unknown, in all probability dead years ago, but who yet seemed so much more real to him than most of the people he met in daily life. A German, like himself, as deeply aware of guilt, as deeply engaged by its complexities, a sensitive and cultured man who had come, as he had come, to this place on the western edge of the continent, landlocked but almost within smell of the great ocean; and who felt as he did that there was a meaning to be plucked from the maelstrom of existence—tragic, maybe, but giving significance, purpose—that he might yet find it, but whether he did or not, the seeking was the justification. Why had he come here? There was no clue in the journal, nor to the work he spoke of. There was much of recollection, and of remembered unhappiness. V., it was clear, had been his wife, deeply loved, her death after many years still resented, still at times impossible to accept. He wrote of her with tenderness and without affectation. This had been a love, Stefan thought, hearing Hanni's gentle breathing, uncrippled by circumstance, a deep engagement of two minds with no barrier between them.

Bridget had said he could tell her what was in the journal when he had read it. It had been no more than a gesture of politeness, but he had intended to do that. He thought now that he would not. There was nothing important to tell, nothing that would interest her; and its intrinsic character, and what he felt

83

about it, could not be conveyed in English. Stefan turned back to one page that had particularly struck him, and read it again:

The strong man creates his own philosophy and moral code; to take them ready-made from another is the action of a weakling. But what meaning do these terms have? For the first makes up his outlook from a great number of small things—events, defeats, triumphs, prejudices—while the second recognizes an excellence in one person with which he would choose to identify himself completely. As I did with V. There were human imperfections in her, as there must be in all, but I embraced them because of the essential rightness, the splendor of her. And knew them to be small, unimportant. I could have lived my life in her shadow, worshiping her gods, acting in accordance with her wishes, expressed or unexpressed. I would not have questioned my life, because to do so would have been to question her, and I could not doubt her goodness.

But she abandoned me. Not of her own volition, but the one left is abandoned even though it is death that intervenes, not faithlessness. And her creed had no power to compel me once she was gone. The fullness went from life, leaving not the emptiness there had been before but a much greater one, a night without moon or stars. What she had believed and wished and sought had no meaning without her. There was no point to anything.

Except work, of course. Work was my salvation at a time when I could have wished to invent a god so that I might revile him. Work made the fatuous minutes and hours and days pass more quickly. Work drained the blackness from the night, leaving no color perhaps but, at least, shapes in somber gray.

I am glad that I have never been tempted to believe that the dead survive. I would not be judged by her ghost.

Stefan stared at the page lying open on the sheet. What, though, if it is the ghost that comes to judgment? "I could have lived my life in her shadow." As I in his. "There were human imperfections . . . but I embraced them because of the essential rightness, the splendor . . ." You were in a happier case than I, my friend, he thought, because you could still say that and believe it to be true. How much easier to fear the other's judgment than one's own. You at least could think and write of what had once been.

Hanni murmured softly in her sleep—a lament? an accusation? —and turned away from him. He put away the book and switched off the light. The wind howled in the darkness, but outside, far away. He was tired, his body exhausted by exercise, his mind soothed by the peace of this soft, rain-bleared land. His leg kicked and he was falling, into sleep, into a dream.

He saw the mountains, the twin peaks dark with pines and between and beyond the great white summit, blinding against the blue, of the one they called Old Lonely. Every summer, as long as he could remember, that had been the first thing he had seen from his bedroom window in the morning, sometimes shrouded in mist but always inescapably there. Except that this was not as one saw it from the gable window. He was at a lower level, he realized, looking out from the veranda. And on that instant it was no dream, but reverie. He was awake and remembering.

In uniform still; there had been no time to change. He had gone up to his mother's bedroom and stayed with her until she fell into a restless sleep. Then he had come down, and his father had poured him a beer, and they had talked in quiet voices so as not to waken her.

"What does the doctor say?"

His father shrugged. "That we must wait and see."

"How long after the news about Karl?"

"Five days. She did not sleep and would not eat."

She loved her sons. It had been bad enough when Johann was killed in France—it had taken her a year to recover from the shock—but this was Karl, and Karl, they had all known, was her favorite. Stefan had never resented that. He loved her, but he was his father's son. And the only one left now. He said, "Did you hear how it happened?"

"A little. They were overrun in the counterattack at Kharkov. His company held out for half a day after both flanks had given way. He is recommended for the Iron Cross, First Class."

"That will not do her much good."

His father shook his head. There was a lot of white in his hair and lines of strain in his face. He said, "There is no comfort one can give her. I managed to get you back here. That was the best I could do."

"It was not possible to get him out of it?"

"Only with his consent, and he would not give that. You know his stubbornness."

"I know."

The beer cooled his throat. In Italy one drank wine, and there was the livid heat, the white choking dust, flies and stench and fear. One dreamed of the cool fresh air of the mountains, of bright flowers starring the scented grass, of this place, a time like this. He saw his father watching him, blue eyes impassive.

"There is one thing we can do—you and I together."

"What?"

"I could have got him back from the front, but he would not permit it. You are the only one she has left."

Stefan was silent. The thought had occurred to him already, selfishly in the first place. There were rumors that the Division's next move would be to the east. He did not enjoy the Italian war, but everyone knew what the Russian front was like.

His father said, "We have lost two sons. And you have done your part in the war. It is no disgrace if you take something safer now. And it may mean everything to her."

"I will think about it." He paused. "What is the news from Berlin? Are we losing the war?"

"No. We cannot afford to."

"That is always said."

"But this time it is true. If it were only the Americans and the English . . ."

He had not intended to speak of it until later, but it had been nagging at his mind more than he knew. He said, "Father. Listen."

"Yes."

"There are stories one hears."

"About what?"

"One of our officers met an old friend of his on leave. He comes from a place called Bergen-Belsen. There is a work camp there, and he says they are using it to murder Jews. By the thousand. Day after day trains packed with Jews, and day after day the sky blackened with smoke from the crematoria where they burn their bodies. Men, women, children even. Thousands every day."

It was enough to have said it. Even though his father did not reply right away, Stefan was reassured, reading the disgust and anger in his face.

"The English are good liars," he said. "In the first war, also. Our soldiers were cutting the hands off virgins, sticking babies with their bayonets, and our factories were making soap out of corpses. This was for their own morale, and for the neutrals, but here in Germany I heard about the soap that was being made from the dead. And in this war . . . We have a continent to hold down—they spread their lies through France, the Low Countries, Italy, Scandinavia, and the whispers travel here, into the homeland. Some knaves spread them, and some fools believe them." The blue eyes stared at Stefan. "You are neither."

"The one who told me did not seem a knave or a fool."

"There are camps, as you know, and Jews are sent to them. They are admitted enemies of the Reich, and the war is too desperate to allow liberty to our enemies. They work, as we all work. When the war is over, they can go back to their stinking ghettos, if that is what they choose, though the camps are healthier. The camp at Bergen-Belsen has a smelting plant, and smelting plants have furnaces; and furnaces fill the sky with smoke. That information, of course, is secret."

Stefan nodded. His father took the empty stein from him and filled it again with beer. When he had put it down in front of him, he grasped Stefan's shoulder with his right hand. He said, "If these murders were happening, I would know of them. That is obvious, isn't it?"

It was obvious. Even before the war Stefan could remember seeing him talk to Himmler on terms of near equality. There had

87

been promotions since then. He said in apology, "One loses touch. And there is so much confusion."

His father nodded. "I know. Come back home. You have done enough service at the front."

Stefan shook his head. "No. I will stay there. I know that job best."

"Think about it."

"I do not need to."

That had been his last leave during the war, the last time he saw his mother, who died two months later, the last time but one he saw his father. Stefan curled his body into a ball in the bed. Even remembering that had been too much. He closed his mind against memories still more bitter.

When Daniel talked at the breakfast table of what he had seen outside, Stefan was puzzled and mistrustful. The reasonableness of the English was only a thin veneer over their incalculability, and their self-confidence was unnerving. Some elaborate joke, he thought, and was inclined to keep his distance. But his curiosity was stronger than his caution. He decided he would remain watchful, uncommitted. He maintained this attitude while they were arguing about the impression in the ground, content to observe the various hostilities between them, and to wait for the explanation of the print itself to emerge.

All this changed when, wandering away from them and their bickering, he saw the hole in the wall. There was no real reason for it to have such an effect; it was an ordinary hole where one of the big stones had fallen out, what one would expect in an old building half ruined and uncared for. But glimpsing it, he became for the first time truly conscious of the footprint and its possible significance. It was no longer isolated, a mystery out of context. The creature that might have made it ceased to be hypothetical and was conceivable. It was fantasy still, but a fantasy which, if one sought to exclude it, left a far less credible void.

The suggestion that it had been used by rats was not to be taken seriously. The bit of thread, on the other hand, was an

88

almost expected confirmation. So, after he had asked about the inside of the tower, was Bridget's reply to his query as to whether anything strange had been noticed. The things missing were precisely what should be missing. Food. String. Candles. And a knife. The apparatus for survival in a giant's world.

He was impatient to set about the exploration of the inside of the tower. Hanni would not go. She understood what it was about, but her reaction was a kind of fear—not so much of the darkness and probable ruin of the place, nor even of what might be living down there, but of the thing in itself, the disruption of the world she knew. Stefan did not try to press her, her fears were sacred. Waring also refused to take part, and with some scorn. Helen, on the other hand, was eager to go. Daniel included himself in the project, and after a slight hesitation Mat did the same. Bridget said she could not spare the time. She provided a couple of flashlights—a large one with a long-distance beam, which Daniel took, and a smaller one, which she gave to Stefan. There would be morning coffee, she told them, in just over half an hour, so they were not to spend too long a time down there.

They went by way of the door at the end of the passage. The stairs wound up to the room with the dolls' houses, which Bridget had shown them on the day of their arrival, and down to a part which only Mat had seen during the time he had been helping her to get the place ready for guests. It was quite black—the beam from the big flashlight picked out isolated circles of light on the worn gray stone, in one place showing a surface glistening with water that had leaked through from somewhere, in another a pair of initials—R.N.—incised a centimeter deep. Stefan used his flashlight to illuminate the steps, which were broken and uneven, the more so as they got deeper. The air was cool and mustily damp, smelling of mud.

The stairs ended. The floor was paved with huge flat slabs, but there were places where smooth rock jutted up; the tower clearly had been built on the foundation of a natural outcrop. They were in a fairly small room whose fourth wall followed the interior curve of the building. Open doorways led off from two of the remaining walls. They were quite small, the lintels less than five feet off the ground. Daniel led the way through one, warning them to duck their heads, and they followed him.

This chamber was a repository for the junk Bridget had spoken of. It was somewhat larger than the first, but more than half was taken up by old furniture, boxes, paintings, and miscellanea. Stefan noticed an old-fashioned mangle with worn and pitted wooden rollers, parts of bedsteads, a cheval glass cracked down the middle, and, half concealed by a stained mattress, a broken spinning wheel. Helen picked up a canvas, and Daniel shone the light on it. Through the dirty varnish one could just make out that it depicted nymphs and shepherds in an Arcadian sunset landscape.

"Isn't this the kind of way people find a Rubens worth half a million dollars?" Helen asked.

"More like a Poussin," Daniel said. "Probably not more than four hundred thousand, even through Sotheby's."

"Worth checking up on, I would say." She gave a small laugh. Her voice was much less strident down here; they were all, Stefan noted, speaking softly. Even so, their voices echoed with strange overtones. While they were looking at the painting, he went ahead into the next room. There was more rubbish here, and in one corner a pile of stone where a wall had collapsed. Mat had followed him.

Stefan said, "How many rooms are there, altogether?"

"I don't know," Mat said. "The place is a warren of them. And some you can't reach."

"Why not?"

"I'll show you. Through here, and then through the opening on the right."

Steps went down from that doorway. His light picked out two and then found something else, the blackness of water. There was a noise of dripping farther in. Stefan bent down and tried to see farther. The whole floor of the chamber was submerged.

"How deep?" he asked.

Mat said, "I've no idea. Nor whether there are any other rooms on the far side. This must be the level of the lake, and the water's seeped in under the foundations."

Daniel's voice came from behind them. "Are you all right in there?"

Mat called back, "Sure." He said to Stefan, "Let's go on."

They went through the other doorway. The whole place was a maze of small chambers, mostly empty but some with heaps of rubbish. Stefan's sense of direction had abandoned him, and he recognized a room as one previously traversed; but there was nothing disturbing in this. It would be easy enough to find their way out, and they would hear the progress of the other two. Another room, and Mat said, "Shine the light over here."

His voice had a sharpness in it. Stefan swung the flashlight around. It lit up a ledge that projected from one wall a few inches above the ground. A stub of candle stood on it.

Stefan felt a wave of excitement at the sight of this small ordinary object. He said, "Candles were missing. Did she not say that?"

Daniel and Helen came through while they were examining it. Helen said, "You think that might be . . ." She laughed nervously. "A street lamp for Lilliputians?"

Daniel said, "It's probably been there for years. It wouldn't be worth taking up—there's less than a inch of candle left. Let's try and keep rational about this."

Mat said, "It wasn't here a week ago."

There was a pause. Daniel said, "You can't be sure of that. One room looks very much like another."

"I'm sure, all right," Mat said. "But if we want to be certain, I can tell you there's a cross carved above the door over there, and what looks like part of a letter S."

Both flashlights found it. The cuts went deep. The cross must have taken many weary hours. He had started on something else—his initials, or perhaps a prayer—and then unexpectedly he had been taken out, for release or execution, or just to be moved to another cell. There were bolts set in the wall, Stefan saw.

91

Daniel said, "In that case, someone must have brought it down here in that time. Bridget, maybe."

"Why should she bring a candle, instead of the torch?" Mat said. "Anyway, she's not been down. She's been too busy."

"I could make the same charge you did up above," Daniel said. "You spotted the candle, you're the one who's so sure it wasn't here a week ago. In which case . . ."

"My God!" Helen said. "Do you have to throw these silly accusations about? Can't you see that we're standing on the edge of maybe the most fantastic, most wonderful discovery?" She put her hand into the beam of the light, holding something—the wrapping off a chocolate bar. "We found this back a way. The candy that was missing, as well."

Daniel said, "It could have been the girl—Mary. She might steal the chocolate and come down here to eat it. Girls of that age do odd things."

"She's as full of fears as a broken-spirited horse," Mat said. "Nothing on earth would get her down here, and you know it."

Daniel said stubbornly, "There's nothing conclusive. A wrapper, a stub of candle. It's very little to go on."

"And a footprint," Stefan said. "Do not forget the footprint."

They were silent. In a flat voice, Daniel said, "I think we ought to be getting back. We told Bridget half an hour."

Helen insisted on continuing with the exploration, but after another five minutes was ready to go up. They had seen the rooms before; there was nothing strange in them. The maze had been more apparent than real. There were eight chambers in all, Mat told them, not counting the one with the staircase leading from it, nor the one that was filled with water. There was no difficulty about retracing their steps. Following behind the rest, Stefan noticed that one of the boxes on top of the old mangle was a file with German lettering. He opened it. There was a mass of papers and a leather-bound notebook like the one Bridget had given him, with the same spiky handwriting inside. Daniel and Helen were already on the stairs, but Mat had hung back waiting for him. He closed the book and slipped it in his pocket.

VIII

WARING WALKED OUT to the walled garden when the expedition set out for the tower. Once inside, one was in a different country. It was possible to see the upper part of the house, and from the elevation of the stepped dais at the center, which held the sun dial, one saw the hills, but otherwise there were only the shrubs and hedges and flower gardens, the walks and arbors, and every vista blocked by the enclosing red brick of the walls. As a young man he had seen a garden very much like this in England; he could almost imagine that outside lay not the featureless desert of the bog, but the rich, rounded folds of Hampshire, planted with fat cattle and prosperous-looking dwellings. And that he might walk out as the young visiting American, bothered by the social nuances, desperately concerned as to whether he ought to send his hostess flowers or nylons or a food parcel. Imagination, he thought regretfully, could not go as far as that. One could almost believe in calling back old places, but not one's old self.

He was disturbed by what he had heard a little earlier. He had been looking for Bridget to tell her about a light bulb that had failed in their room and had heard her voice through the open kitchen door. He had held back, partly to let her finish, partly because she was in the kitchen, not the guests' quarters, and had heard his name mentioned.

Bridget said, "What about Waring?"

Daniel answered her. "No, he's not going."

"But she is?"

"Didn't you hear her? She thinks the whole thing is just terribly terribly cute." He made, Waring noted with distaste, a very bad shot at reproducing Helen's accent. "I suppose that's why he's so determined to have nothing to do with it."

Bridget said, "It's a pity they spend so much time getting at each other."

"Yes. She, I thought, was not so bad in that respect this morning. Trying quite hard to be civilized."

"It's rough on Cherry," Bridget said.

Waring had moved away before they could come out. His first reaction had been one of simple annoyance. Not at their being discussed—one had to expect that—but at the failure to see who was the aggressor in the continuing irregular warfare. They had both been branded equally; Helen, in fact, as far as the morning was concerned, judged the innocent party. "Trying quite hard to be civilized." Oh, brother, he thought, I could have gone in there and told you something about being civilized! The time she set fire to my suits, and nearly burned the house down. Or the time she punched me in the gut when we were doing sixty-five on a crowded freeway. Not to mention all the non-physical aggressions, the insults and sneers at cocktail sessions and dinner parties, the time she met that couple from New Haven who bored her by talking horses, and she said, "Speaking of geldings, I don't think you've met my husband . . ."

In the garden he gradually cooled down. After ten minutes or so he was ready to be objective, to admit that the English couple had no axe to grind, that their observations were honest in intention at least. If he was thought to be as bad as Helen, that must be the impression he had given. And yet he had chosen this vacation to make things easier, had been desperately concerned that first day in case Helen should insist on moving on. He ought to be delighted that she was quite liking the place, that she had now picked up this wild goose chase fantasy about little people to keep her engrossed.

This thought recalled to him the dinner table that second day and swamped him in a new surge of rage. It had been bad enough

94

that there had been the humiliation in the bed. Then, unguarded and confused by finding he had woken her, he had been so unutterably stupid as to tell her what he had thought he had seen. She had told him not to be a silly fool, and to come to bed. He had woken with the apprehension that she would bring it up again, but she had not. Nothing had been said all day, and he had thought she had forgotten the whole thing. And then at dinner . . . He had seen trouble coming when she had asked Morwitz all sorts of damnfool questions about Germany, and he had dodged them and made matters worse by obviously enjoying a discussion with Waring himself. She had tried to come into that one, and Waring had done his best to stay polite while keeping her out. And then the waiting for the momentary lull, and that blaring voice: "You'll never believe what Waring thought he saw last night!"

Anger subsided into sick disgust. There was a bed of roses, but they were in poor shape, the bushes weak and spindly, leaves cankered, flowers small and few in number. Whiffs of a feeble scent came up from them. The soil was probably wrong, he thought, and they had been neglected for years. A bit of tidying up made no difference when things had been let go drift for a long time.

He thought, Is that what life offers me—to tag along after the whims of someone I despise? To accept the kicks, grin at the humiliations, and smile nicely when she decides she's put me through the hoop enough for the time being and marital harmony is now on the agenda? The most monstrous thing of all was that this morning he had known she was trying. That had been nothing to do with the fighting and the acting. In the middle of that crazy argument about the footprint and fossils—Eohippus and the coelacanth and Leakey—there had been a glimpse of her as lonely and wistful. As human. And he had responded with sarcasm and bitterness.

But what other response was possible? It was not just the memory of what the past had been like, but the absolute certainty that the future would be no different. It was like analyzing the results of group surveys. To start with, while you were learning, there was a degree of unpredictability. The more surveys you had to work on, the more the unpredictability ironed out. In the end you had a line on a graph and you knew that any points falling outside it were minor aberrations which could not affect the overall picture. It worked that way with people. The mystery unraveled and eventually you saw clearly. You might love what you saw, or hate it, or be indifferent to it. What you knew was that you weren't going to change it, and neither was anybody else.

The sky was full of separate rounded clouds, some white, some gray, some brushed with black. Since he had come out, the sun had been traversing a line of them, brightening occasionally to a pale disk and subsiding again to a golden milky glow. Now it emerged, coursing a gulf of blue, and everything in the garden was sharp-edged with brilliance.

The last line of the conversation came back to him. "It's rough on Cherry." He realized he had not wanted to remember that, nor to consider its implications. It did not really matter if he was blamed for the war, or whether or not they were right in blaming him. The only ones that really mattered in a war were the noncombatants. The noncombatant. With that in mind, there was no case for self-righteousness or self-justification.

Cherry did not come down until after eleven. Waring asked her if she had slept badly, but she shook her head.

"I stayed awake last night reading a book, and I picked it up again when I realized I'd slept through breakfast."

"Must be some book. What is it?"

"One of those paperbacks I bought on the boat. It's a French classic. Someone called De Laclos I'd never heard of before."

"I know it. Well written and corrupt."

Helen came into the drawing room. She said, "Hi, honey. So you made it at last. Who's that Dad's calling corrupt."

Cherry smiled. "Just a book I'm reading."

She turned to Waring with smiling belligerence. "So you think people are corrupted by books now?"

"No," he said, "I called it corrupt, not corrupting."

He had made a conscious effort to speak mildly. She stared at him for a moment and then, dismissing that subject, said, "You want to know what we found in the tower?"

She was talking to Cherry, but Waring realized he was expected to stay in the conversation, if only as a sleeping partner. Cherry made a suitable response, explaining that she had not heard anything, and Helen told her—about the footprint Daniel had found, the hole, and the trip the four of them had made down inside the tower.

Cherry said politely, "Sounds like it might have been fun. Did Mat go with you?"

"And Daniel and Stefan."

"You should have called me."

She spoke with a mild interest which might or might not be real. Sometimes, watching her and her calmness, almost serenity, Waring asked himself what he was worrying about. It had not touched her. She was strong enough in herself not to be affected by the wild animals her mother and father turned into from time to time. He had a spell of thinking this now, and it ended the way it always did. He was back in that hot August morning, picking up the telephone and hearing the awkward, aggrieved, whining voice on the line. "This is Leroy Biggin of Camp Ashmole. I'm afraid I have to tell you something rather unpleasant, Mr. Selkirk." He jerked his mind away from that, and gave his attention to what Helen was saying.

" . . . something down there. Just one thing you can explain away, but when you take all of them together, you have to admit there's something that needs investigating."

She looked challengingly at Waring. He said, "I guess you're right. Were you thinking of going down again after lunch?" He smiled at Cherry. "What do you say—we might join in?"

Helen said impatiently, "There's no point in that. We've seen all there is to see. If there's anything there, they would hear us coming down the stairs. There are all sorts of holes something could bolt into. The walls are six feet thick in places and probably honeycombed with little tunnels."

"What do you plan to do, then?"

"Things have been disappearing—from the kitchen and the storeroom in the basement. More than Bridget thought. It seems Mrs. Malone has been missing things as well, and didn't say anything about it. There are always fewer potatoes in the sacks than there should be, and there was a sack of flour she thought the rats had been at, but there's no sign of rats. She put poison down, and nothing happened. The bait wasn't taken up."

She was in full flood and excited by it all. Her face was flushed, and her voice got louder as she spoke. She said, "We're going to put a watch on tonight to see what happens."

Cherry said, "The same ones who had a look down in the tower?"

"And anyone else who's interested."

"I think I'll join you," Cherry said.

She was smiling. Waring said, "I'll help swell the number, too."

"Well," Helen said, "that's fine. Makes it quite a party."

She also was smiling. Waring looked into her face, and looked away. Where were the loneliness and wistfulness, the humanity, now? She was openly gloating at having him back in line, the running dog brought to heel. The dots were back on the graph line.

They talked it over after dinner. The longer this went on, and the more seriously it was taken, the more convinced Waring was that it was a hoax, inspired by the talk of the little people, which was in turn started off by Helen's reference to his own experience. That experience, he was now persuaded, had been a hallucination. It was not the first in his life. As a boy of sixteen he had stayed in a strange house, and there had been talk of ghosts, and he had retired late to a small room on an attic floor. Then, too, he had awoken in the night. It was an old wooden house, and he had lain there, hearing the timbers creak above and below and around him. And on the wall opposite his bed he had become aware of a glow, a twisting and melding of light that waxed and waned, shifting, writhing slowly, seeming to come out of the wall and sink back in. His glasses had been beside his bed, but he had not put them on. In the ordinary life of the day the need to see clearly, without limitation or distortion, was urgent, but over and above the basic fear of the glow was a sharper, more desperate fear of seeing its true shape. And the fear that, whatever it was, it might become aware of him, as he was of it. The conscious nightmare had gone on for an immeasurable time, until at last he had fallen terrified into sleep.

He had never spoken of the experience. For a few hours the next morning he had been sure that it had been a contact with the supernatural, and he was glad that night to be back in his own room at home. The feeling faded gradually over days and weeks. It must have been a month later that he looked at it hard. Moonlight, he thought, cast on the wall through the window. The waxing and waning, the writhing? Clouds, and a screen of leafy branches tossed to and fro by the wind. But he could not remember if there had been a wind or a moon or whether the trees outside had been tall enough to shade the attic window. Nor did he want to remember. It had been an illusion; that was enough. It could not have been anything else.

The mind played tricks; no one knew that better than he did. You got them, consistently and predictably, in fevers or by the use of drugs or through alcohol. And, rarely and without warning, they happened apparently spontaneously to well, undrugged, nonalcoholic people. Which meant only that the causation was obscure and no one had done any work on it. It was difficult to see how anyone could—you needed a body of phenomena, a mass of data, before you could start drawing inferences.

He thought back to that moment in the night. Already, so soon, it was a memory of a memory. He could visualize himself standing by the window, but the rest was him recalling the event, the vision blurred and uncertain.

Contemplating the subsequent hoax, he was on firmer ground. The trickery of the conscious mind was well documented and of long and dishonorable history. One could analyze the incident, whittle out the improbabilities, and be left with a high probability of something like the truth. And Helen, he was forced to admit, had turned the key in the lock. It all stemmed from the footprint, and the position of the footprint was vital. No one would have spotted it out there by the foot of the tower without Daniel taking them and rubbing their noses in it. Mat had picked that up, and someone had defended Daniel. Who? He thought back and got it. Bridget! If he had been faking, she argued, he would have left the mark for someone else to find, and would have placed it nearer the house.

Waring thought about that. The counter from Mat—that it would have involved the danger of being spotted—had been feeble; there was little chance of that if it were done in the dawn hours. But there were more cogent arguments. One was that it was necessary to be quite sure that the impression *was* seen, and even if it were left right outside the back door, it was quite possible that they would miss it or fail to identify it. You could go on for days renewing it and not be sure of success. The other was that the footprint needed to be near the hole in the tower wall, where the stone had been carefully rubbed, the earth scuffed, a piece of thread ingeniously caught in a crack. From which point you went, naturally enough, to an exploration of the inside of the tower, and finding a candy wrapper and a stub of candle.

Daniel then, primarily, but not Daniel alone. Mat? He was the one who had been sure the candle had not been there a week earlier. Waring dismissed that. He was not the man for it, and it had been he who had accused Daniel of faking. Whereas Bridget had, fairly plausibly, defended him. Waring gave a small inward sigh of satisfaction. It fitted well enough.

She was a capable young woman and an enterprising one. She had taken on the running of this place as a guest house, and she was putting her back into it. But it must be hard going, and she was making no fortune from it. On the other hand, if a story were to get out into the newspapers and television—a story about little people living in a ruined tower in a wild part of Ireland . . . There would be no empty rooms, and she would be turning them away in droves. If it were handled right, it could be kept going for several years, long enough for the place to become established in its own right, or for clever Miss Chauncey to unload it at a nice profit.

And Daniel was her fiancé. It made a pretty good arrangement.

They were talking, he realized, about this business of keeping a watch. They were taking it with varying kinds of seriousness—Stefan earnest, Helen euphoric, Mat with a dogged melancholy. Credit that, too, to clever Miss Chauncey. It was something to keep the guests interested in a place that had few resources by way of more normal forms of entertainment. Daniel, he noted, was playing it pretty cool, which also figured.

Things had been missing both from the kitchen and from the storerooms below. It was argued that there should therefore be two parties, one on each spot. They argued undecidedly about the best way of splitting up for that.

Bridget said, "Please yourselves." She smiled. "I'm going to bed. I don't think there's anything to see, and I shall be too tired to wait up, anyway."

Which was, Waring thought with admiration, exactly the right way to react. He wondered if some kind of stunt had been dreamed up to carry things a stage further. Daniel was going to be *en scène,* even if Bridget was conveniently out of the way. He decided there was more in it for him than just keeping Helen sweet; it was going to be amusing watching all this.

They sorted themselves out in due course. Helen and Mat plumped for a post in the kitchen, Stefan and Daniel for keeping watch down below. Cherry opted for the kitchen as well. Partly, he thought, because of Helen, but perhaps a little because of the Irishman. She had been staying close to him during the day, talking to him quite garrulously for her, and studying him with what Waring judged to be interest. He was not at all unhappy about that. Mat was handsome enough, but pretty obviously both shy and slow with members of the opposite sex.

Hanni, like Bridget, said she would go to bed. She did not seem at all sure as to what was happening. Stefan explained to her in German, but she still looked lost. Waring himself said he would join the party belowstairs. That, he guessed, was where things were likely to happen.

They agreed there was no point in starting the watch until their normal bedtime. Until then they passed the time talking and drinking. Going downstairs, Waring realized that he had had just about two drinks more than he regarded as suitable for an evening. He was aware of being elated, and found his arm describing a wider than usual arc in grasping the doorknob. They had left the three in the kitchen settled in chairs, with no lights but the smaller of the two available flashlights. Daniel had the other one. Which, Waring noted with satisfaction, gave him a commanding position.

The house, like the tower, had been built on rock. Ribs and outcrops were in evidence, as also were signs of the castle which had been here before it. The cellar floors were paved with flagstones, some three feet by two, and the walls were a mixture of large cut stones and brick. The area taken up was smaller than the ground floor, but like it bisected by a central corridor. On one side, access to the chambers was by means of low but wide stone arches; there were a couple of similar arches on the other side, but for the rest the rooms had brick walls and stout wooden doors. Most of them lacked separate lighting, but there were three light bulbs altogether in the corridor, one in the middle and one at either end.

Daniel said, "Better check first to make sure it's all clear."

Waring nodded. Nothing up my sleeves before the rabbit comes out of the hat. He and Stefan followed Daniel as he walked to the far end flashing the torch into the entrances. Helen had spoken of the amount of junk in the basement of the tower. There was a hell of a lot here, too. Refuse, Waring knew, was disposed of by being carted out into the bog—there was a man who came once a month from the village to dig a new hole for it—and it was understandable that one thought twice before trying to get rid of anything bigger than an empty can that way. Even so, it was staggering how much had accumulated.

Apart from the rubbish, there were a couple of small rooms with wine racks, mostly empty he was grieved to see, and the storerooms. These, as was reasonable, were near the stairs, though the archway at the foot of the stairs gave onto a chamber packed with broken and discarded furniture. The storerooms had lights, which Daniel switched on.

"Seems O.K.," he said. "We could take a room each. Not much point in our sticking together in one spot."

Not, Waring agreed silently, if you are going to have room to maneuver. He nodded.

"Which one are you taking?"

Daniel shrugged. "It doesn't matter. But if I'm having the torch I suppose I'd better be nearest the stairs. We aren't going to be as lucky as the ones up above as far as seating goes. I suppose we could bring chairs down, if you think it worthwhile."

"There are sacks," Stefan said, "and boxes." He pointed to the room next to Daniel's. "This will do me."

"Then I'll go opposite," Waring said. It offered a good vantage point. He found a wooden crate which was suitable for sitting on and dusted it off. "We all ready for action?"

Daniel said, "I'll snap the lights off as soon as you're comfortable. O.K.? Right, then."

There was darkness except for the darting beam of the flashlight as Daniel found his own perch; then that, too, went, and the blackness was absolute. So was the silence. The other men were only a few yards away from him, but he could hear nothing of them or anything else. The dankness of the air was in his nostrils and seemed to lie on his tongue. It would be difficult to keep food from spoiling down here once it was opened.

Someone—Stefan, he thought—coughed once, and the quietness flowed in on the sound like a river. There was no particular point in striving to keep senses alert—with so complete an absence of stimuli, any tiny disturbance would rivet the attention. It was an opportunity for reverie, for pondering fundamentals, like Helen and himself and the messes, joint and several, they had made of

103

their lives. The hell with that, he thought. The subject had taken up too much of his time and energy, and to no good purpose. Think of something good. Think of Cherry.

He was pretty sure she liked the Irishman. It could be that he would be very good for her. She was pretty, intelligent in her quiet, blessedly undemonstrative fashion. She was young, of course, but . . . He side-stepped a thought and reflected instead how good she was with kids—that week Hetty had brought her brood to stay, Cherry had kept them happy and pretty well under control. They had obviously loved her.

Could things still happen in that simple, rewarding storybook way? Mat, although he had not spoken of it, was presumably a Catholic, but Waring had no great objection to that. Everybody chose some kind of myth to live by, and that one had the merit of being well rooted and for the most part positive in its attitudes to life. Cherry could accept it; he was confident of that. And settle here in Ireland? Well, there was not much wrong with that, either. She would be free of Helen once she had a husband. My God, he thought, so could I be! What was there to keep him, once the hostage had been set free? He should be able to get a job on this side, in England if not in Ireland itself. Near enough to see her from time to time, and for the rest to live peacefully and alone . . .

The sound jarred him out of that dream. He felt his head jerk around, his body tense. It was a small sound, unidentifiable. Mechanical? Something being dragged—shifted? He wondered if the others had heard it. Then he realized he had been treating it as genuine. Probably Daniel had caused it. It came from a different direction, from the end wall, but that didn't mean anything. He could easily have taken his shoes off and sneaked across there in his stocking feet. He was the one with the flashlight. On the other hand, there was nothing to stop Stefan or himself from moving fast and getting to the light switch. No, wait, he thought. Let the program get under way.

There were other sounds, louder and more purposeful. Stefan

must have heard them as well. The little men shifting furniture? And a whispering, too small and sibilant to be comprehensible, but without doubt meant to be communication. Waring's skin prickled with a sudden cold fear. But that was nonsense. Anyone could fake sounds nowadays. You plant a battery tape recorder in among the junk, fiddle with the speed control . . . As fear subsided, irritation took its place. Did he have to be so goddam elaborate? And what kind of fools did he think Stefan and Waring were to stay rooted in the dark while this racket went on a few yards away? Abruptly Waring got to his feet.

Light came before he could do more than that. The shifting oval projected from the flashlight swung fast along the wall, exposing old brick, a broken wooden rack, the heap of junk by the wall. And they were there—against all reason and logic, but there. Two of them, reacting fast as the beam revealed them, darting into the shadows of the tunnel which had been made through the rubbish, gone almost as soon as glimpsed, but the images in that instant seared on the mind beyond any possibility of doubt. This was no trick of light or fatigue, but grotesque reality. He heard Stefan cry out something, but in his shock and bemusement failed to take it in.

Daniel switched on the light. He said, "A bit of bad luck there. I should have let them get further into the open, but when you moved, Waring, I thought it would alert them."

Waring said, "I'm sorry."

"Not important. At least we've seen them. Three of us. Whatever they are."

He said, still numb, "Then what I saw in the moonlight . . ."

"I should think so. Except it looked feminine to you, while those two—well, that was male dress they were wearing."

"So you think . . .?"

Stefan interrupted. "Look."

His voice was thick. Turning to him first, Waring saw his jowling face tensed in concentration and perhaps in awe. He followed Stefan's look.

She stood in the far corner, pressed hard against the angle of the walls.

As they advanced on her, Waring was expecting her to cry out or try to dart away. But she stayed there, silent, motionless, her little eyes staring up into their giants' faces.

IX

BRIDGET TOOK A BOOK to bed with her but after a page—the lines blurring into one another, followed by the sudden small shock of realizing that she had no idea who the character Joe was nor what had made him angry—she replaced the marker, put the book down, and snapped off the light. She snuggled down into her sheets, warm and luxuriously tired. The thought of Daniel and the guests on watch down below was a refinement of her present well-being. She was a little surprised that Daniel should have got himself mixed up in this, since he must be pretty tired as well, but relieved in that it meant she could get off to sleep without an argument or a foray in lechery. She decided she would not have him called in the morning. He could sleep on. Which would mean, unfortunately, that he would not be the least bit tired *tomorrow* night. Ah well, she thought with a small sigh of exhaustion, sufficient unto the day. Let tomorrow night take care of itself.

She was pleased and relieved that they had got on so well after their separation. Not the bed part—she found it difficult to imagine that going wrong—but there had been the awkward, inescapable fact of Daniel's disapproval of the entire thing, of which she not only had the memory of the hot words and cold feelings back in February, but the continuing awareness of it as a shadow over their correspondence and his occasional telephone calls. To some extent, her own stubbornness and determination had surprised her. She had been expecting him to arrive with a degree of truculence. She had also, she was now willing to admit, cultivated Mat as relief. And insurance? No, surely she could never have had that seriously in mind. He was pleasant enough, but there were too many things against it, and a yawning absence of the important thing that should be for it. Poor Mat, she thought.

And she had, she was forced to accept, almost certainly hurt him. These lapses into melancholy, into surliness even, had come with Daniel's arrival, as had the drinking. She remembered and was rather ashamed of her brisk offer of Contac and codeine for his mythical cold. Of course, she had never hinted for a moment that there was anything wrong in her relationship with Daniel. He had known she was engaged from the time they first met, and so only had himself to blame for any subsequent involvement. She looked at that honestly, and found she was not being entirely fair. She had just possibly been ever so slightly amiable beyond the line of duty and mere acquaintanceship. But I liked him, she thought, and still do. It was all very difficult. Perhaps he would simplify things by falling in love with the pretty little American. She hoped so.

Drifting fast toward sleep now, her thoughts went back to Daniel. It was lovely having him here, even though tiring. But something had changed, or at least swum up into recognition. Having rejected his lead in one important thing, she no longer took it for granted in anything. She loved him—she was quite sure of that—but her eyes were wider open. She had not, of course, been serious in her veiled threat that morning about carrying the place on after the end of the season. But certainly she was not prepared to be taken for granted.

And he, bless him, appeared to accept that. He really was, she thought contentedly, something of a honey, and a honey, praise the Lord, that could be handled. Sleep claimed her on this self-satisfied and self-congratulatory note.

She was so deeply asleep that the light did not wake her; she was only roused by the hand on her shoulder shaking her gently but with the clear intention of bringing her back to consciousness. She opened an eye, which ached in protest, and saw Daniel standing over her. At that moment she loathed him. She rolled over, away from him, burrowing down.

"Go away. Please go away."

"No," he said. "Wake up, darling. It's important."

"Not to me."

"But I tell you it is."

She realized furiously that she was awake. She sat up abruptly and stared at him, blinking her eyes. The light still hurt, but he swam into focus.

She said, "Now listen to me. I *told* you I had to have a night's rest. I meant it, too. You are not getting in this bed under any circumstances, and if you carry on with these apelike pranks, that's going to become permanent. Now you can run along back to your own room ... "

Daniel said, "You look delicious."

Belatedly she scooped the edge of the sheet up to her neck. "I don't feel delicious. I feel absolutely bloody livid. If you had any consideration for me at all, you would realize ... "

"I'm not trying to make you. That's important, too, but it can wait. We've caught one of them."

"One of what?"

"The little people."

Bridget drew a deep breath. "My God. There's some excuse for honest lust, but to wake me up in the middle of the night for a practical joke beats everything." She stared at him. "You must be mad. Or drunk?"

"There were three of them," he said. "They came through the heap of rubbish down in the cellar. There's a hole in the wall that leads into the tower. They must have been using this tunnel for some time, keeping stuff in front of the opening so that it wasn't spotted. Two of them got back before we could get hold of them, but the third was either too far out, or ran the wrong way when the alarm was raised. We captured her. She's quite docile."

"She?" He had the look on his face she associated with important and difficult cases in law, a brooding absorption. It had been one of the things that had first attracted her. With alarm she understood that he was being quite serious, that he was talking about something that had actually happened here in the house.

She said quietly, "How big is she?"

"A foot high, or a little under."

"And what . . .? I mean, what does she look like?"

"Come and see." He went to the door and brought her housecoat. "You'd better put this on."

She heard Helen's laugh as they went into the library, and wondered suspiciously if her first guess could have been right and this be part of some lunatic and unpardonable joke. They were standing by the billiard table with their backs to her, and she could not see what they were looking at until Mat glanced around and moved silently to one side. Then she saw. The doll-like figure was standing almost in the center of the expanse of green baize, head bowed, minuscule hands limp by her sides. Ludicrously, she was dressed in green, too, in the old country dress of Irish girls. She wore nothing over her glossy jet-black hair, and no stockings. On her feet she had sandals, a green cloth band across the instep and what looked like miniaturized rope soles. Not rope, but string. Of course.

"Have you got anything out of her yet?" Daniel asked.

Stefan said, "Nothing. She will not speak."

"Maybe she can't," Helen said. "She may be dumb."

"They were whispering in the tunnel," Daniel said. "But I couldn't make out whether it was in English or not."

Cherry said quietly, "She's probably dumb with fright, poor thing. She's trembling."

Bridget saw there was indeed a slight tremor from time to time in the hunched shoulders. Her hair was done in two braids, one lying behind and the other twisted and falling over her breast. She wondered how old she was, or if that word had any meaning. The face did not have the roundness of a child's but the lines rather of a young and almost beautiful woman. Not quite beautiful—the nose was not perfectly straight, and something else was wrong. After a moment she got it. The head was tiny, but not quite proportionately so with the body. It should have been smaller. A young woman, just past girlhood? But her breasts were scarcely in evidence. Her figure at least had a child's purity of line.

Helen said, "Why should she speak English, anyway? She probably talks Gaelic. Mat, you try saying something to her. Ask her something."

He looked as though he would refuse, until Cherry reinforced the request. Then he spoke a few words rapidly in Erse. The little figure gave no sign of having understood, or even of hearing him.

Helen asked, "What was all that?"

He said awkwardly, "Nothing, really. Asking her did she know what I was saying."

Daniel leaned forward and rapped the table hard with his knuckles. She started, and her head jerked up to look in that direction, but then dropped again. He said, "Not deaf, at any rate."

Bridget asked, "The others—were they the same?"

"No. Little men. But wearing green." There was a baffled note in his voice. "That's why one has the feeling it's all been put on for our benefit. But that's nonsense, of course. Freaks from a circus? But she's a miniature rather than a dwarf."

Waring said, "Not a dwarf. She's too well proportioned. You get pygmies from time to time, but nothing so small as that, I would say. Who was that at the court of Charles the Second? They called him Tom Thumb, something like that, and he fought duels. But he was two or three feet high, as I remember."

Daniel said, "And three of them."

With a touch of irascibility Helen said, "Isn't it obvious? You have all the legends of the little people. Not just here, but all over —all over Europe, certainly. So the legends were true, and here's the living proof of it. My God, you want to disbelieve what your own eyes show you!"

Waring said, "Not disbelieve, evaluate. O.K., so she's here and she's real. I accept that. But why, and how? Little people? It's like having a banshee stretched out on the dissecting table."

Her voice had been loud, and his had risen in replying. It would be like the rumbling thunder of the gods, Bridget thought, tossing their insults at each other like thunderbolts across the vastness of heaven. She was wondering how to say this tactfully, when Cherry reached forward. She stretched her arms across the green baize and took the small figure gently between her hands. There was a tensing, but Cherry ignored that and lifted the little one and brought her to her. She made a crook of her arm, and settled her in it as best she could. The eyes had closed, Bridget saw; the trembling was more violent.

Waring said, quietly now, "I should watch her."

"Why?"

"She might bite or scratch."

"I don't think so."

"Watch it all the same."

With a finger of her free hand, Cherry touched her, making small stroking movements. The figure did not resist, but did not relax, either. She was trembling still. Cherry said, "Isn't she lovely?" Her voice was soft. "Don't be frightened, lovely. No one's going to hurt you. You're going to be O.K."

The others watched for a moment or two in silence. Stefan broke it. As though talking to himself, his voice not much above a whisper, he said, "*Sie ist so schön. Wie eine Puppe.*"

Bridget saw the small eyes open, staring. They were brown, with long black lashes. Then the little one spoke. Her voice was shrill and tiny. Bridget could not catch a single word, but with a shock of surprise she realized she knew what language it was. She turned to Stefan. "That's . . ."

His astonishment mirrored and magnified her own. He said slowly, "I know. She is speaking German."

Daniel asked impatiently, "What did she say?"

"I could not tell. It is so fast and high-pitched, and also garbled." She was watching him from Cherry's arms, the alertness fading back to dull resignation. Stefan bent toward her and spoke again in German. Bridget gathered he was asking her to speak slowly. The brightness flowed back again.

A conversation developed. Helen started to ask something, but Stefan hushed her with a wave of his hand. Communication was uncertain—each had to repeat things, sometimes more than once—but it was communication. All the time Cherry cradled her in her arms. When after some minutes there was a break, Daniel said, "Can you tell us anything now?"

Stefan shook his head. "Not much. They live in the tower. They have always lived in the tower, she says. There are seven of them, five boys and two girls."

"Seven!" Waring said. "But where do they come from? Their ancestors, I mean?"

Cherry said, "What's her name?"

Stefan said slowly, *"Wie heissen Sie, kleines Fraülein?"*

They could all hear the silvery disyllable: "Greta."

"That's cute," Cherry said.

"Also German," Waring said. "It makes no kind of sense, does it? Ask her, Stefan. Ask her about her folks—how they got here. You know."

He put a question and was answered. He said to Waring, "She only knows they have always been in the tower. There are no parents. Only what she calls the Big One—*der Grosse.*"

"In the tower," Daniel said. "But perhaps not down in the cellars all the time. In the upper room? Did they live in the little houses?"

Stefan spoke to her and said, "Yes. They lived higher up, in the houses."

"And der Grosse . . ." Daniel said.

Bridget said, "Cousin Seamus! He wasn't just playing dolls' houses. There were live dolls, too."

Waring said, "So why did they leave the houses?"

"It's understandable," Daniel said. "I suppose he was a kind of combination of father and god as far as they were concerned. He had that heart attack up there. They saw him crawl away and down the stairs. It must have been a pretty severe shock. They might not want to stay in the place where the god had been stricken. So they went down to hide in the darkness."

Helen said, "Or went back to the place they'd come from in the first place. There must have been a race of them living down there. Ask her again about parents. Maybe she didn't understand you."

Stefan spoke to her and listened carefully to the answer. He said, "No, no parents. And they have always been there, in the room with the houses. None of them can remember a time before that."

"So he captured them as babies," Helen said. "And maybe not here. Some other part of Ireland."

Mat said, "And taught them to speak German?"

"In Germany, then. He found them on a trip sometime. In the Schwarzwald, maybe. They have some pretty wild parts in Germany, too."

"He was Irish," Mat said. "He never said anything about Germany to my father, and he had a Cork accent a yard thick. Why should he teach them German and not English?"

"Just a minute," Daniel said. "Ask her about that. Ask her if der Grosse spoke to them in their own tongue."

They saw her shake her small head, the braid of black hair moving on the immature breast. She answered, and Stefan said, "No. He spoke to them in a strange language. He did not say much—only gave commands. In English, I think. One thing she remembers he said sounds like 'Do this.' "

"Which leaves us," Waring said, "exactly where we started. They've always lived in the room with the houses, they had no mothers or fathers, and they speak German."

Helen said, "She may be lying."

"Why should she?" Cherry asked.

"To put us off the scent. If there's a tribe of them down there, or out in the bog or somewhere."

"The houses are there," Daniel said. "The room had a lock on the door and barred windows. We know who der Grosse was. And she speaks German. The only thing she could be lying about is this business of parents. I don't see why she should."

There was a silence while they thought about this. Helen broke it. "Anyway, what are we going to do about her?"

It was a fairly obvious question. Bridget realized she did not have a clue about answering it. The event was staggering enough in itself, without speculating on possible results.

Waring said, "Your fortune's made, Bridget."

"My fortune?"

"Headlines in the newspapers. TV news cameras blocking up your driveway. The Little People of Killabeg."

She said sharply, "Oh, no!"

"No?"

Her reaction had been instinctive. Loving privacy and seeking self-effacement as she did, the thought of being exposed to the shriveling heat of publicity was an agony tasted in advance. But not only for herself. She thought of this little creature—of the others in the tower—and agonized for them. She was not a doll, she saw, but human—miniature but no less sensitive for being tiny. She said, "We have to avoid that. Think what would happen to them."

Waring gave her a lopsided smile. "Before we caught Greta here, I thought that was the setup you and Daniel were working. My apologies."

Daniel said, "One will have to be realistic about it." She glanced up at him, and he went on quickly: "I'm not talking about making fortunes out of the newspapers. But the news is going to get out, isn't it?"

"Need it?"

"Seamus kept the secret for years, and so well that it died with him. But that was one man, with a locked room to which he had the key. Are you going to put them back in the tower room and keep them locked up?"

"Well, of course not."

"Then there's Mrs. Malone and Mary. And tradesmen. Not to mention your guests. Even if everyone here keeps quiet about it, what about the next batch? And will everyone keep quiet? It's a great deal to ask."

Waring said, "Surely, the point is to get them into the right hands."

"What hands would those be?"

"Scientists. People who would know how to look after them and treat them properly."

Helen said, "People like you, you mean." The hostility was back in her voice, edged with naked contempt. "So they can be put in cages, or little study rooms with one-way mirrors. Weigh their food, weigh their excrement and urine. See how they copulate —how many times and who with. X rays and blood tests and urine tests and lumbar punctures. And then their minds have to be tested. Stanford-Binet and Rorschach and look at the pretty EEG lines. And good old Waring Selkirk pulling the strings and collecting material for that really big thesis, the one that's going to get his name in colored lights on the wall of the Smithsonian."

He looked at her with dislike, but said mildly, "Not quite as bad as that. And do you think the alternative's any better? What else are they likely to be but freaks in a circus?"

Mat said, "I don't think you've either of you got it right."

He was staring at the little one, and at Cherry who still held her in her arms. He had been drinking again. His face was flushed and set in hard angry lines. He spoke with a bitter emphasis that secured their attention. Even Greta was looking at him. Bridget wondered what thoughts could be passing behind those small delicate features. The realization of her humanity was fading; she was so tiny and puppetlike.

Mat went on: "They're not animals. They've got immortal souls the same as we have. And that means they've got rights and privileges. They can vote, once they've registered, for Fine Gael or Fianna Fail. Or they can go to England and vote Labour or Tory. Or to Germany and have a wider choice. But they won't need the vote, because they've got something to sell."

Bridget said, "To sell?"

He gave her a quick look. "Ah, not the pot of gold, that turns to dead leaves the moment you've let go of them. They have themselves to sell. And all they need is a good lawyer and a business manager and a press agent, and they're in business with a million the first year and a steady income after. The money will pour in. From the television, the magazine articles, the advertising . . . A hundred guineas for opening a bazaar, a thousand for their names and pictures on a breakfast cereal packet. And after that they can teach themselves to play the guitar and form a pop group. The Stunted Seven. They would only be small guitars, you understand, but they have the wonderful amplifiers to make up the noise. And if that's too difficult, they can hire someone else to play the music, and just open and close their mouths at the right time. Did I say a million? I meant a million each." He said to Bridget in contemptuous appeal, "You wouldn't stand between them and a future like that, would you now?"

Cherry said, "What would they want with a million dollars?"

"Pounds, not dollars." But his voice softened, Bridget noted. He went on more quietly. "They're human," he said. "With souls. And so to be tempted. What would she like, do you think? Diamond rings on her fingers, and platinum bells on her toes? Or the biggest doll's house in the world, with three hundred rooms and wall to wall carpeting—priceless Persian rugs cut up small—in each, and little golden baths and golden lavatories, and golden television sets, built to order with a five-inch screen? And perhaps a miniature Rolls to drive around the two-feet-wide roadways she has laid on her estate? Or maybe she would like to collect paintings? You can spend a lot of money on a Nicholas Hilliard. Or she could buy a Rubens and cover the ballroom ceiling with it."

Daniel said, "Point taken. We're going to have to give this some thought, aren't we? But I suggest not now." He looked at his watch, yawning. "One o'clock. We'll think more clearly after a few hours' rest."

Waring said, "And Greta? What do we do with her?"

Cherry said warmly, "She can come to bed with me. I'll look after her."

"And the moment you're asleep," Daniel said, "she slips out from the sheets, slides down the leg of the bed, and is off back to her brothers and sisters. We wouldn't catch her so easily a second time."

"Lock her up somewhere," Helen said.

Bridget said, "Do we have any right to do that?"

"That's something else that needs talking about," Daniel said, "and the same considerations apply." He was talking in his thin Gray's Inn voice. "Meanwhile, on the assumption that we had any right to catch her in the first place, I propose we also assume that we can keep her in comfortable duress until the morning." He looked at Bridget. "Any ideas about that?"

She said unwillingly, "There's the big clothes hamper; it has a strap that can be fastened around it."

"That will do. We can put something soft in for a bed, and to be doubly sure, I would suggest locking it up somewhere. The downstairs cloakroom, for instance. That should be enough to frustrate any rescue operation her friends decide to go in for."

Daniel looked around the group, receiving some signs of assent, none of objection. He said to Stefan, "The important thing is: Can you explain to her what we're doing? That she's not going to be hurt, now or ever, and this is only a short-term measure. Can you get that over?"

Stefan nodded. "I think so."

Cherry said quickly, "And ask her if she wants anything to eat and drink. She may be thirsty."

Stefan spoke to her slowly, repeating phrases and sentences where she showed signs of not understanding. At the end she stared at him blankly, but the small head nodded. She spoke a few words.

"Not hungry, she says, but she would like some water."

Bridget said, "I'll get that."

Daniel left her at her bedroom door with just one long kiss, which had the effect of increasing her drowsiness. She let her housecoat fall by the side of the bed, kicked off slippers, and climbed back between the sheets. They were cool and secure. Her thoughts were affectionately of Daniel, the Lilliputian captive only touched on as a marginal wonder, a problem for which the new day and Daniel would provide a solution. She slept almost at once, and heavily.

Mrs. Malone was by her bed with a cup of tea when she woke

118

again. Her gaze darted to her clock. Quarter past seven—she had slept through the alarm. She struggled up and pushed the sheets back.

"You're tired enough," Mrs. Malone said. "You're needing the rest after all you've been doing. Now don't fuss, for there's no cause for it. The breakfast's cooking."

Yes, Bridget thought grimly, and the bacon's burning, and the eggs are leathering, and the coffee doesn't bear thinking of. She gave her sweetest smile.

"You're a wonder, Mrs. Malone. You look after me too well."

"Ah, it's a pleasure," she said, blushing. She turned at the door. "Now don't you be rushing yourself."

She was down in ten minutes, dressed but, she was sure, disheveled—there had only been time to run a comb quickly through her hair. At a time like this, she thought, it only needed Daniel to wave a special license under her nose and she would drop the whole thing and run. But it was not as bad as she had feared. Mary was attending to the cooking, dreamily but quite effectively, the only casualty a pound of cindered sausages. The coffee had not been made, but the water was boiling. Bridget slapped grains into the Cona and started it off. Within quarter of an hour it was a normal morning, things were running on schedule, and she was able to think more than a few seconds ahead. At that point she remembered the prisoner with a pang of guilt. She should have been all right in the basket, but still . . . She looked for the cloakroom key, which she had left the night before on a high shelf by the door. It was not there.

Mary, when asked, denied all knowledge of it. Bridget thought of calling Mrs. Malone from the dining room, but decided it was quicker to go along to the cloakroom and see. Was it possible that the others had come back, found the key, rescued her? It seemed downright improbable, but that was a poor argument in the circumstances.

The cloakroom door was partly open, and as she approached it she saw that the hamper was open, too, its lid thrown back. She rushed in and saw that there had been no rescue or escape.

Greta sat in the hamper on the cushion she had put for her. Bridget realized at the same moment that someone else was in the cloakroom. She looked and saw Stefan.

She said in relief, "So you took the key?"

He nodded, and she saw his face. The expression was one of tormented wretchedness. She said, "What is it? What's wrong?"

He tried to say something, but the words did not come. She thought there were tears standing in his eyes. He was staring at Greta, who stared solemnly, blankly, back.

"To do with her?" Bridget asked. He nodded again. "Then what?"

She waited for him to answer, beginning to be afraid, hearing the water in the pipes, the distant rumble of the generator. He did, at last, in a flat strained voice.

"It is that I know."

"Know what?"

"I know now who the parents were."

X

EVEN BEFORE Mat saw the footprint, he believed. He trailed along with the others to the tower in a daze, almost reluctant to see what was there and yet longing for the visual proof. What outraged him most was Daniel's casualness, the detached way he pointed it out, and the clipped English voice: "The only thing that makes any sense is that some one of us came out early and made it." It was this which made him, a little later, turn the accusation against Daniel himself. Then Stefan found the hole, and he forced himself to repeat the jibe. But he knew this was real and true, and the most important thing that had ever happened in his life.

Every year, as a boy, he had gone to his grandfather and grandmother in the summer. There had been the long, slow train journey, stopping at stations that were no more than two platforms, with a few houses huddled together beyond, cows tossing their heads against the flies, the green of pasture and the long purple potato fields under a sky that was gray or blue but either way hot and still. And being met by the pony and trap and his grandfather giving the whip a flourish, and letting him give Betsy the lumps of sugar he had hoarded, and laughing and telling him not too much or her teeth would be falling out. And the leisurely clopping ride up to the farmhouse, and his grandmother coming out in her blue flowered apron with the cats after her.

He had loved them both consciously, aware even then of his mother's apartness from all humanity, his father's surface cheerfulness and absorption in work. This, he knew, was the way people ought to live together, happy and at ease. Even after the shock of the first time his grandfather came back drunk from a race meeting, he believed that. The belief did not change, except to become desperate.

The pattern grew familiar, as did his own reaction. It was one of mixed anticipation and fearful apprehension. From the moment his grandfather went off in the morning, all was different. She would do a special treat for his dinner, brew the chicory-flavored coffee whose smell deliciously permeated the house, make the flat cakes of soda bread which he loved. And more important than all that was the closeness, the extra squeezes and caresses, the realization that for these few hours it was he who met her deep need for love, and fulfilled it. At ordinary times she was fond and kind, but now, abandoned, smarting where she had thought herself accustomed to the hurt, she turned hungrily to him, and he glowed with that.

The best of it was after tea when, with the day's work done and his grandfather's supper keeping in the oven, she told him the tales. Sometimes they were of relations or people she had known —stories strange and fanciful and often grim—like the one about the aunt who married into the Protestants and when she died, the boys twice dug up her body at night, leaving it once at the crossroads and once on her husband's doorstep—but more often they were of wonders, of the leprechaun and the banshee and the little folk of Connemara, which had been her home as a girl. Those were his favorites. He would listen, sitting on the rug with his head against her knee, with the hiss of the kettle on the hob, and the cats asleep, seeking the glow of the fire even in the summer. So, listening, he would grow sleepy himself, too sleepy sometimes to have his cocoa and biscuits. Afterwards he would lie in his bed, watching the bats dart across the gray-blue square of sky, and think of all the things she had told him.

And later still, there would be his grandfather's drunken return, smashing the reverie, perhaps waking him from sleep. The voice shouting or singing in the distance, the heavy floundering footsteps, the banging and crashing, and his grandmother's voice protesting, and the roared answers—ugly in volume, ugly in tone, ugly above all, in that every other word almost was that word which he knew to be terrible, the currency of the Dublin slums. And his grandmother's voice, louder and shriller: "Think of the boy up there, if you won't think of me! Will you talk filth like that when a boy can hear it?"

And the savage answer, laced with the same obscenity, that he would talk the way he liked under his own roof, that the boy was his own grandson and would need to grow up to be a man who would have something to say for himself and not be put under by women. To and fro, surge and countersurge, till he wanted to scream, half from a need to stop them, half to join in. And finally the lumbering progress to bed, and her sobs, and so something like peace.

The next day there would be a silence, almost as bad, short replies to anything he said, his grandmother withdrawn and brooding, his grandfather making awkward gestures at reconciliation and then stomping out to the animals. And the day after, all would be well. Until it happened again, in two weeks' time or three.

But even after he grew to dread all this, he still looked forward to race days, to the smell of coffee, the day at once peaceful and exciting, to the stories about the little people. The serenity was there, and the magic, even though the night must come to sully them. This went on from year to year until, between one visit and the next, his grandmother died, and he dreamed that night of her body being dug up by the little people and set up in the doorway of the farmhouse when his grandfather was coming back drunk from the races. He screamed then and woke himself with screaming.

He did not think of the stories after that. They ended badly, as most things did. He drank heavily as a young man, in sessions lasting for days on end, and then by an act of will stopped completely. Until these last few days. Now there was this revelation, a triumph of good over evil, calm day over monstrous night. He was dazed by it, and exalted.

Mat took no more whisky that day. He followed the lead of the others, going with Daniel and Stefan and Helen down into the cellars of the tower, but with no expectation that they would find anything. That was not the way it would happen. What the next manifestation would be, or when it would come, he had no idea; but he knew that the only thing to do was wait. He was jolted out of this mood for a moment by the sight of the stub of candle, but that passed. Wait, he thought, and whatever was to happen would happen. He felt happy most of the time, only occasionally tired and sad. The suggestion of the night watch and his own participation in it he accepted with the same lack of interest. The English, he thought with unsmiling mirth, and the Americans and the Germans. They would chase ghosts with butterfly nets.

When there was the commotion from belowstairs, he assumed that was what was happening—that, with their nerves frayed by the dark and the quiet, they were flailing the empty air. Even when they came up, Waring shouting in his excitement, he was sure that it was a flurry about nothing. He was sure until he saw her, so small in the clutch of Daniel's hands. She was the way his grandmother had described her, even to wearing the green. It was not possible—it could not be possible—that she had been caught like a rat in a corner. And yet there was nothing else that was possible, nothing at all.

What followed was worse. He stood by in silence while they talked and argued. Helen asked him to try talking to the little one in Gaelic, and he stared at her with mute contempt until Cherry asked him, too. She made no answer. Why should she? There was only a dull surprise when Stefan spoke in German, and the small lips moved, replying. They went on putting questions to her, debating it among themselves, and it was all meaningless. He even contributed a couple of remarks himself, hearing the emptiness of his own voice. The world had jarred out of gear again, and nothing mattered.

And yet, he found, something did. His anger stirred with the talk of newspapers, rose higher with the interchange between the Selkirks. Scientists, he thought with horror and disgust, and circuses. He told himself to stay silent, to ignore them all, but in the end burst out. He parodied their arguments and mocked them, and beneath the mocking there was the bitterness of knowing that he meant what he said. All the time the little one rested in Cherry's arms watching. It was not until Cherry said, "She can come to bed with me," that he was shamed.

He left to go upstairs while they were still talking about how to keep her trapped for the night. He poured himself a strong whisky in his bedroom, drank it, and poured another. The anodyne did not fail him. Closing his mind on what had happened, he began to get undressed.

Cherry came in with no more than a flick of her fingers on the door. He was naked apart from his underpants. He felt the shame of being a comic sight and of her seeing him and the shame of her embarrassment. But she was not embarrassed. She stood in front of him with the faint, pure smile on her face, so innocent that embarrassment could not touch her. She said, "I wanted to be with you again."

He wondered how he could ever have thought of her as dull. It was just that she was simple and direct, a contrast to Bridget's smiling complexity. He felt a great need to protect and comfort her. But he could not stay awake in the chair another night. He said, "I'm tired, Cherry."

She nodded, accepting that. "Can I just kiss you good night?"

She did not wait for his answer, but came to him and, standing on tiptoe, pressed herself to him and tightened her arms around him, her fingers hard against his naked back. Her face turned up to him was open and trustful, like a child's.

He kissed her lips very quickly, just brushing them with his own. Then he took her arms, gently broke her hold, and stood back.

"Good night," he said. "Sleep well."

XI

STEFAN WAS SURPRISED that in the discussion about the little
Greta, and the fact that she spoke German, no reference was
made to the journal. The degree of probability that a connection
existed between the two things must be very high. He realized,
though, that Bridget might be the only one who knew of the
journal—there had been no one else present during their conversation about it—and certainly for her it had held no importance.
Nor had he discussed it with her since. He did not raise the subject
while the others were arguing, from a reticence that he only partly
understood. It concerned his feeling for the man who had written
those lines, lonely and far from home. It might be necessary
eventually to talk about him, but he wished to avoid it as long as
possible. There was also the second volume which he had found
that morning in the tower and not yet read. He was all the more
eager to read it now, but he wanted time to reflect on it in private.

Hanni was asleep and did not wake when he went up. He
undressed quickly and got into bed. Settling himself, he drew the
book toward him, and opened it.

It has rained almost continuously for three days, not heavily but
with a thin monotony that tires the soul. I have not been out
today at all. After lunch I sat a long time in front of the fire which
Mrs. Rafferty had banked up high. The coals glowed bright yellow,
almost white, and I remembered being a child and believing that
a salamander lived there in that scorching splendor, and wonder-

ing what it must be like for him when the fire burned low, and if he died shivering among the dull embers, the cooling ash.

I awoke in the night again with the sharp pain in my stomach. I took one of the pills, and it eased after a time, but it was long before I got to sleep. One cannot help wondering that it may be serious. This doctor here is plainly a fool, his usefulness to his patients on a level with water from Lourdes and the priest's prayers. It would be sensible to go to someone in Dublin or, better, Berlin. From that point of view sensible, from another an unwarranted risk.

It would have been V.'s birthday tomorrow. I do not think about it, but I remember it all the same. She had such great courage.

The rain comes down still. The damp cold of this country is in my bones. I am a salamander; the world grows chill about me.

Stefan read on. There were dates of days and months, but no years; nevertheless, this volume plainly was written after the other one. The note of melancholy was more marked and more frequently evident. He wrote less about his work and its importance in keeping him active and contented. It was almost as though he were disillusioned with it. Near the middle there was a passage concerning it.

News on the radio that Frausig has been given the Nobel. Little chubby Frausig, with his passion for white sausages. He can eat them by the hundred thousand now if he wishes. He and I were the only ones in our year that Merkenheimer accepted as showing promise—and my promise was the greater. I chose the wrong field. Nonetheless, under other circumstances—if it had been possible to publish—my fame would have been enormous. I do not believe that I mind not having that. What I mind is that the work itself, from so incredible an achievement, must dwindle into ordinary observation, such as any third-rate naturalist could carry out. I go on, keeping the record. After I am dead, perhaps . . . There will be objections, inevitably, but the greatness of the accomplishment must be recognized. The papers are there. One day they may be published.

* * *

Stefan was very tired. The spiky letters danced in front of his eyes. He read more quickly, taking in the gist only. He could read it more carefully another time. But there was a page near the end which, having glanced over, he paused and reread.

F. and G. both running temperatures this morning, F. flushed and lethargic, G. complaining of throat, both refusing food. It seems almost certain that they have the feverish cold which I contracted last week from S. Without his trips we would be free of this nuisance, isolated as we are. This is the first time any of them have taken the germ. I suppose I could have prevented it by wearing a mask. As it is, it is of minor interest. It will be interesting to see if it develops in the others also.

Stefan closed the book. F. and G. Greta? "I could have prevented it by wearing a mask." So S.—who would be Seamus—was not in contact with them, whoever they were. The little people in the tower room, speaking German. Der Grosse, she had said— only one. But the one might have changed. After the chronicler died and Seamus had the place to himself, he must have gone up to the tower room and taken over. But not, any longer, in a spirit of scientific experiment. Instead they became toys to a middle-aged man, a means, along with whisky, of passing the lonely years.

And the papers—the record of the great accomplishment—what had he done with them? Burned them, most likely. They would mean nothing to him.

Stefan awoke in the early morning. The light was still on, the journal lying where he had dropped it on his bed. He had vague memories of a troubled night and bad dreams. Hanni was sleeping peacefully. He looked at his watch and saw that it was not long after six o'clock. Time enough to sleep again himself.

The papers, he thought. Seamus might have burned them, but he had not burned the journals, or at least not all of them. In which case . . . It came back sharply to him—there had been papers in the file from which he had taken that second volume. And there had been other boxes amid the rubbish whose contents might have been similar. It would be worth while to investigate them.

The idea, once it had developed, engrossed him. He lay thinking for a few minutes more and then got out of bed. He went about the business of dressing quietly so as not to wake Hanni. And ineptly—his fingers fumbled badly at buttons. The growing excitement in his mind was a sensation he had forgotten—he had not known it since those days just before the war when the world and life had seemed to be opening out to him. That had been an illusion; the aspirations probably had been too large and too vague. This was local and actual, a single problem with the possibility of one solution.

There was no one about in the house, no sound except for the heartbeat of the generator. Stefan went downstairs to the kitchen and found the key to the tower. It was big and heavy, with the satisfying massiveness of keys to locked doors in fairy tales. He weighed it in his hand for a moment. What story? He found he could only think of Bluebeard, which was absurd. He closed the kitchen door behind him, grinning. Then he remembered he would need the flashlight and went back to get it.

He had a moment of wondering whether he might surprise others of the little people by going down into the tower at this unexpected hour, but the sound of his footsteps echoing from the walls of the staircase demonstrated the unlikelihood of that; if they were about, they would have plenty of time to scatter. All the same, he flashed the beam of the torch ahead as he reached the foot of the stairs. There was nothing there but bare dripping walls and the glimpse through the doorway of the pile of junk. The light hit on the cheval mirror and briefly dazzled.

His first objective was the file from which he had taken the book. The papers were jumbled, some typewritten, some covered in the spiky handwriting which by now he knew so well. He picked one out. It was headed "Report on Trials of Stearan with Seven Dogs." He glanced over it, but could not understand it on that quick impression. It was, in any case, difficult to read, holding the flashlight. The sensible thing to do, he decided, was to take them all upstairs where they could be read more easily and at leisure. It was bulky, but he was able to get it under his arm to carry it.

There was still no evidence of activity in the house. He took the file through to the library, tipped the papers out on the table, and drew up a chair. Some that should have been clipped together had come apart. He started trying to sort them out in some sort of order, but while doing so his eye caught a sentence on a page, and he paused to take in its context. He read the whole of that page and after putting it down stared for some time into the distance. His chair faced the window, and he looked across the lawn to the walled garden, the wilderness of the bog, the far hills. The air was clear and still, a bright morning of a bright day.

After that he read the papers methodically, but in no order. Some he could only partly understand, others hardly at all, and they were not in chronological sequence, which confused things further. But a picture emerged. He had been right to think the solution might lie here. When he had read the last of the papers, he dropped his head in his hands. He thought of Old Lonely, white and clear in the days of his boyhood, mantled with the purity of snow, limned against blue heaven.

He thought, too, of the last meeting, across a bare table in a cell, an armed American guard a few feet away staring contemptuously at the wall above their heads. It was not the change in his physical appearance that had been so shocking, though he had aged so much. What he could hardly bear to look at was the helplessness, the pitiable weakness in one whose strength had been beyond doubt or question. He put his hand out, and his father took it, and there were tears in the blue eyes, and the fingers trembled as they pressed on his.

His father said, "I am sorry."

The silence filled the cell, pressing on both of them. He tried to find words, but what words were there? At last he managed to say, "Is there anything I can do, Father?"

"No."

"Any message to give anyone?"

The white head shook in negation. There was a scar on the side of his face which was new. It was known that prisoners were roughly handled, occasionally tortured. Some of the American guards were Jews. He felt on his mind the unbearable weight of not being able to be angry, the sickness of acquiescence.

His father said, "There is no one to give a message to now. No one except you." He paused, searching, as helpless to express himself, Stefan saw, as he had been. "And I can think of no message that I can give you."

"It doesn't matter."

The silence came down again. Desperately Stefan wished that the American would do something—shift his feet—to make some noise, but he continued to gaze blankly ahead.

His father said, "One thing. My property is confiscated—you know that. Nothing comes to you. But what your mother left is separate and cannot be touched. Lasser will be writing to you about it."

"I do not want it."

The words came out more roughly than he had intended. His father's grasp on his hand weakened as he spoke. After a moment his father said, "It is not mine and never has been. It came from her father, your grandfather. He was a surgeon, as you know. It is clean money. She would wish you to have it."

Stefan said, "I'm sorry."

"There is nothing to be sorry for." The blue eyes searched his, and he forced himself to look back. "One thing."

"Yes?"

"You might be allowed to come again. Do not. Go away if you can. Do not read newspapers or listen to the radio. In a few weeks it will have happened, but for us it happens now, when you go out through that door. This is easier for me, also. Do you understand?"

There, for a moment or two, the strength came back, and all this, which he had accepted, turned into a grotesque nightmare, something which even the dreamer knew to be a dream. But as he

131

nodded, his father's shoulders dropped, the hands, after one last pressure, released their hold. The nightmare, he knew again, was real.

He had done, he remembered, as his father had asked, wandering for nearly two months through the stinking ruins of the Reich. During that time he had met Hanni, who had lived out the war, untouched but insecure, in the care of her Aryan uncle and aunt. They were married before the snows covered the rubble. The previous day he had told her of his father, and she had nodded her dark unknown head in acceptance.

He said, "This does not shock you?"

"I recognized the name. I thought it might be—some relation."

"And you can bear it? Bear taking on that name yourself?"

She paused before she said, "You could have seen him again. Why didn't you?"

"He told me not to."

"That was for your sake. You should have gone."

With some bitterness he said, "It was his order. I always obeyed his orders. I was a good son, a German son."

"You should have gone to him."

He stared at her in wonder. "How can you be so saintlike?"

She shook her head. "It is not that."

But it had been that, he knew, which pardoned him, brought him from despair and gave him a justification for going on living. In her, and her alone, lay his absolution. And yet this knowledge faded. At first he sought its renewal. On the anniversary of their wedding he asked her, "Do you hate me for what I am?" And she smiled at him and said, "I love you always," and he believed her and was comforted. But it did not become easier to believe as the years went by. This, he understood, was not because of any change in her, but through the sapping and deepening of his own despair. It was impossible that she should love him, tainted as he was, and so each avowal was a lie, made for the sake of keeping the peace, or even out of fear. There had been times when he had imputed still worse motives to her, the thought of which in more balanced moments sickened him. It was easier to stop demanding assurances, easier to live with unspoken rejection.

Stefan stared across the wilderness to the sun-sharpened hills. Had it all the time been simple goodness, simple love, and was there enough in that to forgive and absorb all evil?

Bridget said, "Tell me, then. Whatever it is you know."

He had taken the other key from the kitchen, had gone to the cloakroom and opened up the hamper. She had been lying on the cushions, but awake, and when she stared up at him he had wondered how he could have missed seeing it before. Small though the features were, the lines were unmistakable. He had no idea how long he had stayed there before Bridget came through the door. All that time there was silence between him and his small accuser.

He said, "I found papers in the tower. Among them the certificate of a marriage in 1929 between Veronica Chauncey of Cork and Karl Hofricht of Munich."

She screwed her face up, remembering something from long ago.

"Veronica . . . Grandfather spoke of her, but not much. She was his sister. She sided with Sean when the two brothers fell out. And she married a German? Do you mean, the diary . . .? The man who wrote it was my uncle?"

"It seems so."

"But she was never here?"

"She died in Germany before the war. Of cancer, I think."

She looked down again at Greta. "You said you knew about the little people—about their parentage. You're not trying to tell me that this is something to do with them?"

"Not with them. Him only. Except that perhaps her death led him to the study of growth, both normal and abnormal. And affected him, perhaps, in other ways."

"Study? You mean, he was some kind of a scientist? But how could he work here?"

"He did his main work in Germany."

"And had you heard of him? Was he famous?"

He shook his head. "Not famous."

"Growth," she said. There was a pause. "And lack of growth? He was responsible for the little people?"

"Yes. He was responsible."

"But how could he be? No one would be allowed to conduct experiments of that sort on human beings. Not in any civilized country."

He said heavily, "I agree. But she is older than you think, you see. She was born in 1944. In Germany."

"The Nazis . . ."

"He had a laboratory hidden away in the Schwarzwald. It was a nursing home before he took over. He did not go short of funds, I think. They supported him well from Berlin. Cytology is a wide field and can be made to cover many things. Aging, for example. There is a report which bears that out. Perhaps someone thought he could make Hitler live as long as the thousand-year Reich. Perhaps he thought so himself, or was merely willing to deceive them while he continued with the work which interested him. At any rate, they sent him money and equipment. And everything he needed to further his experiments."

"Everything? Prisoners?"

"Guinea pigs and white rats. And cats and dogs. And Jews. Or Jewesses."

Bridget was silent, staring at Greta. After a few moments he went on, speaking precisely, unemotionally, because no other way of saying it was possible. "There was a screening point at a camp. Females coming through were tested for pregnancy. If they were pregnant and at the right stage, they were sent to him. It had to be an early stage, you understand. It seems there was a—a critical moment."

"What did he do?" She added quickly, "Unless it's too awful."

Stefan said, "There are many papers, and a lot of them I do not understand. He had discovered a drug, which he called Stearan. You remember thalidomide? There was a critical moment for

134

that, also. Past a certain stage of pregnancy it did not harm the child in the womb. But when it was taken at a certain point of development, some limbs did not grow, so that the child might be born without fingers, or without arms or legs. A local effect, one might say. This other was general. Growth is controlled by the pituitary gland, or by a part of it—the anterior lobe. It was this that the drug affected, and permanently. The two-month fetus is a fish, or a reptile, but the four-month fetus is almost a miniature of humanity. For more than half its time in the womb it hardly changes except to grow. These did not grow. At birth they were only a few inches in length, less than five hundred grams in weight."

Bridget said, "But why?"

The simplicity of the question was self-defeating. Saying it would not help her to understand, but all the same he tried.

"Because to be a scientist is to be human still, and the grown man keeps much of the child. There is curiosity in all children, an urge to pointless destructiveness in many. Most people do not hold strong standards; they do as their society advises them or conditions them. The society in which he lived . . ."

He had been speaking as flatly as possible, but he found that suddenly he could not go on. He put his hands up to his face, feeling the tears well against his fingers. A blind man lives in a world of horrors, smiles and is happy, not knowing what surrounds him, what he accepts. Given sight, he does not want to live. But finds strength to do so, because the horrors are done with and dead and were not, he tells himself, his fault. Also, there are good things in the world, which he now sees more clearly—things of light and hope. And yet, long years after, the horrors are alive still, and part of him.

Bridget said, "What happened to the mothers?"

"After giving birth they were returned to the camps."

"To be murdered?"

"What else?"

"And he kept the children. I still don't understand how they came here."

"He left Germany in '44 and went to Spain. They gave him papers and, one supposes, money. This could not have been Hitler, but presumably one of the others who could conceive of the war being lost and had made his own plans to survive defeat. Perhaps Bormann? For him, as for all men, old age lay ahead, and the man who could produce a race of little people might also create Methuselahs. From Spain he must have come here. They were neutral countries, both Catholic, and there was commerce between them."

"With the children?"

"One supposes so. It would not be difficult. They could be drugged for the journey, and they would not weigh much or take up much space. Once here, he would make contact with his cousin by marriage, your relation also. One does not know what story he told him, but one knows he had money. So Seamus bought this house, and the two of them lived here, and in the end died here."

"How pointless."

"Is that not true of most lives? Probably Hofricht felt that somewhere at some time he would be able to relaunch his experiments. In some dictator country in South America, perhaps, where an aging tyrant could be persuaded into giving his support. Perhaps he made overtures, discreetly, and was rebuffed. Meanwhile, he could observe the little people. A coda to the great work, but part of it."

"The great work!" Bridget said.

"Yes."

He felt a great weariness. The problem had been solved, a dreadful line drawn under the answer. He wanted to sleep and, thinking of that, thought of Hanni upstairs in bed. With a fresh wave of sickness he realized that telling the story now had been nothing. He must still tell it to her.

XII

H E HAD A DREAM which was mostly to do with Helen, but all confused and mixed up. For one thing they were both in the Vermont house, which they bought the summer Cherry was three, but in the dream they were not married yet and her father was somewhere around, though the coronary had finished him before he saw his only granddaughter. It was Waring's own sensations, however, that were really weird, because in some way he had both his present feelings and knowledge about her, and the feelings and knowledge of their first dating days out in the Gulf. He was a divided man, loving and loathing at the same time, at grips with a divided woman. Finally she delivered to him the speech she had made the previous night over the little one, the diatribe about scientific method and his cheap, conniving ambition. That really set him going. They were alone in the dream, with no social considerations to worry about, and he weighed into her as he had been unable to do at the time. She bit back furiously, and he woke himself shouting.

From her bed Helen said, sleepily resentful, "If you're going to have nightmares, can't you keep them quiet, for God's sake? You must have one hell of a subconscious."

She awoke properly as he was getting dressed. "What's the hurry? It's early yet."

"I'm going down to see if Greta's still there and O.K."

"My God, I'd forgotten." She pushed the sheets back and got out of bed. "Wait for me."

The confusion of the dream lingered. The anger of the argument had died down, and the other memories were stronger. He could almost see through the distortions of the woman to the simple (so it had seemed) artlessness of the girl. That night with the moon and the stars and the camel bells when they had got away from the others for the first time. And she had talked about the stars and told him the trick she had picked up as a girl. You took three stars, fairly close together, forming a triangle. There should be one brighter than the other two and you visualized that as the nearest. Then, as you looked, they were no longer bright points against flatness but suddenly took wing and soared away into infinity—lamp beyond lamp, ranging back into the incredible dark. She had said shyly, apologetically almost, that she knew, of course, that the brightest star wasn't necessarily the nearest, but it was a way of making the trick work. And he had loved her for that and told her so and heard her quick indrawn breath above the wind's sighing in the palms and the faraway slap of the sea.

Waring looked away from her toward the window. "O.K. I'll wait."

They ran into Daniel on the stairs and found Stefan with Bridget in the cloakroom. He saw at once that Greta was still there, her little face surveying them all impassively. Stefan, on the other hand, was showing a lot of emotion. He excused himself almost right away, and when he had gone, Bridget told them the story she had heard from him. They listened in silence.

When she had finished, Daniel said, "Do you think it's true?"

"He said the papers are in the library."

"I think we ought to go and have a look at them."

"They'll be in German."

"We can probably get something out of them, even so. And we might as well take her out of here."

Bridget put her arms down to the little one. She neither responded nor cowered away, but allowed herself to be picked up and carried. Bridget talked to her, telling her not to worry, that no one was going to hurt her. The tiny features did not change.

They found the papers scattered over the table in the library. Waring, like Bridget, had a smattering of German. The papers were there, and they related to experiments involving pregnant women.

Daniel asked, "What do you make of them?"

"Not much. But they're here, aren't they, and there's no reason why Stefan should make up that kind of story. I guess we have to take it as true."

Bridget said, "I don't understand how the news didn't come out after the war. Wouldn't there be captured documents and all that?"

Daniel said, "Not necessarily. Stefan seems to think it was a private show, probably dependent for funds on one man and answerable only to him. Not all the relevant documents were captured, by a long chalk. On the other hand, Hofricht's continuing to hide out here makes it look as though something did turn up, or he was afraid it might. But it need not have been anything more than evidence that experiments were conducted on human beings. It's quite likely that he kept the results even from his man in Berlin. After all, the funds were intended for work on preventing aging, not creating a race of pixies."

Helen was unusually subdued, Waring thought. She had made no comment on the story Bridget told them and said hardly a word since. He wondered whether the inhumanity or the humanity had shocked her more—the experiments, or the realization that there was no magic here after all. He was conscious of a conflict in himself, between horror and relief. But the horror was long past and done with. There were limits to human sympathy, none to the delight of discovery. He felt a fierce cupidity, which he knew he must dissemble. He had to have this one, and the others, to study. He said, "We're still going to have to decide what to do about them."

Daniel said, "Which brings us back to our discussion last night, or early this morning. We now know that Mat's fine peroration was exactly and legally right. She is human, and has human rights.

As far as nationality goes, I can visualize something of a three-way tussle between Germany, Eire, and the State of Israel; but on the personal level she has to be accepted as independent."

Waring said, "O.K. But discovery confers responsibility, wouldn't you say? We can't throw her into the sea of twentieth-century life without making sure she can swim, or at any rate has some kind of life belt." Cherry came in from the corridor, and he smiled at her and got her faint but transforming smile in reply. "What I mean is, no newspaper reporters, no television camera-men. Not yet awhile. We agreed on that?"

Daniel said, "I imagine we are agreed. Though there may be difficulties." He glanced at Bridget. "Mrs. Malone, for instance, and Mary."

"I think they'll be all right," Bridget said.

She had put Greta on the table, from where she watched them with the same impassiveness. Cherry now came toward her. She put her hands down, and the small arms opened to her.

Bridget said, "She remembers you!"

It was a contact, Waring thought, which gave them all a glow of pleasure. Cherry swung the little one up into her embrace. She said, "The first thing is to give her some food. All she would have last night was water. What's the German for breakfast, Pop?"

"*Frühstück.*"

Cherry bent her head down, smiling. "*Frühstück,* Greta. O.K.?"

The dark head nodded. It was a contact, all right. But there was, Waring noted, no answering smile.

Among the equipment Bridget had laid in for possible use by guests was a baby's feeder chair which could be hooked on the back of an ordinary one. It was still grotesquely large for Greta, but the addition of a couple of books provided her with a seat within the seat which she could manage. Her approach to food and drink was entirely reasonable and natural; she tasted or sipped and then ate and drank, for her size, heartily. Bridget put before her scrambled eggs and chopped kidneys on a coffee

140

saucer, with a silver spoon from the saltcellar. She coped almost as well with the matter of drinking coffee from a liqueur glass. It was proportionately larger and she handled it more clumsily, drawing her hand back from the heat at first and returning to it as soon as Bridget had put in more cold milk.

Mrs. Malone watched this with wide eyes and a right hand automatically going through the motions of crossing herself. Bridget had told her and Mary of what had happened, and of the need for present secrecy. The girl had apparently accepted the situation more easily than the woman, perhaps because she understood it less. For her the story of experiments and strange births meant nothing beside the living presence of legend. But Mrs. Malone, Waring noted, was acutely, tremblingly afraid.

Although he watched all this with interest, Waring was inwardly preoccupied with more important things. He had no doubts as to the rightness of the course of action he proposed—it was nonsense to think of letting them out of the care of properly qualified observers, for years if ever—but he was fully aware of the delicacy that would be needed in bringing it about. His first notion, of a transatlantic telephone call to Dean Matthews, he had reluctantly rejected. A transatlantic call, outside Dublin at any rate, was something that would attract interest and probably eavesdropping, and Matthews was a man who would need to have it all spelled out to him, probably three or four times, before he would initiate any kind of action. Moreover, if he did fly over, his intervention, as an American, along with the fact that Waring had betrayed the secret, would have the worst kind of effect. Short of a kidnaping operation, which would neither be practical nor do any good, they would only be ensuring the reverse of his intentions.

He brooded over the problem throughout breakfast, regretting his own lack of imagination. The situation needed a creative approach, which he realized he lacked. And yet it was unthinkable that the little people should be handed over either to an Irish government official or the exploitation of the publicity machines, which were, he clearly saw, the only alternatives to his own project. A way out had to be found and in that instant, despairing of finding one, he thought of McGredy, and wondered how he could have missed seeing it before.

That was it, exactly. No American takeover bogey: Sir Patrick McGredy lived in London, was a Fellow of the Royal Society and talked of as the next President. He was world-famous as a biologist, a TV-screen and after-dinner speaker, and a man of integrity. Although not a pacifist, he had refused to be nominated for the Nobel prize on the grounds that the award derived originally from a tainted source. No man should take profit, even at several removes, from instruments of death and destruction. Moreover, as a graduate of Trinity and a supporter in his salad days of the Revolution, he was even more revered in Ireland than in England. There could be no objection to McGredy, and there was bound to be tolerance over admitting him to the secret.

He was also a subtle and imaginative man. Waring had met him on two or three occasions, and they had got on well. He would not need to be bludgeoned into dropping things and coming over; a hint would be enough. It was, Waring admitted, a further consideration that he was entirely scrupulous about the rights of prior discoverers and colleagues. He would respect Waring's special position. It would be cooperation, not domination.

McGredy was the answer. The only remaining question was when and how he was to be brought in. He had to get hold of the telephone when he was sure of not being overheard. That might not be easy, and going into the village to telephone would attract attention. The main consideration was to avoid rushing things. It would keep for a day or two if necessary.

He looked up to see Mat coming into the dining room; he also saw, and was pleased by, the affectionate exchange of glances between Cherry and him. The Morwitzes followed close on his heels. Stefan was holding his wife's arm, and she looked pale and uncertain. Hanni stopped at the sight of Greta, and he stopped with her. Her mouth quivered, and the tears came, a silent flooding from her eyes which she made no attempt to disguise or wipe away. They stood like that for a moment or two, with no one willing or able to say anything. Then Stefan put his arm around her shoulders and, turning, led her out.

Hanni stayed in her room that morning, but Stefan came down again, though he would not have anything to eat. He explained that his wife was not feeling well. He did not look well himself. One could understand that, Waring thought—German, and with a wife at least partly Jewish—but sympathy was subordinate to a more urgent consideration. They needed him to communicate properly with the little one. He put this to Daniel, who agreed. Daniel did the asking, allowing Waring to stay, as he wished, in the background. Stefan, drinking a black coffee, nodded his head with neither enthusiasm nor reluctance.

"I will talk to her for you."

They got him to repeat the assurances that she would be well cared for and in no danger. This Greta accepted with no change in her impasssiveness. The next part, Waring judged, was going to be the tricky one. Daniel proposed, and Stefan passed on the suggestion in German, that it would be a good idea for the rest of the little people to come out of hiding. She listened carefully and answered in shrill quicksilver tones. Stefan said, "She agrees. She will call them for you."

"And they will come out?"

He shrugged. "It seems so."

Daniel considered that. "I suppose we ought just to let her go and bring them, if we're to treat her as human and an equal."

Waring said quickly, "I'm not in favor of that. We don't know how they're likely to treat her, for one thing."

"In what way?"

"We know, or we're pretty sure, that the antecedents are human, but we know nothing about them as they are. She seems quite intelligent, but things like behavior patterns . . . We have absolutely no data on that. And remember they've not been raised as humans, but first as special laboratory animals, later as playthings. If she just goes back, they might harm her, in the way some animals do with one of their kind that's acquired an alien taint."

143

Cherry said, "Do you think they would harm her?"

"Surely she would know that," Mat said. "As you said, she's intelligent."

"*Seems* intelligent," Waring said. "And the position's an entirely new one for her. She's bound to be disorientated."

Helen said, "Let her go."

It was the old automatic opposition and defiance, but there was less heart in it. She was still depressed and quiet.

Daniel said, "I think Waring's right. We need to go carefully. Stefan, tell her we'll come down to the cellar with her. Can she call them from there?"

They spoke together again. Stefan said, "Not the cellar here. In the tower. They will come from there, she says."

"Fair enough," Daniel said. "We might as well go right away, if there's no objection. Are you carrying her, Cherry?"

Cherry nodded. Waring said, "Hold her tight, sweetheart, in case she gets frightened and jumps."

Cherry smiled. "She won't. *Nicht wahr,* Greta?"

The little face looked up at her, blank but incurious. Waring felt a sudden prickle of uncertainty, almost of apprehension. What he had said—about knowing so little of her, her mental processes and behavior—had been off the cuff, its simple object the frustration of the suggestion that she should be let go. But, of course, it was literally true. Humanity was not merely a genetic inheritance, but the product of mixing that with a culture built up over a hundred thousand generations. And a culture predicated on a certain minimum height. It was impossible to guess how important that one factor could be.

He adjusted his spectacles on his nose. Uncertainty, yes—that was reasonable. Apprehension was nonsense.

Bridget was busy seeing to things and Hanni was in her room. The rest of them trooped down the stairs in the tower, Daniel and Mat with the flashlights, Cherry carrying Greta and talking nonsense to her in a low voice. Waring wondered how she would call them and if they would really come. The previous night reality

144

had followed too close on cynical disbelief for there to be any build-up of excitement, but he felt it now, a tingle in the blood. Would they come? He wanted it too desperately to believe it.

Greta and Stefan spoke together again, and he said, "We need to go to the place that is flooded. They have hidden themselves beyond that."

Daniel said, "How do they get across? Swim? It's a couple of feet deep."

Stefan did not bother to pass on the query. They were almost there. The light flashed ahead, found the oily blackness of the water. In a moment they were by the doorway.

Daniel said, "All right, Cherry. Put her down."

"No!" Waring said. "She can call while you hold her."

Cherry, not answering, stooped, and he saw her set Greta gently down on the stone flags. Waring had an impulse to snatch her up, but there were others in the way. He tensed himself to plunge if the little one attempted flight.

But she moved, with a strange graceful deliberation, only to the top of the steps that led down to the water. Her head lifted, and she called out. The cellar's resonance deepened her voice, making it more articulate.

"*Komm! Ich bin hier. Greta.*"

Nothing happened. How could it? They would be fools to come, Waring thought. But she was still there. Then the ray of the flashlight moved farther out, and Helen beside him drew in breath.

Waring looked and saw it. A child's toy boat moving across the still waters, with doll-like figures bending to the oars.

XIII

IT WAS MORE RAFT than boat, Daniel saw—a flat piece of wood, roughly boat-shaped and about three feet in length, with crude gunwales nailed or glued in place along the edges. The oars were crude, too, one of them no more than a splinter of white wood from an orange box or the like. But his attention, after the first quick glance, was on the occupants rather than the vessel.

They were wearing green costumes, like Greta. These, in the artificial light, the spotlight surrounded by blackness, gave the scene a harsh Disney-like unreality—the cinema's ultimate 3-D achievement after all the fumblings with Cinemascope and Cinerama and the rest. Who in God's name could have dreamed up that one? Surely not the little people themselves, nor the scientific Hofricht. Seamus, then—a national dress for his puppets to wear. And it was not so unreasonable, he saw. They *were* puppets. Whatever one said about human ancestry and human rights, there was no way of taking seriously creatures bearing man's shape but only twelve inches high.

Man's, and woman's. There were six of them, as Greta had said, five male and another female. She sat surrounded by the little men—four rowing, the fifth handling what looked like a rudder at the stern—looking directly into the light that dazzled her. And, reflecting from her, dazzled the eye of the beholder.

She was a triumph of beauty in miniature. Greta had seemed pretty, the prettiness magnified by the scaling down which hid

146

minor imperfections, but this one was different altogether. To start with, she was a blonde, the hair that hung loose about her shoulders a rich, cornfield gold, thick and gleaming. Her eyes were dark—brown, he thought, though he could not be certain yet—large and well spaced under brows just a little darker than her hair; her face was comparatively broad, high cheekboned, the skin less pallid than Greta's, as though no amount of darkness and confinement could dim a refulgence stored from long centuries in the sun and the open. Jewish, he thought? The immediate reaction was of skepticism, but he had seen this kind of Jewish beauty before in refugees from the great snowy burning plains of Russia and Poland; though never such a beauty as this.

The boat reached the steps, grating against the stone, and Daniel stooped down, putting his hand out to her. She did not flinch or draw back, but lifted her arms. His hand embraced her waist, and she looked up fearlessly into darkness as he raised her. Through the dress his fingers felt the throbbing warmth of her body, the curves of hip and breast. He straightened up, holding her. They could look at each other now. She stared at him with no change of expression. Her mouth was wide, the lips red and slightly parted, showing even teeth. Parted, but not in a smile; it was a look of calm regard.

They had the open trust of puppies, not merely permitting themselves to be lifted and carried, but expecting it. The hesitancies were on the part of the others. Cherry scooped up one of the men, along with Greta, and Waring also picked one up. Mat, after a moment, followed suit. Helen and Stefan simply stared down at them, their expressions in the darkness and shifting torchlight impossible to read. Two small men remained standing on the steps. There was a cord attached to the stem of the boat, Daniel saw, and a nail low down in the doorway which had probably been used as a mooring post; but they had not bothered to secure it and the boat was starting to drift away. They were unconcerned about this. From skulking in the dark holes of cellars, sneaking out at night to steal food and other necessaries, they had apparently swung around to a complete unquestioning accept-

147

ance of the giants' world. It was an odd mental process, but their mental processes were bound to be odd.

Waring said to his wife, "Aren't you taking a passenger? They'll be a long time climbing up that staircase if we don't give them a little help."

She said, "I suppose so," and stooped to pick one up.

Waring looked at Stefan, who turned away. He shrugged and gathered the last himself. He said, "No point in hanging on down here now. Let's take them up where we can see them properly and talk to them."

He walked forward, one of the little men resting on the crook of each arm. Cherry giggled, and he stopped and looked back.

"Seven of them," she said. She began singing the Dwarfs' marching song from *Snow White*. "Heigh-ho, heigh-ho! It's off to work we go . . ."

Waring took it up with her. Their voices echoed and re-echoed as they went through the cell-like rooms and onto the staircase. It was not the resonance, Daniel thought, that gave the sound a sinister note, so much as the silence, except for footfalls, of the others—the utter silence of the little people. He was relieved when they had come through the door from the tower and closed it behind them. Daylight came through the fanlights over the doors and from the hall. It was not bright, but it was blessedly ordinary and natural.

The others headed for the library. Daniel stayed behind to push open the kitchen door and call to Bridget. She looked up across the big deal table, her hands and bare arms floured and a patch of flour on one cheek. She stared at the little creature in his arms.

"So they came . . ."

"Right away." Daniel creased his brow over the sudden improbability revealed. "Almost as though they were waiting for us."

"She's lovely," Bridget said. She shook her head, marveling. "No. Exquisite. I've never seen anything the word properly fitted before. And the others?"

"They've taken them into the library."

"Wait till I rinse my hands. I'll come with you. Mrs. Malone, the filling's ready. Put it in the pie and pop it in the oven, will you?"

Mrs. Malone was in the far corner of the room. She stood with her back to the end of the drainboard, pressing herself against it. Her face was white, and she was almost shaking with fear. Bridget, washing her hands under the running tap, said, "Now, there's nothing to be afraid of. I've told you, they're little people, but not the kind they tell stories of. More like those in a circus. Can you see to things for a few minutes?"

"Yes, ma'am." Her voice was choked.

Bridget said, "Pour yourself a dram of brandy if you're feeling nervous. The bottle's over there in the cupboard." She came to Daniel and touched the little one with her finger. "It's so hard to believe she's real, isn't it? And breathing." She slipped off her apron and hung it up behind the door. "I want to see the others."

They stood on the big table in the library. Among the people watching them there were signs of different emotions; a wave of reactions, from simple delight in the case of Cherry to Stefan's fascinated horror. These feelings showed themselves in various ways—nervous laughter or movement, Helen's voice booming, a twitch of hand or face. By contrast, the little people were completely calm, almost motionless. Their movements, when they made them, were quick enough, somehow fluid, but in between actions they were weirdly at rest. It was disconcerting. Daniel set the fair-haired beauty down with the others; she offered him one fathomless look and looked away.

He said to Stefan, "They don't seem to need reassuring, but perhaps you'd better do that. And you can find out their names at the same time." He hesitated. "I suppose you'd better tell them ours. We have to make some sort of personal contact."

And yet it was absurd. One called a cat by name, and these were bigger than cats, or at any rate stood higher, but a cat was not human in shape and wearing clothes, and a cat did not call you back.

149

Stefan said in a dry voice: "Must I?"

"You're the only one who can talk to them. Except Hanni, I suppose."

"I will do what I can."

Their voices all sounded the same. That was reasonable, Daniel supposed, since they operated in a fairly narrow band at a frequency unfamiliar to the human ear. There probably were distinctions, and one might eventually pick them up—those between the men and women, at least—but not yet. Their physical appearances were more distinguishable. One of the men stood an inch taller than his companions, and another was short and squat. The latter was called Berthold, the former Dietrich. The other three, of roughly the same height as the women, were Fritz, Christoph, and Adolf. Adolf was very thin, practically emaciated, while Fritz and Christoph could be recognized by their hair, Fritz's deeply black, Christoph's blond—a thinner, lighter color than the golden straw of the girl Daniel had carried. Her name was Emma. The remaining men had dark brown, undistinctive hair. None of them had a beard. It was possible that they had kept their faces shaved but more likely that they were hairless. All their skins were delicate, pale, apart from Emma's, and with the bloom of softness.

Daniel asked Stefan, "They understand that we will look after them? That there's nothing to be afraid of?"

"I have told them." He shrugged. "They do not seem to have any fear."

This was true and still surprising. Daniel tried to envisage himself in the charge of beings who stood higher than a house and found his imagination would not make the leap. What was really staggering was that things had gone so easily. One could not have guessed after capturing Greta that the others could so easily have been persuaded to come out of hiding, nor with such seeming nonchalance. He felt his mind prickle, remembering what he had said to Bridget in the kitchen. "Almost as though they were waiting for us."

Waring had picked up Emma. She lay in the grasp of his hand quite unperturbed, and he ran the fingers of his other hand over her.

"One would need to make proper tests," he said, "with instruments, but I have a suspicion that the pulse rate is higher, and perhaps also the body temperature. I had that feeling about Greta."

The sudden irritation he felt surprised Daniel. He found himself saying quite sharply, "I should put her down." Waring looked at him in mild inquiry but complied. A gloss, Daniel thought, was called for. He added, "There's bound to be a tendency to treat them as—well, as dolls. I think we ought to resist that."

Helen said, "He wasn't thinking of her as a doll. More as a subject for experiment." The flush of excitement had left her and her voice was dully resentful. "Don't think he's given up the idea of the great thesis on the little people. I know him."

Daniel said, "It was sensible to carry them up from the cellar, but I don't think carrying should become a habit."

"They have human rights," Mat said. His voice was melancholy and, even so early, barely perceptibly slurred. "The life stories in *Life,* with all the pictures, and a commentary by Patrick McGredy, telling how it happened." Daniel saw Waring's head jerk up as though startled. "Their own little TV program once a week—a discussion panel, maybe, and they could call it 'Think Small.' Not to mention the pops. With voices like theirs they'd leave the Chipmunks standing, and the Chipmunks can't do TV except as cartoons." He put on an elaborately vulgarized Irish accent: "It's a great future they have in front of them, it is, an' all, an' all." Speaking normally again, he bent down close to Emma's golden head and whispered, "Remember me when you come into your kingdom."

While Mat had been talking, Daniel had had time to think about his own reactions. The irritation with Waring—stemming from what? His mind supplied an answer, but it was so ludicrous that he could dismiss it with amusement. Jealousy? On account of a creature less than a foot high? He said, "Something else you had better ask them, Stefan. Greta's had breakfast, but the rest are probably hungry."

They ate as willingly as Greta had done, unconcerned about surveillance. They knelt beside the coffee saucers containing scrambled egg, taking it in turns, two at a time. Bridget had found another saltcellar spoon, and they seemed to grasp the point about lack of implements readily. Daniel wondered how they had managed before. With fingers, probably, but now they adopted this usage quite naturally. Mary, who had brought in the tray with the food, stared at them wide-eyed and bemused but without the terror Mrs. Malone had shown. She had a child's mind. These were the creatures of her fantasies come to life. She probably jumped the gulf toward acceptance more easily than any of them. Except, he thought, the little people themselves. They drank their coffee from the liqueur glasses with the ease and aplomb of old men drinking brandy after a good dinner.

Bridget could not stay, having the lunch to see to. The rest remained, fascinated by the little people, who were put down now from the table. They stayed in a group on the carpet, most of them standing but Emma and the short Berthold sitting, propped by one arm, with legs drawn up beneath them. Daniel and the others sat in chairs around them, and Stefan put questions for them and relayed the answers.

The picture did not, at the outset, greatly differ from that which they had got from Greta. One of the men—Fritz—had a vague memory of a time of long darkness, but otherwise they recalled only the tower room, living in the little houses, being visited by der Grosse. Waring asked them if there had not been two Big Ones, but drew blankness in reply. It had always been der Grosse, always until the time that he fell down making strange noises and crawled away from them, and they took the things they needed and went down into the cellars.

"Because they were frightened?" Daniel asked.

Stefan said, "I suppose so. They do not say that." He hesitated. "It is not easy to communicate with them, you understand. Not only because of their voices, or because their speech is garbled, but because I do not think terms always means the same to them as to us."

Waring said, "They would be bound to. It's a different universe they live in. But it must have taken guts to live down there in the dark."

"I agree," Daniel said. "What about rats?"

Cherry shuddered. "Rats!"

Stefan put a question to them. It met lack of comprehension at first, but understanding came as he explained it further. Fritz, who did more of the talking than the others, rattled off an answer. Stefan said, "Yes. They did not know the name, but there were rats. They killed them."

"God Almighty!" Waring said. The awe in his voice, Daniel thought, was well justified. "Size for size, that's something like tackling tigers. And in the dark. And with what kind of weapons? The missing penknife, maybe. Ask them what weapons they used, Stefan."

His question drew another blank. The reply he got when he put it another way semed to baffle him.

Waring said impatiently, "Well?"

"He says—whips."

"Whips? I don't get it."

Daniel saw that Fritz was observing the interchange and appeared to have grasped Waring's bewilderment. The little one's own face remained expressionless, but with a quick sure movement he put his hands inside his belt and stripped off the green shirt. Naked from the waist up, he offered his back to Waring's scrutiny. The whiteness was seamed with thin dark lines that crossed one another. Without the reference to whips, Daniel did not think he would have recognized the marks. As it was, the implications were plain, though still not making sense.

Waring said, "Rats don't . . ." Breaking off, he leaned forward to pick Fritz up. He looked closely at the bared back. "Scars," he said. "From whippings? But how? They whipped each other? Some kind of ceremony? Initiation, maybe?"

As though taking a cue from their leader, the rest of the little people were stripping off their upper clothing. Greta undid a fastener at the front of her dress and slipped first one shoulder out and then the other. All their backs carried the crosshatchings that they had seen on Fritz's. Only Emma, Daniel saw, did not join in this display, but stood, austere and beautiful, watching the others. Daniel heard a shocked exclamation from Cherry, something like a groan from Mat. They were all shocked, as he was himself.

"*Aber warum?*" Stefan whispered. "*Warum?*"

Waring put Fritz down with the rest. He chattered on in high, fast silvery tones, and Stefan listened. He put occasional questions, and waited for the answers. At last he turned from the little one, but did not look at anyone else. His gaze fixed on the window, he said, "It was a misunderstanding. They used the whips to harry the rats, but I still do not know how they killed them." He spoke like someone very tired or sick at heart. "When I was puzzled, he thought I did not know what the word meant, just as they do not know what some of my words mean. They have left the whips behind in the cellar. So they tried to explain by showing the marks on their backs."

Helen said, "But why? What are you trying to tell us? That they're a bunch of sadomasochists?"

Stefan said, "Sometimes he whipped them himself. More usually he compelled them to whip each other."

"He?" Helen said.

"Der Grosse."

"Seamus," Mat said quietly. "May his soul rot in hell forever."

"There were other—torments," Stefan said. His voice had a dreadful blankness. "I did not seek the details. But Fritz spoke of being squeezed in the hand, crushed to the point of unconsciousness."

Waring looked at the palm of his open hand, and from that to the black-haired Fritz who stared up at him from the carpet.

"And after that," he said, "they came into our hands quite willingly—with no signs of fear? How could they?"

Daniel said, "It amazes me, too. One can see why they ran as soon as they found a door open with no one to guard it, and why they hid in the dark. But surely after that they could never make willing contact with the human race again."

The human race, he thought. I am still making a distinction. But could any group of human beings have done that?

Cherry said, "It was because of Greta. She knew we were different, that we would not harm them."

Waring objected. "But she had had no chance to tell them."

"She called them," Cherry said. "That was enough. She would not have called to them to come if there had been any danger. Can't you see? They trust one another."

"I suppose," Waring said doubtfully, "they could have got as far as the cloakroom door during the night, and while they could not get her out, they could talk to her."

"Trust," Cherry said. She was looking at the little people, her face more animated than Daniel had seen it. "They have complete trust. No arguments, no rows—just knowing that no one's going to let anyone else down. Knowing it."

Daniel saw Waring glance at his daughter and look away. If she were right, he thought, the distinction was a valid one and worth bearing in mind. Not human. Most certainly not human.

For lunch Bridget had found an arrangement which permitted dining *en masse*. She had brought a card table into the dining room and put a very short-legged coffee table on top of it. Books made bench seats for the little people, and the men made do with coffee spoons, which were large for them but not entirely unwieldy. She had put their meat through a mincer and crumbled their potatoes, but left the peas whole. It was fascinating to watch them eating these one at a time.

Hanni had not come down, and Stefan had taken lunch for her up to their room and stayed with her. The atmosphere was a cheerful, lighthearted one. The things which had shocked and disgusted them earlier had been put behind, not forgotten but ignored. Stefan was absent, and Mat gave the impression of savoring, to some extent sharing, Cherry's simple delight in the little ones. They, as usual, showed no particular emotion, but their imperturbability had in part a mirror surface. It reflected ease and high spirits now as earlier it had reflected incredulity and nausea. Reflected, Daniel thought, and heightened. It was almost as though, themselves without vagaries, they were a catalyst to the run of human feelings.

Daniel found himself alone with Waring in the library afterwards drinking coffee. They talked about the little people, and Daniel found the American, on his own, far more impressive than he had previously thought. He was intelligent, and he talked sense; his character, with no others intervening, was without the ragged nervous edge that was generally in evidence. One other person in particular not intervening—Helen was in the lounge with the rest. Daniel could not restrain a slight feeling of contempt for someone who permitted his mind so to be dominated by conflict with another, but it was very slight. Chiefly, he admired Waring and found him interesting.

What he said made sense. Their discovery presented a problem which they by themselves were not equipped to solve. The little people could not just be loosed on the world, or rather, Waring amended, the world could not be loosed on them. The rats by comparison had been no more than a minor nuisance. It was very important to look at this as rationally as possible. They had rights, of course, and their rights must be protected, but what was the best way of protecting them? Some kind of tutelage and care was obviously necessary in the first place, whatever happened eventually, and it was essential to work out who would be best qualified to organize this. One could call in a government department— the Irish government, presumably—but the most likely immediate result would be confusion, and quite possibly the letting in of exploiting commercial bodies. Decisions were going to have to be made, and you were unlikely to get swift and rational decisions from government departments.

"Especially," Daniel suggested, "Irish government departments."

Waring grinned. "Especially. I would say we need somebody who is disinterested, who can study the whole thing intelligently and dispassionately, and who has a high enough reputation—a world reputation—so that he can stand up to the politicians and officials. Despite the emotive prejudices"—his voice briefly took on a sour note—"that sounds to me like a scientist."

"Anyone in particular?"

Waring shrugged. "Not so far. How about you?"

"My mind's a blank. I'm not very well up on scientists."

"We can think about it a bit. We don't need to rush it. The main thing is that we should agree on general principles. Someone's got to look at this straight, and with Stefan the way he is and Mat on the bottle, it looks like maybe we constitute a quorum."

"Yes," Daniel said, "I suppose it does."

"They are fascinating." Waring's voice was absorbed, contemplative. "Absolutely fascinating."

"I suppose there's no doubt they were created the way Stefan told it? I don't know enough about biology to get the picture."

"I don't know much, either, but enough to know that it makes sense. Growth is controlled by the pituitary, and the fetus is completely formed by the time it's three inches long. Except for fingernails and such. And the head being disproportionately large. Which it still is with them to some extent. Miniatures have been born before, by accident, though not so small. It's not basically unreasonable, granted the intention."

"It takes some granting."

"Well, yes."

"Another fascinating quirk of the German mind."

"Nazi."

"Is there a difference?"

"Einstein was a German. So was Schweitzer."

"Yes," Daniel said. "One was thrown out and the other left voluntarily."

Waring grinned. "You English can keep a hate up."

"You don't think it's justified?"

157

"I was thinking that we're in Ireland, and the Black and Tans were not long before the storm troopers."

"That's quite a different thing."

"Is it? I guess so." Waring stood up. "I think I'll go and take another look at them. You coming?"

"Not just yet."

The door closed behind Waring, and Daniel was alone. He was glad of that. He had enjoyed the conversation and the company, apart from the trivial jibe at the end, but there was gratification in being alone in a spacious and well-appointed room on a day like this. There were some clouds in the sky, but they had had long spells of sunshine and were in one now. The French windows stood open, and a breeze came in, but too slight a one to move the heavy curtains. The air was warm and soft, conducive, he thought pleasantly, to sensuality. Bridget had promised she would come and join him when she had finished the necessary supervision of Mrs. Malone and Mary. He could enjoy the thought of that with a relaxed anticipation. They might take a walk together. There was a garden, and they could wander up one of the paths that led to small oases of long grass in the bog. His mind was running cheerfully on this when he glimpsed a movement in the corner of his vision. He looked there and saw Emma.

He had thought she was with the rest, but they were so small and moved so quickly and lightly that they were difficult to keep track of. She must have slipped in here directly after lunch and sat, quiet and out of the way, while Waring and he were talking. She came toward him across the carpet, and he marveled again at her bright, calm diminutive beauty. He racked his mind for the few German words he knew and said softly, *"Komm, Emma. Komm zu mir."*

She came and stood beside the chair, her golden hair almost touching his leg. She put her arms up to him, and he lifted her onto his chest; he was lying back in the club chair. Her warmth and tiny weight were charming, and her loveliness delighted the eye. Holding her lightly with one hand, he touched her face with a finger of the other.

"*Schön*," he said. "*Sehr schön*."

Her response first surprised then amused him. Her hands went to the front of her dress and loosened it. Minutely feminine, she lifted the dress over her head and freed her arms from the sleeves. Like a little girl, he thought, childishly vain of the beauty of her body, wanting to show her prettiness to someone who admired it. At the same time it was disconcerting. She was quite naked, her nudity almost but not entirely sexless.

"*Schön*," he repeated. He picked up the discarded dress and offered it to her. "But you'd better get dressed again, there's a good girl."

With a swift twisting movement she slid down from his chest to his lap. He thought she was getting down to the floor, that with a child's willfulness she wanted to continue showing off, to dance perhaps on the carpet, a teasing, innocently sensual fairy princess. The awareness of the small probing fingers—the realization of her actual intention—came as a greater, more physical shock than anything that had happened here so far.

"My God!" He found himself gasping for breath as he abruptly sat up. "My God."

He lifted her and set her on the carpet and put the dress beside her. He was still trembling. He said, "Get dressed. Put your dress on."

She could not understand the words, of course, but he thought the harshness of his tone conveyed his meaning. She looked up at him, the dark eyes inscrutable under the summery hair. Then, submissively, she picked up the dress and wriggled into it. She fastened it and stood there, demure, watching him and waiting.

It was only at this point, with her whiteness clothed again, that Daniel was aware of having noticed something about her body, a difference. Her back. The skin delicate and unblemished. There were no marks of whipping there.

He stared down at her. All that, and despite it such beauty and serenity. How could it be possible?

XIV

KEEPING MRS. MALONE from hysterics was proving a more arduous and more continuous job than Bridget had thought. When she had first told her about the little people, her reaction had shown traces both of doubt and anxiety, but had not been extreme. She had not accepted Bridget's offer to show her Greta, and her first sight of one of them had been when Emma was brought into the kitchen by Daniel. She had plainly been shocked and frightened, but Bridget had hoped that a little time for reflection, helped by a drop of brandy, would enable her to absorb the experience.

She had returned from the library to find that she had been too optimistic about this. Mrs. Malone was going about her duties after a fashion, but she remained chalk white and trembling. Bridget made her sit down and gave her a long and careful talking to. In reply to this, Mrs. Malone whispered, "But it's not natural, ma'am. It's not natural at all. I can't . . ." Her voice trailed off.

Bridget said briskly, "No, it's not natural. They're not natural, if you like. But the point is that they're entirely harmless. They're not going to hurt you. You must stop being frightened of them."

She said, "My uncle Ben saw something once, coming past a churchyard, when he was only a boy. And he never spoke a word after, though he'll be seventy-one next Easter." She shuddered. "I can't abide the thought of them."

Bridget paused. "Do you want to leave?" she asked her.

It was a bluff, she admitted, and a not entirely fair one. She had learned that this house, and latterly she herself, represented a desperately needed security to Mrs. Malone. Her nervous garrulousness and brashness on that first visit to Killabeg back in February had disguised a fear that she would be put out and have to seek a position elsewhere. The fear was not rational—she was, under proper supervision, a reasonable housekeeper—but stemmed from a background in which callousness and contempt had far outweighed what little affection came her way. She had gone at thirteen from a hard home life to a harder one of domestic service, and had been married at seventeen to a groom, who first got her pregnant and then through a bout of physical violence caused her to have a miscarriage which also prevented her having further children. He had died after five years of misery for her, and she had gone back to service. Two years later she had married a second time, a man whose cruelty was cold and spiteful rather than brutal, and who had spent eight years systematically undermining what little confidence she had in herself. He had then abandoned her—she had no idea where he had gone, except that he had talked sometimes about South America—and she had gone into service for the third time. Her experiences there had not been much happier—her timidity had been found and exploited —until she had come to Seamus Chauncey at Killabeg. Seamus' attitude—one of complete indifference provided his meals were cooked after a fashion and he was not troubled—had come as blessed rain after drought, and Bridget's succeeding regime of patient supervision with no unkindness or hectoring had been the sunburst that set the flowers growing in the neglected soil. She had responded, Bridget thought smugly, astonishingly well. And the world outside, now that she had known some warmth, was all the colder and more cheerless.

Mrs. Malone said, "Ah, no! It's the last thing I would do." She paused and added with a desperate honesty, "And where would I go if I left?"

"Then stop worrying," Bridget told her. "They're strange little things, but nothing to be frightened of. You should pity them, rather. They've had a hard time of it."

"Will you be keeping them long here in the house?"

"Not long, I should think."

Mrs. Malone nodded. "I'll try to pull meself together. I know I'm not being sensible."

"After all, they've been in the house all this time, remember. They were here before you came."

"And it was them himself went up to play with in the tower each day?" She shuddered. "He was a queer man, but I didn't think him to be as queer as that. As to them being here, I didn't know of them, did I? There's a lot of things you can live with easily enough until you know about them."

"But you know they're not likely to harm you. If they were going to murder you in your bed, they could have crept up and done it any time in the past four months, instead of stealing pathetic bits of food and things from the kitchen. Don't you see that?"

She had shuddered again and more violently at the reference to being murdered, but the force of the argument seemed to have penetrated at last. She said, "I'll try to keep a hold on meself, ma'am. I'll promise you that."

The hold, however, slipped over lunch, the equilibrium nudged perhaps by the sight of the seven little people eating at the double table. Bridget came back into the kitchen to find Mrs. Malone sobbing uncontrollably in a chair, with Mary holding one of her hands and making ineffectual sounds of comfort. Mrs. Malone looked up with streaming eyes. Her voice a gasping howl, she said, "I'm ashamed of meself, ma'am. Oh God, I'm that ashamed! And the more so with Mary here not troubled at all. It's just that . . . I'm so ashamed." The howl increased in volume. "Oh, so ashamed . . ."

Bridget said, "All right, Mary. You can be seeing to the clearing. Now, Mrs. Malone, stop that at once."

"I can't help being afraid, ma'am. And when I set eyes on them, it's worse."

"Here. Drink this."

She had poured her a very stiff brandy indeed. Mrs. Malone

made feeble protest, but allowed herself to be overruled. Gradually, with a combination of bullying and coaxing and the assistant effect of the brandy, she calmed down. In ten minutes Bridget could leave her. She was not entirely sober, but at least she was not hysterical.

Bridget went from the kitchen up to the Morwitzes' room. Stefan had insisted on taking the tray up himself and had said that Hanni was all right apart from a headache, but Bridget felt responsible all the same. She knocked, and Hanni's voice bade her come in. Hanni was in bed, Stefan lying fully clothed on the other bed. The tray stood on the table, the food untouched. Seeing her look at it, Hanni said apologetically, "I am so sorry that we have wasted such good food."

Bridget asked, "How are you feeling?"

"Better. I am sorry about—all this. I have not behaved well, I think."

"There's no question of that." Bridget hesitated. "It must have been an unpleasant shock for you."

"It is not easy to explain. Except . . ." Her voice was steady, the only appeal that of her eyes. "I lost many people during the war. All my family, many of them young women. They could be my cousins—the little people."

Bridget had not thought much about her. Stefan had been so obviously the dominating partner in the marriage, Hanni retiring and acquiescent, that she had concentrated her attention on him, taking it for granted that what made him happy would satisfy Hanni also. This might still be true, but Bridget was suddenly aware of the deep strength in the woman. It shone the more clearly through her present unhappiness: a strength that had faced and overcome despair. "They could be my cousins." It was a frightening glimpse into an abyss, whose existence had been known, but whose vertiginous depths had been beyond her imagination.

She said, "Don't hurt yourself by talking about it."

"Thinking is enough, and one cannot avoid thinking. But I know it does no good to talk. It does not help to tell of horrors."

"It's not that. If talking helps . . ."

Hanni shook her head. "No. There is nothing to say, except recite names. And the names by themselves are meaningless."

There was a silence. Bridget said, "Is there anything I can get you?"

"No. But thank you. Do you need Stefan to help you talk to them?"

Stefan, remaining silent, looked toward his wife. It was a look difficult to fathom. Unhappiness, a call for help—but more than that, Bridget thought, much more. She said, "There's no hurry about that."

"He will come down later," Hanni said.

"If you would like to leave . . ." Bridget said. "If you think it would be better to go away . . ."

The suggestion this time was sincere, but Hanni gave it the same prompt answer that Mrs. Malone had done.

"No. Where would one go?"

She had told Daniel she would see him in the library when she was free, but before that Bridget went to her room to freshen up and tidy herself. She thought of Hanni and Stefan at first, of what it must be like to carry that sort of burden for a quarter of a century, with as long a time ahead, but the exercise was futile. To set oneself a task of agonizing over another's misery had an obscene quality—was, she felt, a kind of insult to the victims. They had suffered and died, and it was best for the memory to fade. If she had been one of them, she thought, she would have wanted that.

It was different with the legacies that were inescapable—the memories that the Morwitzes shared, or didn't share. One could do nothing to help them. And, of course, the little people, a living breathing legacy, a monument in flesh and blood. That was different altogether, a problem that challenged and had to be answered. Putting on fresh lipstick, she thought of the various suggestions which with varying degrees of seriousness had been put forward. Scientists, circuses, publicity agents. They struck her

164

as dreary or unpleasant or absurd, and in no case likely to contribute to the happiness of the little people. They would be better off staying here.

Working her lips together to spread the lipstick, she thought about it. Was there anything wrong in that? It was the place they were used to, the only place they knew. Now that the days of torments by Seamus were over and done with, there was no reason why they should not be entirely happy here. It was a place easy to protect from the world, from the TV men and the reporters. People would have to be told about them—it was not the sort of secret that could be kept indefinitely, or even for very long— but that did not mean that they would have to be exploited. She remembered reading about two sets of quintuplets of much the same age, of which one had been completely private and out of the world's eye. There was no reason why that should not be done in this case. And obviously it would be to their good to do so. It was the only way, really, in which there could be a chance of their leading something like natural lives.

To their good. Her mirrored face had been looking at her, but suddenly she became conscious of it in a sharper way. The well-brushed, slightly waving auburn hair, the good brow, candid gray eyes in a broad, quite handsome face—and behind that fine façade, small, selfish, self-deceiving thoughts crawling. An exclusive arrangement, for the good of the little people, but under whose management? And so to whose chief benefit? One would need to keep the place going as a hotel, of course, to pay for their keep and their protection, and just think how exclusive that could be. No need to advertise the principal attraction; the difficulty, whatever the rates were, would lie in selecting the ones to be chosen for the privilege of paying them.

With a surge of self-contempt she remembered the previous night and Waring saying that before Greta was caught he had suspected she and Daniel were working some sort of trick to obtain publicity. What she had just been contemplating was worse, far worse.

In a bad temper with herself, she quickly finished her makeup and went downstairs, slamming the bedroom door behind her. She checked the kitchen and found Mrs. Malone subdued but apparently under control, and went along to the library. Daniel was sitting in one of the chairs, alone in the room except for the little Emma, who stood motionless a few feet away watching him. She had realized on the way down that her annoyance with herself had set her, as far as Daniel was concerned, in the center of a seesaw. She had been afraid that, out of sorts as she was, he might say something which would make her angry with him, too. It was unreasonable, but she knew herself well enough to recognize it as a genuine danger.

But the first sight of him dispelled that. He was looking unhappy, she thought, and she felt a wave of sympathy and affection for him. Poor Daniel—how much had happened since that letter came from O'Hanlon and O'Hanlon, and he had suggested that they should go over to Dublin for the weekend. First deserted by his fiancée; then when he has patiently followed after her, summarily thrown out of her bed. And now enmeshed in all this, which must be worrying the careful legal side of his mind no end. No wonder he was looking a bit miserable. She contrasted his unobtrusive nondemonstrative strength with Mat's naked emotions. There was a lot to be said for an Englishman, however infuriating the unimaginativeness could be at times.

Going to him, she stooped and kissed him. There was constraint in his response, and she realized that his attention was not entirely on her. He was looking past her at Emma. They were, it was true, under surveillance, though it was not a surveillance that Bridget felt she could take seriously. All the same . . . She put her hands to his neck, and whispered, "Let's go out."

Obediently he got up. Bridget took his hand and started toward the open door. He took a couple of steps and hung back. She said, "What is it?"

"What about Emma?"

"Well, what? You don't want to take her along with us, do you?"

"No." He made it very emphatic. "Most certainly not. I was

166

wondering . . . do we just leave her here? With the door open?"

"What else? We're not treating them as prisoners."

"No, I suppose not." He followed her through the door. "How are we treating them, though? How ought we to treat them?"

"Let's not worry about that for half an hour." She drew a deep breath of the soft warm air, its scent compounded of grass and flowers and the peaty smell of the bog. "It's good to get away from things for a little while."

They walked hand in hand across the lawn. It needed cutting, she saw. When Danny Moore came in from the village, she would have to get him onto it. Mat had done it the last time, but it was not terribly likely that he would volunteer again. She said, "I've been thinking."

"About them?"

She said impatiently, "No. Not about them. Do you think you can find out the best place for advertising the house? The *Irish Times,* I suppose. And where else? *Country Life?* Isn't there something that deals particularly with guest houses?"

She had thought the suggestion would please him, but he merely said in an abstracted way, "I think there is. I'll look it up when I get back to the office."

Bridget released his hand and took his upper arm and squeezed it.

"Look," she said, "is something worrying you?"

He was silent, then, said, "What are they?"

"What do you mean—what are they?"

"It's not merely a question of size. Not even of their conditioning by—that pair of madmen. There's something else, something very odd."

"Does it matter? Can't we forget them for a bit? They're not our problem."

"Then whose?"

"I don't know." She thought about it. "I suppose they are, damn them. But not right at this moment. This is time out. My holiday half-hour. Let's just watch the grass grow."

He said, "Waring thinks it's important that they should be

handed over to someone properly qualified—rather than getting involved with government departments, or the press and television. I'm inclined to agree with him."

"I'm sure you're both right. Are we going through into the garden?"

It was quiet in the garden, the air hot and still and brushed with the smell of rose and honeysuckle. Bees embroidered the silence, and Bridget wondered where their nest was. It might have been worthwhile putting in a few hives for honey. They walked on along the winding paths, hidden, as they penetrated deeper, from the entrance. No one else was here. They reached the bower at the far end. Approaching it, one could see nothing of the inside; from within, though, one looked out between slats and the green tendrils of honeysuckle, and the path was plainly visible for quite a long way—visible and empty. Footsteps, moreover, would be heard. The paths were laid with gravel which crunched underfoot.

A place, in fact, Bridget reflected, where one could scarcely be surprised by an intruder. She lay back and waited in pleasantly languorous anticipation for Daniel to do something about that.

Instead, he said, "They don't smile or laugh. Isn't a sense of humor one of the essential human features? I don't think they can laugh."

Bridget stood up. "I don't know," she said. "But do tell me when you've worked it out."

He said, "I'm sorry. You're not going back already?"

"Yes, but you stay here and meditate."

He reached out for her hand and pulled her back beside him. The strength was there all right, well remembered and altogether satisfactory. He started kissing her, and that was satisfactory, too, up to a point. Realizing just what the point was, she experienced frustration and annoyance and equally strongly a determination not to let the annoyance show. After a time she gently disengaged herself and smiled at him. The smile might be an essentially human feature, she thought, but it did not always have anything to do with a sense of humor.

She said, "Darling, I do have to go, I'm afraid. I've just remembered—I've been so mixed up with all this business that I haven't got Mrs. Malone started on the stew for tomorrow, and if I don't remind her, she'll never remember herself."

"I'll come with you."

She pressed him back. "No. If I can manage it, I'll slip out again."

And smile nicely, she thought, as you grit your teeth. How long since you were congratulating yourself on having got this one all for your own? As she was going, Daniel said, "There's something I want to tell you."

She turned and stared at him. "What?"

He looked back without speaking for a few moments. "No," he said finally. "It can wait." He chewed his lip. "You're not the only one who feels mixed up at the moment."

"Never mind." The smile came on again. Or grimace? "We'll probably both feel better later on."

On her way back to the house she saw Mat and Cherry walking together over toward the lake. They made a handsome couple and from a distance of a hundred yards looked happy and at ease. *Venus à sa proie,* she thought. In which case, *bon appétit.* There were, it was perfectly true, things that needed seeing to, and although Mrs. Malone had been warned about the stew, a little checking on that point was desirable. She went in through the library windows. There was no sign of Emma, but the door to the passage stood open. Someone must have opened it. She realized again the helplessness of the little people in a world where door handles stood at least three times their height, and needed far more than their strength to turn. They required and deserved sympathy, and if Daniel had become somewhat deeply engrossed in the problem, that was to his credit. While you, she informed herself, are a selfish and oversexed bitch. Depressed by this unflattering insight, she pushed open the kitchen door, calling for Mrs. Malone.

Mrs. Malone, she saw at once, was not there, but Mary was. She was doing something at the sink. In reply to Bridget's question, she said no, she did not know where Mrs. Malone was. She had been down to the kitchen garden gathering peas, and the kitchen had been empty when she got back.

The stew had been started. There were sliced onions and diced carrots and turnip on the chopping board, and a piece of fat in the stewpot on top of the stove. She felt a slight unease at the sight. One of Mrs. Malone's better qualities was an ability to concentrate on the job on hand; it was not like her to break off at a halfway stage. The most likely explanation was that her nerves had got the better of her again. In which case she might have taken refuge where? In her room, or locked in the bathroom? The obvious thing to do was look for her.

She went through the house, starting on the upper floor, calling Mrs. Malone's name. There was no sign of her and no response. None of the bathrooms was occupied, and her room was empty. Coming down, she found the Selkirks in the lounge arguing about something. They had not seen her, either. Waring asked if there was anything he could do; she thanked him, but said no.

The unease was fairly considerable now. The thought that sprang to mind was that she had panicked after all, and fled the house. She would surely make for the road and not the bog—any sane person would. But was a woman unhinged by fear sane in that sense?

She decided she had better go out and look for her. Before putting that into effect, she remembered that she had not yet checked the cellars. It was scarcely likely that she would have gone down there—since the discovery of the little people the cellars had provided one of the focus points for her dread, and Bridget had had to get supplies up herself that morning. Nonetheless, she supposed she ought to make a quick check. She went to the stairs door, opened it, and snapped on the light. Then, herself rooted by fear and nausea, she stared down at the huddled and motionless figure that lay at the bottom.

She stifled her first impulse, which was to scream. The second —to turn and run for help—took rather more mastering. She was still uncertain of the outcome when something happened to decide her. A moan or a groan came up from what she had assumed was Mrs. Malone's dead body. At that, Bridget ran down the steps. She remembered as she reached her that one had to be careful about moving someone before one knew what, if anything, was broken. Mrs. Malone lay on her side with her legs curled up and her hands covering her face. Kneeling by her, Bridget took her hand as gently as possible and said, "Tell me where it hurts."

A series of shudders, starting at her shoulders and working down to her legs, shook Mrs. Malone's body. She whispered, "Where are they? Are they after me still? Ah, God and His Mother and His Holy Saints preserve me from them."

The possibility came to Bridget that there might be nothing physically wrong with her at all. Her voice had not sounded like that of a woman with a broken leg or ruptured spleen or the like. She stood upright and, holding on to Mrs. Malone's hand, said in a brisk, peremptory tone, "Try standing up now. I'll help."

Mrs. Malone got to her feet, the other hand still covering her eyes. Bridget prised it loose.

"You're all right. What happened? Did you slip on the stairs?"

Mrs. Malone looked fearfully up the stairs and then around her. She said, "Are they gone, then? Are you sure they're gone?"

Now that she was reassured of her safety, it was impossible not to feel irritated. Bridget said sharply, "Look, be reasonable. You slipped and fell. It's got nothing to do with the little people."

She grasped Bridget's arm, her fingers digging in almost painfully. "They threw me downstairs."

"That's nonsense. They're only a foot high and not much heavier than a cat. They couldn't throw you downstairs. You're imagining it all."

"I was upstairs in the passage when they came after me. They harried me, and they took my voice from me so that I could not cry out. The stairs door was open, and I made for that. And they threw me down. I heard them laughing up above, and I lay as though I was dead and prayed."

"It's ridiculous. They don't laugh at all. They don't even smile. I suppose you saw them and were frightened again, and you came running for the steps and missed your footing."

Not to mention, she thought, the brandy; the stale smell of it was nauseating.

Mrs. Malone said, "They took my voice and threw me down. Ah, Jesus, preserve us all!"

"Come on," Bridget said wearily. "Let's get you to your room. You've been shaken up badly, you need to rest."

But the little people had disappeared. This became clear by the end of the afternoon. Bridget herself was too busily engaged with doing Mrs. Malone's work as well as her own—Mrs. Malone was lying down in her room with the door locked on the inside—to bother much about this, but the others were concerned. They conducted searches, and she heard their voices from time to time calling through the house. When she managed a break of five minutes for a cup of tea, Daniel and Waring came to talk about it.

"She must have frightened them," Waring said.

Bridget drank her tea, feeling a little bit of herself come back into her drudge of a body.

"Mrs. Malone put it the other way around."

Daniel said, "I suppose she came across some of them in the passage—probably screamed and ran for it."

Waring shook his head. "I didn't hear anything from the lounge."

"Ran, anyway. And fell down the stairs. They saw that and saw her lying still, apparently dead. Seamus used to whip and torture them for small offenses—for nothing. They must have been frightened to death of what would happen."

Bridget said, "The door was shut."

"The door?"

"At the top of the stairs."

"Probably the wind blew it shut."

"There hasn't been any wind."

172

"A bit of breeze from time to time. It could gust enough to blow a door shut."

Could it? Bridget was chiefly aware of feeling tired. It had been a long and exhausting day, and she doubted if Mrs. Malone would be in a mood to lend any help with the dinner.

Waring said, "We must find them and reassure them."

"They'll come back," Daniel said. "When they've got over the shock of it. It's probably wiser not to make too much of a performance of looking for them—it's more likely to prolong a state of fear."

"Do you think so?" Waring asked. "I suppose you could be right."

The five minutes were up. Reluctantly Bridget got on her feet and headed toward the kitchen. The little people were, she supposed, important, but at the moment she would have far preferred a way of reassuring Mrs. Malone.

This she did not find, but somehow she got through the evening. She made her excuses just before ten and took her weary way to bed. The little people still had not returned. Well, she thought, dragging her clothes off, that was just too bad.

XV

During the day the clouds thinned and vanished; by sunset there were only a few, high and far in the west, of rose bruising to purple as the sun sank into the Atlantic. Stars began to appear; first the evening star close to the horizon and then more and more as the sky's blue deepened to indigo and at last to the black of night. Across it arched the cloud of light that was the Milky Way: the lamps of a city unimaginably vast, unimaginably remote. There was no moon, and the breeze had gone with the clouds. The earth quivered with stillness.

Out among the encircling hills the commerce of life and death followed its customary patterns. The gravid vixen patiently enlarged a hole in a fence, wormed her way through and, with only the briefest fluttering and squawking, brought down a sleepy hen from her perch, bit through her throat and feasted on blood. A field mouse, following the scent of the female, thought itself hidden by the dark and moved carelessly over a patch of open ground; but the watching owl saw the starlit flicker of movement from a branch above, plunged, and took him. The otter by the riverbank dived after the hint of a ripple in the river's still deeper blackness, and a moment later came out, shaking its head and the still living fish it held between its jaws.

It was a land and a life from which man was absent. Gentleman and farmer and laborer, housewife and child and priest, slept in their beds, within walls. The brief time of prayers and copulations and vagrant daydreams was over. A very few were still awake—a woman hating her heavy-breathing husband, a boy worrying over an examination—but exhaustion had claimed nearly all of them. Doctor and midwife slept within earshot of silent telephones. Even the poacher slept, his battered tin alarm clock set for the rising of the moon.

Within the circle of the hills stretched the bog, which at one time had been the bed of a great lake, and at another time a forest. Acre upon acre of desolation, its waters for the most part brackish, its miasma rank. But the patterns held here, too. On a patch of turf fifteen feet square, two rabbits nibbled grass, mated, and nibbled again. A mole surfaced, sniffed the dark air, and burrowed down once more in search of worms. An army of this year's frogs, newly transformed, marched over muddy ground, and a heron, planted on the edge of a small pool, waited till they were under its stilts, and dipped its beak, scooping up the tiny delicate morsels with greedy relish.

The house lay at the heart of the wilderness. Small creatures moved in the lawns and gardens, fish cruised in the lake. In the house itself, mice came out from holes and wainscots and fed on crumbs, vaguely aware that things were easier, now the cats and the rats had gone. For the rats had gone indeed. They had come to this place a millennium and a half ago, with the first men who settled here. For fifteen centuries man had waged war on them, and the rats had survived. They had survived the periods of man's absence, too. Now they were gone, killed not by starvation or poisons or traps, but by a new, strange, subtle and deadly weapon wielded by creatures who still did not know the nature or the extent of their powers; but who were learning. The cats, who had been their hunters, died with them. The mice lived on, undisturbed, because they posed no threat to the new masters.

In their bedrooms men and women slept and dreamed their ordinary dreams. Elsewhere in the house figures, human in form though not in stature, moved silently and quickly. Sometimes they talked to one another, mouthing a guttural tongue in high liquid voices, but speech was a habit, not a necessity. They had long known what it was to share one another's thoughts, but now they

175

were aware of other minds, of territories open, and vulnerable.
This was not like the rats or the cats had been—they had no
sense of danger. More from curiosity and interest than malice,
they made their forays, conducted their manipulations.

B RIDGET was very conscious of the act of waking.
There had been a dream, a confused one centered around
her schooldays. The subject was not unfamiliar and always depressing. This time it had been more so than ever. She had been
on the hockey pitch, dressed in those hateful clothes, on a bitingly
cold winter's morning, with twenty-two female figures screaming
exhortations and encouragement around her. She had woken with
the usual feeling of relief at being twenty-five and her own mis-
tress, but with the awareness of an odd hangover—she could still
hear cries in the distance. She reassured herself of her wakeful-
ness by drinking from the tumbler of water by her bed and listened
more closely. Screams, but of pain not exuberance. She put the
glass down quickly, banging it against the wood, and felt for her
light switch. She pressed it, but nothing happened. Another
scream, muffled and distant but very clear, scored the night's
silence. It came from—the north wall, she realized. But that was
absurd. There were no other rooms that way, only the tower.

Bewilderment and anxiety had banished the clinging heaviness
of sleep. She was quite awake and very frightened. Getting out of
bed, she went to the door and tried the switch there. Nothing
happened. A fuse gone? And the flashlight, which she usually kept
in her bedroom, had been taken down to the kitchen the other
day and not brought up again. The cry of agony came again.
Wasting no more time, she opened the door and began feeling
her way with what speed she could along the landing.

Daniel did not respond when she called from the door, and she
had to go over to the bed and shake him. He made a yawning
inarticulate reply to that, but came awake immediately after.

"What? Who's that? Brid? Put the light on. What is it?"

"The lights aren't working. A fuse must have blown."

"Well, it can wait till morning, can't it? You didn't wake me for that, surely." His hand probed, caught her shoulder, bare but for the nightdress strap, and rapidly moved down to her breast. He made an appreciative noise. "Mm. Come on into bed where we can talk."

"No. Listen, Daniel. I'm frightened. I can hear someone screaming."

"Screaming? I can't hear anyone."

"Nor can I, here. But I could in my room. It seemed to be coming from the tower."

"But there's no one in there."

"I know."

"And the walls are feet thick."

"It came from that direction, all the same."

"You've been having a nightmare." His hand tightened its hold. "Come on in and get cozy."

"I wasn't dreaming. I know I wasn't." She tried to steady her voice, which was trembling with the recollection. "Come with me and listen. Please."

Daniel said with amiable resignation, "O.K. Hang on while I grub for my slippers. I suppose one bed is as good as another. I take it I'll be allowed to stay for a little while, in case the voices come back?"

She was shivering more violently than when she had heard the screams. "Hurry," she said. "Please hurry, darling."

They walked hand in hand, with Bridget feeling the wall with her free hand. The landing was pitch black and, apart from their own footfalls, silent. They reached her room and stopped just inside the door.

"Not a thing," Daniel said. "Or are your ears keener than mine?"

She listened, straining. The silence was supreme and inviolate. Generally the wind made some noise, rattling the warped window frames, or howling loud or soft along the eaves or through the interstices of the tower. Tonight there was complete stillness.

177

"Nothing now," she said. "But I did hear it. I wasn't asleep."

"Well, there's a simple solution." He tightened his hand and moved toward her bed, taking her with him. "We'll lie down and wait for it to happen again. There ought to be some way of passing the time. Pity it's so dark. You don't have a luminous pocket chess set, by any chance?"

She allowed herself to be taken to bed, and Daniel got in with her. The shivering returned even more violently as he put his arms around her. He said, "You really are upset. It must have been a shocker."

"I *was* dreaming before, but quite an ordinary dream. But I was awake, standing over by the door, when I heard the screams. Honestly."

"Delayed effect." His hand stroked her body gently and reassuringly. "I knew a chap at school who used to dream the wall was opening up and monsters were coming through to get him. He used to wake screaming, and someone would put the light on, and he'd be sitting up in bed with his hands over his eyes. When you'd dragged his hands away and made him look, he still swore he could see them. Scaly things, he said they were, with large black teeth."

Was it possible? A hallucination of some kind? The memory was still vivid, but Daniel's hand, his lips on her throat, moving down to her breast, were the nearer reality, overlaying and blotting out the other. The deep sense of fear remained, but the warmth and strength of Daniel's body against hers was a shield protecting her. She felt a wild gratitude for that. Holding his head with her hands, she pressed him to her.

He mumbled against her, "Sorry about the nightmare, but I'm really very glad you came along and woke me. You must do it more often—the waking, not the dreaming."

She whispered, "Yes."

"Better now?"

"Much better."

It cut through their warmth and ease like a knife, small but sharp and diamond-hard. Gasping, she felt his body stiffen as he heard it, too. It was the same cry, but even more desperate with pain.

Waring was wakened by Helen. Her bedside light was on, and she was standing over him, shaking him. He blinked up at her.

"What's the matter?"

"You were snoring."

"You woke me to tell me that?"

"It woke me up in the first place."

He sat up and glared at her. "I've got a cold coming. How can I help that, for Christ's sake? I've put up with you snoring often enough."

"You could have helped it by choosing a country with a decent climate to take a vacation in."

"Ah, for God's sake!"

"It's all right for you. You never get bad colds. With my sinuses, I suffer hell for weeks, months sometimes."

"Your damn' sinuses are psychosomatic—you live for them. If you could get your mind off yourself for an hour or so, you wouldn't have them. Hour? I should have said minute or so."

"Listen," she said. "We're leaving. Tomorrow."

Waring realized she meant it. He stared at her. "What about the little people?"

"They've gone, and I don't give a damn if they come back or not."

"Well, I do."

"Sure." She laughed. "Daniel told me about that chat you and he had. I hit that nail right on the button, didn't I? Who is it you're planning to bring in? Matthews? No, I guess not. Someone bigger than that. A real eagle to carry the little wren way, way up into the sky. You know what? I think you've admitted it to yourself at last."

"Admitted what?"

"That you're a failure. You're not concealing the conniving

from yourself any more, not even trying to. You're just as much a failure in your work as you are as a human being. And by God that's failure, all right."

She had gone back to her own bed and sat down. The taunting voice came from a hazy face, the features blurred and indistinct. Waring found his glasses, and she came hatefully into focus.

"I'm not a failure," he said, "in anyone's eyes but yours. You want to be married to a big success, don't you? But not the kind of success that's based on any sort of merit. It just needs to be a big enough shine to reflect on you. And the funny thing is you don't know how goddam ludicrous you are when the spotlight's on you. You have no grace at the best of times, but public functions bring out the worst in you. You talk too much and too loud, and however much powder you put on, your face gets covered in sweat, and everybody—*everybody*—who's standing there smiling politely is laughing like hell inside—and openly the minute your back's turned. The only hope for you is to lead a quiet life. You don't look quite so ridiculous that way."

It had gone home; he had hit her where it hurt. He saw the lines tighten around her eyes and braced himself for her throwing herself at him, a fat soft mass but armed with nails, not to mention teeth. But she controlled herself. She said quite softly, "You stinking bastard. All I have to say to you is that we're going tomorrow. You heard that? We're leaving tomorrow."

Waring found himself a cigarette and lit it. He did not offer one to Helen. She came over and helped herself, and he was ready for her to attack him again, but she did not.

He said, "Wanting to be the Big Chief's Lady is only part of it, isn't it? The other and more important part is that you have to knock down everything and everyone around you, because you're so lousy jealous. This is a break for me, a big break. I admit that. In this world you need hard work and ability, and you also need luck, even as an academic. Well, this is where the little white ball clicks into my slot, and you know it, and you're determined to foul it up if you can. So that's why you want to get me out of here. Isn't that right?"

"You're too little to understand," she said. "Little people? There couldn't be anything smaller than you."

"Which means I am right."

"No." She stubbed out the cigarette from which she had taken no more than a couple of draws. "You won't understand, but I'll tell you. The little people—that footprint, the hole in the wall, the candle and the candy wrapping in the tower—those were signs, signs of wonders. You laughed at the whole thing, which shows how small you are, because it was like Columbus' men seeing land birds and knowing that a new world was just over the horizon. Then we found them, the wonder was a reality, and what did it mean to you? It meant a soft option, no more than that. You said it yourself—the little white ball clicking into your slot. That's what it means to you, and that's why you disgust me utterly. And why we're leaving in the morning."

"You, if you like. Not me."

"Stay then," she said indifferently. "I said we're leaving. Cherry and I. You do just what you want."

"Cherry." Waring picked a flake of tobacco from his lip. "The same old blackmail. Only this time it isn't going to work. Cherry won't go with you."

"You think she'll stay with you?"

"Yes. But not because of me. Because of Mat."

"That doesn't mean anything."

"Doesn't it?" He grinned at her. "Then try it out."

She was unsure. "It couldn't be serious. She couldn't have any real interest in a man like that."

"Couldn't she? You'd know better if you could get your eyes off that imaginary mirror you carry around with you."

"A boozing Puritan. And if he knew about her—if he had any idea—he'd run a mile. A mile? He wouldn't stop this side of Dublin."

Her voice had regained confidence. Waring stared at her with bitter hatred. He said, "My God, I believe you would!"

"Would what?"

"You'd tell him about her to break things up. You'd betray

her, the way you've betrayed me. You bloody heartless bitch."

"You swine!"

She had frozen with anger. Their gazes held in mutual recognition of detestation and contempt. And it was at this point, in the concentration of pure hostility, that it happened. There was a brief spasm of dizziness, and he was not looking at her any longer, or rather, not just at her. His disembodied vision was above them both, looking down from somewhere near the ceiling. And this was real immobility, the view fixed, unwinking, unchanging and unchangeable. As he watched, the figures beneath him broke their silence. His own voice, and then hers, in a babble of vituperation that went on and on. He was as unable to avoid listening as to avoid looking. There were no eyes to close, no ears to shut. The two creatures, one of whom he knew with horror to be himself, went on savaging each other with words. He tried desperately to will himself back into his flesh, but it was no good.

And he became aware of something else, which intensified the horror. It was not through any of the senses, but he was conscious of a near presence, a fellow spectator, trapped as he was. It was Helen. He tried to call to her, but there was no way of calling. Beneath them both the puppet show continued. The voices were shouting now.

Stefan lay awake for some time watching the window and the three stars, one bright and two dim, framed by it. Only gradually did he realize that Hanni's even breathing was not the breathing of sleep, that she was awake, too. He called to her softly, and she answered him.

"Can't you sleep?" he asked.

"I'm not tired." She paused. "Don't worry. I am not being unhappy."

He put the light on and looked across to her. She lay on her side, her face toward him but buried in the pillow. Her right eye watched him under the cloud of dark hair. It was so small a distance between them. He had an impulse to bridge it, to go to her, touch her, take her, comfort her and be comforted. But he could not. Small as the distance was, it held all the past in it.

He said, "Shall we have some music?"

"If you like."

"Since we are both awake." He reached for the Grundig and switched it on. "There will be no Irish stations at this time, of course."

Moving the dial, he first found a French station giving a news bulletin—something to do with farm prices—and then a station broadcasting Bach: a sonata for violin and cello. He remembered another occasion and wondered if Hanni did, too. As though reading his thoughts, she said, "Do you think they still play it together? I suppose not. They are no longer alive, perhaps."

It had been the first holiday after they were married. He had managed to afford a week in Switzerland. They had stayed *en pension* at a chalet in Canton Freiburg, a chalet standing near a river in the middle of a broad valley in which even Nature seemed to bask in Swiss prosperity—there was so much grass and leaf and all orderly and in good heart. Every day the sun had shone as they had walked through the valley—together, he remembered —or climbed the wooded hills to see the Alps beyond. And in the evening there had been a richness and abundance of food unbelievable after postwar Germany. Then coffee, good strong coffee with cream, and sitting out on the veranda, listening to the music as the valley filled with shadow. Dufour, the proprietor, had been the cellist, and his wife, Trudli, had played the violin. They were both in their late fifties. Hanni was right—they would most likely be dead by now. Too old, at any rate, to make music.

There had been such joy there, such peace. The sun had burned up doubts to a dry ash, which the snow-cooled breeze from the great southern peaks had blown away, to be lost in the wide, bright skies of this peaceful land. There again, for that space, he had known he was loved, and trusted the knowledge. Or thought he had known. Because the doubts fastened on him once more as they went north, and seemed to bite deeper for their brief absence.

Yet the assurance and contentment had been real and lived again in the music. This was a bridge, which he could use if he had the courage. Go to her, take her hand . . .

The music stopped.

It was the end of the sonata. The announcer identified it in German. There was a silence, followed by more music. But not Bach. He listened, incredulous, trying to make sense of what he was hearing. It was not possible. But those chords, that stridency, were unmistakable, unforgettable. The notes marching like storm troopers . . . He wanted to turn it off, but could not, and did not know if the paralysis which gripped him was of the body or the will. And there was fascination also. The voices—surely they would not come, too. But they did, bellowing with the old military precision and unison:

> *Die Fahne hoch,*
> *Die Reihe dicht geschlossen,*
> *Marschieren auf, mit ruhig' festigem Schritt . . .*

He looked at Hanni and saw her face frozen with fear; yet still could not move to end it.

> *Kameraden die Rotfront und Reaktion erschossen*
> *Marschieren im Geist in unseren Reihen mit!*

"No," he heard her whisper. "Oh, no."

A joke, he wondered, an unbelievably bad joke? What else? But how was it possible? The music crashed to an end, and he waited. What could they say?

The announcer spoke again: *"Hier ist Deutschland, hier ist Berlin."* The tone was sharp, portentous. *"Jetzt bringen wir— unser Führer!"*

He broke through the paralysis then, reached out to the radio and slammed it to the floor. But it did not stop them hearing that other voice, harsh and unlovely and indelible in the minds of those who had heard it more than twenty years ago. Hanni was weeping, and the voice went on.

184

*   *   *

Mat woke to find her sitting on the bed watching him with grave eyes. He smiled up at her.

"Couldn't sleep again?"

Cherry nodded. "I like looking at you when you're asleep."

"I like looking at you at any time."

"I do, too. I mean . . . You know. I wasn't going to wake you. Just sit by you for a while and look at you."

"How long have you been here?"

"A few minutes. Five, maybe. You didn't wake when I put the light on, so I thought you weren't going to. If you're tired, I'll go away."

"No, I'm not tired."

"I didn't come straight here. I went downstairs first. I was looking for them."

"The little people?"

She nodded. "But no sign. I called Greta, but nothing happened. Do you think they'll come back?"

"I don't know."

"You don't want them to come back, do you?"

"No."

"Why is that?"

He said slowly, "It's hard to explain."

"Because you think they'll be exploited?"

He started telling her, hesitantly at first and then more confidently, about his grandparents. Everything: the feeling of peace and security, the special warmth when his grandfather went to the races, and the stories of the little people that she told him then, and so at last the culmination of savage ugliness. It was something he had never talked about, nor thought he ever could, but the telling was not only easy but in a strange way nourishing. The small buds of bitterness, all these years folded and clenched, uncurled into blossoms—black, ragged, but capable of being looked at. It was her innocence, he thought, that did it, her lovely innocence.

When he had finished, she nodded. For a time they remained

at ease in a companionable silence. Her hand had come toward his, and he had taken it, covering it and holding it on the sheet.

Cherry said, "I know what you mean, I think. I used to go on holiday in the summer, too. I mean, to a real home. It was my uncle and aunt, and there were these cousins. Four of them, sort of in two batches. When I was eight, there was a boy eleven and a girl ten, and then another boy and girl six and five. My uncle was a medical doctor, and they lived on Long Island about fifty miles from New York. They had this big old house and three dogs and a gang of cats and a pony and rabbits and half a dozen hens that were kind of pets, and the beach was less than a mile away."

He smiled at her. "That sounds good."

"Was, too. But it wasn't the animals or the beach or anything. It was just that it all seemed so happy. Meals were a riot—they all had this crazy sense of humor, and one of them would say something and they'd all take it up, even the little ones, and all around the house all day you'd hear them singing—a lot of them completely screwy songs with crazy words and tunes mixed up. They were so happy with each other. Of course, the kids used to fight sometimes, but that never lasted long. And there was no question of the big ones against the little ones, or girls against boys —that sort of thing. They all went together, and when I was there, I fitted into the middle of them, and they treated me like one of themselves, and so did my uncle and aunt. I used to lie awake with excitement for a week before it was time for me to go there." She was silent, remembering.

Mat asked, "What happened?"

She nodded. "Something always has to happen, doesn't it? Only it's not like yours—nobody died. They're all alive, though I haven't seen any of them for years. What happened was my uncle and aunt got divorced. They sold the house and moved different ways, and he took the two bigger ones and she took the others. I don't know what they did about the pony and the dogs and cats and hens and rabbits. They both married again, and they've both got children—she's got one and he's got two. They're all very happy, probably."

186

"You needed it too badly."

"Like you."

She gave a small shiver, and he asked her, "Cold?"

"Not exactly. It's just . . ."

She broke off. The house was somehow rocking underneath them, swinging along an axis in progressively wider arcs. And yet silently. Nothing crashed to the ground, there was no rattle or reverberation.

She said, "What is it?"

"I don't know." He tightened his hold on her hand. "An earthquake, maybe. But a strange one. Maybe we ought to try to get outside into the open."

"No." She gave a quick shake of her head. "Let's stay."

"Then let me hold you."

She nodded, smiling. She came to him, and he opened the sheets for her, and she slipped her small slim body into the bed. Her right arm burrowed under his waist and the left came around to join it, so that she held him tight and pressed her body against his. And he felt the leap of desire, with no shame or disgust, only joy and an awareness of peace. His hands felt for her, learning her with love.

The wild incredible seesawing went on. Over the curve of her shoulder he saw that a picture, a painting of an Alpine scene, clung unmoving to the wall. Incredible and absurd. Her face moved up to his, the warm lips pressed and opened. Let the world end.

Bridget said, "There! You heard it."

He was still tingling from its impact on the senses: a cry so small and distant but capable of electrifying, it seemed, all the nerves in his flesh. With what? Shock only? No, something more than that. He waited intently for it to come again. An animal outside, perhaps, a rabbit caught in a snare. Their cries were supposed to be almost human. The moments passed. Bridget said, "You did hear it. I felt you jump."

Her breath was on his throat. He was conscious of her body again, but very differently. This was not an accomplice, but a fellow witness, neutral, possibly even hostile. He said, "I heard it. I don't know what it was, though."

"Someone hurt and in pain."

"I'm not sure. It could be an animal outside."

"You know it isn't."

"Listen, then. One cry like that doesn't tell you anything. If it comes again . . ."

"Can't we do something?"

"There isn't much we can do until we have some idea what it is and where it's coming from."

"I've told you, from inside the tower. I listened at the wall."

He wanted time to think, time to make some kind of sense of it. A cry of pain, if it had been of pain, and from the tower, if Bridget's assurance were to be trusted. So many uncertainties, and the conclusion one that only posed further and still more baffling problems. Her persistence irritated him. He said, "Wait and listen. I wasn't ready for it."

"But they're hurt now!"

Daniel put a hand over her mouth, only half playfully. She tensed against him and then relaxed, acquiescing. They lay together as close as lovers but in no communion. In part he was hoping that the cry would not come again, that the silence would stretch into the ordinary silence of night and that chill sound fade from the memory. But he was waiting also, in a tension that nagged more and more rawly, for a resolution.

There was a series of cries this time, and there was no mistaking that they were human and an appeal. Words could be sensed before they were articulate. His heart pounded, and he found himself shivering as Bridget had done. She lay very quiet, holding him, offering the comfort that he had thought to give her. But although he felt the weight of her breasts, the pressure of thigh and knee, he could not reach out far enough to take it. The far voice shrieked, and after that the words were clear enough to make out: "Mary, Mother of God, help me!"

The words, and also the identity of the one who had spoken them. Bridget said, "It's Mrs. Malone."

"It can't be."

"It is." She disengaged from him, and he felt her getting out of bed in the dark. "We must go and do something for her."

Daniel got out himself. He was shivering still, so violently that he was not entirely confident that his legs would bear him. He said, "Where are you? Put your hand out."

They linked hands and that was a little better. The cry came again, formless but plainly from the direction Bridget had told him. How could she be in the tower? He said, "It's an illusion. She's in her room having a nightmare, and the sound is being carried round the house. A sort of echo effect."

"Do you think it could be? We can go and see."

"Which is her room?"

"Just on the other side of the landing."

The cries had stopped. They felt their way out and to the door. Bridget knocked, and there was no reply. She pushed it open, and called, "Mrs. Malone? Are you all right?"

There was no reply. Daniel could see the bed near the starry dark of the window. It looked empty. Bridget led the way, and he followed. The bed was empty.

He felt, paradoxically, a great relief, because at that instant a solution occurred to him. Granted that it was Mrs. Malone who was crying out, and that she was in the tower, there could still be a rational and only moderately unnerving explanation. She had been badly shocked by the little people, quite possibly into temporary insanity. There could have been some sort of dual-mind thing working, like the woman he had read about who had two personalities that were not only separate but hated each other, so that one of them, knowing the other was desperately afraid of spiders, would use a period of temporary dominance to send herself a box of spiders through the mail. Perhaps one Mrs. Malone had gone through to the tower looking for the little people, and the other had suddenly found herself there alone and in the dark. Or simpler still—she could be a sleepwalker.

He outlined this rapidly to Bridget, who listened and said, "Whatever it is, we'd better go and get her."

"Of course." It was the darkness that undermined one. Why did the bloody fuses have to choose this night to blow? "There's a flashlight downstairs?"

"Yes."

"Well, if we can get hold of that, we'll have a better idea of what we're up to."

They heard the voice again as they came out onto the landing, faint, at the other end of a bad telephone line, but intelligible.

"Ah, no . . . Don't . . . Don't do that to me, for God's sake!"

The impulses, from nerve ends to brain, and so to nerves again. This time he was forced to recognize it in himself for what it was. Shock, but more than that. Fear.

The terrible thing was that it was not a dream. Helen had a trick of getting herself out of bad dreams. She could always recognize them for what they were, and if they were really bad she could shout and wake herself up. Generally she woke up Waring as well, and he cursed about it, but the important thing was getting clear. She had had bad nightmares as a child, of old men with grasping hands and herself trying to run away and her legs getting heavier and slower all the time, but nothing like that since she had learned the knack of freeing herself. She was generally conscious of the good ones as dreams, too, and did her best to prolong them, though with less success.

But this was altogether different. This was real powerlessness, a sense of complete helplessness and futility, though without danger. She was watching the past and the scenes and people had the iron edge of reality; only she herself was insubstantial and formless.

It was the night of the Club Ball, the last one out there. She knew that because she could see the Townshends dancing together, and they only arrived the year she left. Her younger self was dancing with Pete Stryski, who, she remembered, had brought her. It was a shock and not altogether a pleasant one to realize how pretty she had been—maybe just a slight heaviness of chin, but faultless otherwise. And a hundred and thirty pounds, give or take five.

Knowing that she was there, and seeing it, she looked first for her father, and was lost in a spasm of love and anger. He was with Maisie Dewar, not dancing but talking to her in a low voice over drinks. She had known for years before that he was an indiscriminate lecher, but the reality could still surprise her. How could he talk to, look at, touch a woman like that? In three years the talking and looking and touching would be over, finished forever for him; and Maisie would be in the beginnings of agony from the cancer that was to kill her within four. But she could still feel fury for this scene, this moment.

And Waring? Getting a drink for the Hogan girl. He was handsome, too, she admitted—probably the most handsome man in the place, as she herself was the prettiest girl. A splendid pair, but not at this moment. There had been that terrible row the week before, when she had thrown the engagement ring off the veranda, and laughed at him as he grubbed for it in the dirt. That was why she was with Pete, who had been glad enough to pick up where Waring had interrupted him. She looked at the slim dancing figure and found there was another dimension to this reality—she could be her as well as watch her. But as a spectator still—she could read that alien mind, but could not alter it even in one tiny random thought.

She was talking to Peter now, laughing up at him as she danced, and giving him altogether about twenty per cent of her attention. The rest was concentrated on the covert angry search for Waring. Doing that, she saw her father with Maisie, and covered the swiftly boiling resentment with a darting smile to Pete. He looked pleased and flustered and missed his step. She did not chide him as she usually did, but laughed and squeezed his hand.

It was about ten minutes later that she got her father alone. There was no sign of Maisie—most likely she had gone to the john—and he was standing with his back to a pillar by one of the big palms with a small, self-satisfied smile on his face that made her want to hit him. She said, "Hi, Pop. How's it going?"

"Not bad. You look pretty tonight, lollipop."

"Thanks. You don't look so bad yourself, for an old man."

"Hey, a compliment from my beautiful daughter! I should buy you a drink for that. What'll it be?"

"Nothing." She looked at him, smiling still but letting the steel show. "There's only one thing that gives you away."

The smug expression changed to one of slight wariness. "What's that, then?"

"The quality of the women you go for. I see you're in the Maisie Dewar league now. That qualifies you as old, as well as dirty. Who comes next—Lucy Steele? I hear she's pretty good with jaded appetites in the senile."

She saw his face tighten as she spoke and knew she had got him on the raw. Lucy Steele was in her sixties, blousy but indefatigable. When her first husband had died the year he was due for retirement, she had married old Steele, the British Vice-Consul, following, it was said, a slow but relentless rape, and had then resumed her former promiscuity. With a good deal of difficulty recently—her wickedness had lost charm and the seesaw had tilted.

He did not, as she expected, lash back. Instead, he said, "I see you're with Pete tonight. Had some trouble with Waring?"

"You look after your affairs," she said. "I'll see to mine."

"Sure. Sure, you will. I can give you some advice, though. As a father, as well as an old man."

His voice was mild, but she watched him in suspicious silence. He went on: "I think you should stick to Pete. He's a good boy. Intelligent, good-looking, great future with the company. Above all, though, he's sweet-natured. Of course he'll work out, as soon as he's managed to lift his attention higher than your mons Veneris, that he's married a shrew, but he won't turn nasty. Eventually he'll probably take a little girl on the side, but he'll pick someone in contrast to you—someone nice and straight and softhearted—so she'll stand no chance of taking him away from you. You'll keep him until you've picked the flesh from his bones."

He pulled a long, thin leaf from the palm and pointed it at her like a rapier. "Whereas if you were to marry Waring, you'd be getting someone who could be as mean and nasty as you are, and with a little encouragement from you, will be. Lollipop, I see a long life of murderous in-fighting ahead of you in that case. Of course, you might break up quite soon, but I don't know. You're both looking for something to hate, and you'll have each other. Think of me on your golden wedding anniversary."

He made a dueling gesture with the leaf, smiled, and left before she could get in a riposte. She was minded to go after him, but Maisie was heading toward him, too, and she could well imagine what Maisie would make of the fracas that was likely to follow. Having spent years polishing up the image of the dutiful only daughter, she was not going to spoil it now.

But Waring was standing nearby and alone. Going to him, she said, "We've got to talk."

His look showed resentment, but unwilling fascination as well. Saying "Please," she hunched her shoulders slightly forward. The front of her dress would drop with that movement; only a fraction of an inch, but it brought his eye down.

He asked, "Now?"

"Yes, now. Ann will be all right. I won't keep you from her long."

The night air was cool after the crowded dance floor. She led him to her father's Buick in among the mass of parked cars. They walked in silence a foot or two apart. When they reached it, he opened the door, and she got in. He went around to the other side and got in himself behind the wheel. She looked out through the windshield at the heavy brilliant stars, the gaudy moon. She said, "I'm sorry about last week."

There was a very small pause before he said, "So am I." She went on staring ahead. The night sky had fascinated her as a child and did so still. All that immensity, for nothing. He said, "Look at me. Look at me, Helen."

Her face turned to his. The watching Helen behind the Helen that framed the tremulous smile saw the other familiar face, close and coming closer. Two masks approaching to touch, masks of earnest love with deceit and selfishness and anger behind them.

Helen whispered, "What about Ann? I promised not to keep you from her."

"Ann? Who is Ann, anyway?" Touching, meeting, sucking at each other. "I love you, Helen."

"I love you."

Thanks for the advice, Pop. And now it's like this, within five minutes, and on the front seat of your own car. It hurt her more than she expected, but there was bitter triumph in the pain.

Although she did not understand how she had got there, Hanni knew the place right away.

She had gone there once when Stefan was away for a fortnight seeing to the opening of the shop in Frankfurt. She had gone by train, and then from the station there had been a bus. There were only half a dozen people in it, all foreigners, she thought, except herself, and they had to wait for the driver to come out of the Gasthof across the road. He came, wiping a broad hand across a fleshy mouth, and stared at them all before getting into the driver's seat. She thought his gaze lingered on her, but told herself that was silly. The time of that sort of looking was over, and he could not see the small bunch of flowers wrapped in tissue paper inside her bag.

The drive across flat country parched with the heat of a dry summer seemed endless. The other passengers—the French couple and the four Americans, a man and wife in their fifties and two women rather older—whispered together, their voices a meaningless accompaniment to the noise of the engine. She wished they would talk normally, not as though they were at the funeral of someone they thought they ought to respect.

At last they arrived, and the driver, picking his teeth, looked them over reflectively as they got down. The fences stretched away, with rough grass around them and the high wooden towers set at the corners. Right ahead the gates stood open as they had done for seven years, with the old derisive lettering still there above the entrance. And yet, it touched her heart with an ache of love. They had seen it, she thought, as she went forward herself. Where my eyes rest, theirs rested for an instant all those long years ago.

It was the only place at which she felt contact. She went inside and trailed around with the others, but it meant nothing. Even the shower rooms and the ovens meant nothing. This was just a place like any other. They were not here, and their spirits would not linger in this barren ugliness. She could not find anywhere to lay her flowers and brought them back to the front gate with her. There she put them down and straightened up to see the driver looking at her. She walked to the bus under his scrutiny, and he stood aside, his expression blank, to let her enter. The two American women were coming back, as well.

"You just can't imagine it, can you?" one of them was saying. "You can't picture it."

But now there was no question of imagining and picturing. This was how it had been, and she was there amid it. She stood in line for roll call with the others in the cold wintry dawn and heard their voices answer as the names were read. She did not hear her own; perhaps it had been called already. And a woman in uniform moved along the ranks counting. She was a thin, gaunt woman, at first sight as starved-looking as the others. But the gauntness was not that of lack of food; her face for a moment stared into Hanni's, bleak and strong, consumed by its own hatred and contempt. In the line in front a figure was being supported by those on either side of her. The guard came to her, stared, and then jabbed suddenly with the stick she was carrying, and the figure collapsed onto the frozen ground. The guard moved on in silence, and the figure stayed where it had fallen. She was dead, Hanni saw, the eyes staring sightlessly up at the dark heavens.

After, there was another lining up for breakfast, for the hot water soup and the small square of gray bread, and then a short space of time before they would parade again for the day's work

195

parties. She used it in searching for the faces she remembered from childhood—Tante Miriam, Tante Sarah, Tante Eva, Evchen and Ruth, and Sophie and Esther. They would be changed, skin drawn tight over bone like all these around her, but she knew she would recognize them. A face cannot change to deceive the eye of love.

She searched frantically, aware of the shortness of time, of the impossibility of checking every face in this shifting cloud of anonymity. It must be for that she was here—what else? To see them, if only once, if only for a moment. What other need could have brought her back through space and time to this desert of life in death? A tall stooped figure from a distance looked like Tante Sarah—she remembered her standing just like that at the time of Benni's Bar Mitzvah—and she raced toward her, but the woman turned and was a stranger.

The wind howled through the wires and between the huts. Hanni held her hands together in front of her, pressing them for warmth against her breast. She was cold like the others and, she knew now, emaciated as they were; she felt her own ribs under the thin cloth. Perhaps she had been wrong. Perhaps it was not to find them but to be with them, to suffer here and die here, even though for them it had been last month, or next month. She did not mind that. Except for . . .

Remembering him, as sometimes she remembered him on waking after a bad dream, she felt a great lift of gladness. Not that anything changed about her. This, however it had happened, was no dream. But thinking of him she knew with an unswerving certainty that he was here, somewhere in the camp with her. He was here, and she could find him. In the men's camp? She ran toward the wires. There was a no man's land between the two enclosures, but at least she could look through at him, see him, smile.

He saw her at the moment she saw him. They went toward each other, with the two lots of wires between them, and she knew that he had only just come here, that her need had drawn him to her. He looked happy at last, and his happiness halted her. Because it meant that he still did not know what he was or what uniform he was wearing.

She saw him read the horror in her eyes and then look down at himself with a terrible despair.

The house had stopped rocking by the time she drifted up from sleep. The only sound was Mat's breathing and her own, comically out of phase. Her right arm had woken her. It was under him, and the weight of his body pressing on it had numbed it. She opened her eyes, saw that he was awake and looking at her, and wriggled it free.

"You've been asleep," he told her.

"I know. Long?"

"Not long."

She massaged her arm. "Pins and needles. Apart from that I feel good. In fact, I feel tremendous."

"I've been working something out."

"What's that?"

"I may have fifty years in front of me. That's seventeen thousand, two hundred and fifty days and nights. It's a lot of nights to look forward to."

"You don't have to say that." He looked puzzled, and she smiled. "What about nights off for illness?"

"Say fifty. It still leaves seventeen thousand, two hundred."

"I guess we're both pretty fit. Do you mean it?"

"Mean what?"

"That you want to marry me?"

"What else?"

She put her fingers up to his ear and pulled at the lobe gently for emphasis.

"Well, what people are going to *say* is that the whole thing is *crazy*, we hardly *know* each other, we come from different *backgrounds*, different *countries* even, so that it's nothing but an *infatuation*, the effect of sex on a couple of *simple minds*. That's what they're going to say."

"Does it matter what anyone says?"

She stared at his strange and yet familiar face. What was so different was being able to look at him now with love and trust and hope. She saw his innocence, his complex simplicity, and felt the weight of what she had to tell him. But it did not crush her, and it never occurred to her for a moment to keep silent. She said, "I'm not the first, am I?"

"No."

"How many?"

He answered her simply. "Two." He hesitated. "One of them was a prostitute."

"Five boys had me in one evening."

His face did not show horror, but bewilderment, and then the beginnings of anger. But not against her. He said, "You mean . . ."

"No, not rape. I went with them willingly. Statutory rape, I guess. I was fifteen."

He said, "Tell me."

She understood what he meant. There was humbleness in the demand, and faith. She said, "I don't know that I can explain it. Maybe the analyst could. They had me go to an analyst, and I was pretty impressed at first. He talked kind of like God. And then one hot afternoon I went in there with the top buttons of my blouse undone, and I could see him sitting there wanting to tear it right open, and the terrible thing was knowing why he didn't—not to protect me, but to protect himself and the money and professional reputation and all that. After that it wasn't a lot of use going on. He wrote me off as uncooperative."

He had not shrunk from her, and now he took the hand that had been up against his chest and held it in his own. She said, "It's been happening for three years. They wanted me, and I wanted them to want me, and once they knew . . . They just don't leave you alone then. I went to summer camp, but so did one of the boys from school, and he told others, and in the end I was the scandal of the year and they sent me home. That's when my parents knew about it. And when school started, it was worse than ever, naturally. So this year they brought me here with them for a quiet holiday. Where they could keep an eye on me."

He said, "But this is not the same."

"You know that? Nothing like. This was the first time, the very first."

"I know."

She saw the lights first in reflection on the wall—brightness and shadow leaping in a strange dance. He said, "Look at the window," and she turned, though reluctant to take her eyes from his face. The sky was alive and moving with brilliance, flashing and writhing in greens and blues and pinks. She said, with no more fear than when the house had rocked, "What is it?"

"I don't know. The northern lights? I've never seen anything like it."

She said contentedly, "Quite a night."

They watched in silence for a time. Then Mat said, "It must be pretty fine outside."

"Shall we go look? Get dressed?"

"Dressing gowns and slippers."

"O.K."

They went out quietly, but there was no sign of anyone else stirring in the top part of the house. They did not switch lights on; enough brightness came in from outside. From the stairs, St. George in stained glass killed an iridescent dragon, himself shifting through strange hues. From the hall, Cherry looked up the stairs again and caught Mat's arm.

"They're back."

The little people stood at the top, staring down at them. She could see both the women and at least three of the men. She waved, and they gazed down without moving. She said, "Perhaps the rocking frightened them. Or the lights. It's funny no one else is awake. Don't you think so?"

"I'm glad they're not."

She hugged his arm. "So am I."

They went out into the night. The air was warm, and the sky was full of angels.

* * *

Bridget said, "We'd better get a move on. Sleepwalking or dual personality or whatever it is, she's in bad trouble. Let's go and find her."

"No."

Although he was standing beside her, she could only dimly see him, could not read his face. His hand gripped her arm with a strength that surprised her. She said, "Why not?"

"I need to think."

"What about? She's in pain, even if she is only imagining it."

"That last cry—'Don't do that to me'—it was directed at someone."

"Well?"

"The earlier one was a general cry for help. Someone in distress—finding herself alone in the dark, perhaps. But this time she was speaking to someone. Who?"

"Does it matter? As you said, imagining things."

"I'm not sure."

"Whether it's imaginary or not, the obvious thing is to go and help her."

"The obvious thing isn't always the best." He sounded angry in the dark, and it shook her confidence. Men, after all, were much better at this sort of thing, surely. He said, "If she's in real danger, it's important to think matters out first."

Bridget said, "I still don't see . . ."

"The little people. She told you earlier that they harried her, threw her down the steps. We didn't believe her. What if it were true?"

"But how could they? They're so small and helpless."

"I don't know. I don't *know*. But there's something very odd about them."

"And why should they?"

"That's easier to grasp. Look, they went to earth when Seamus died. Then we caught Greta, and the next day the rest came out. I suppose they had realized that all human beings were not the same, that there was nothing to fear from us."

200

"And there wasn't."

"No. But remember their conditioning. Laboratory animals to Hofricht, toys to your degenerate cousin. Toys to titillate him, and toys to be tormented. The whippings, the tortures—all that. Master and slaves, with the slaves fearing the master. So what happens when the master dies and the slaves are free, and then they find creatures like the master but without, as they see it, the master's brutality and strength?"

"You're saying they would torture Mrs. Malone—to get their own back for what happened to them?"

"Mrs. Malone in the first place, because probably they sensed her fear. But once they've acquired the taste for it . . ."

"I can't believe it. Greta?"

"Yes, Greta." His voice carried a ring of utter conviction. "Greta isn't at all what she seems. She's been conditioned as they all have. They are not human. You have to remember that. It isn't just a matter of size. Being human means being raised as human, with human values. They were not."

"But even if one grants that—I mean, they *are* so small. How could they be a danger?"

"I wish I knew. But I would prefer to have some sort of weapon before getting ready to tackle them. They're small, and they move fast. Bigger than rats, and infinitely more dangerous because intelligent."

She said slowly, "There's an old gun downstairs, but no cartridges for it."

"It would make a club. Though there might be something better in the kitchen."

The cry came again, inarticulate, pitched higher and higher until it was a wail of agony. Bridget said, "We mustn't wait any longer. God knows what they're doing to her."

"How did they get her there?" Daniel said. "They couldn't carry her."

"Never mind that."

She groped her way to the door, and he followed her. The darkness on the landing without the starlight from the window was even more impenetrable. They felt their way along toward the head of the stairs. Stopping there, Bridget was aware of his rapid breathing, the beating of his heart near her own. Something impalpable but real came to her from him. It communicated as love communicates, a sensing without senses. But it was not love, it was fear.

Her nerves crawled with the consciousness of it. It was biting into her own mind as she knew it dominated his. She had to be free of him. Action was as necessary as breathing. She started running forward, down the stairs in the dark, and heard him call her but paid no heed. She had passed the turn in the stairs, had almost reached the hall, when something caught her foot. She fell forward, putting her arms up in an effort to protect herself. And as she fell she heard the laughter, thin, tittering, inhumanly evil, about her.

For a time she lay there winded and faint with pain where her left elbow had hit the floor. She heard Daniel call to her and heard the laughter double in reply. She could see nothing, feel nothing but the hard boards against her face. Wincing from the pain, she tried to get up. But her limbs did not respond. It was as though she were Gulliver tied to a thousand tiny stakes with threadlike ropes. Was that possible? Of course not. Then was she paralyzed? She called out to Daniel for help. He replied, but it was lost in the laughter.

"Help me!" she cried desperately. "Help me!"

The laughter was a flood which it seemed he could not cross. She called again and again and after that fell silent.

What was he doing here, Waring wondered? What conceivable point was there in this?

He had stopped actively rebelling against being a disembodied presence, finding that rebellion did no good, but the irrelevance of the present scene bothered and annoyed him. He was in a small room on a sunny afternoon; a broad beam of light came in through one of the windows and fell on a carpet of weirdly pseudo-Oriental pattern. He knew at once that he had never seen this place before. In the distance there was the boom of surf; the only other sound was the noisy, almost grunting exhalation of breath by the fat woman in the armchair. She was grossly, disgustingly obese, and dressed in a white costume that exposed her fat calves and, under a vee neckline, enormous leathery brown breasts beaded with sweat. She had some kind of instrument jetting cool air at her, but it did not seem to be having much effect.

The carpet and the instrument were not the only details that were troubling. There was what seemed to be a television screen, but it was a rectangle hanging flat against the wall, and the telephone was a contraption of sinuous curves with no sign of a dial. Furniture was a mixture of short and squat with tall and spindly, as though the room was used by two quite different races, and there was something on a table by the window to which he could not give the hint of a name. It was shaped roughly like a large shell, but made of steel and plastic in an eye-wrenching mélange of colors.

He was still wondering about this when he heard another sound, a door opening. There were footsteps, the weary tread of an old man. The fat woman stirred and called, "Waring!"

He recognized her as the room door opened and his own self, seared with age, came in. Once you had the key, he thought with horror, it was all too easy. And this later Waring—honed to a creaking thinness of flesh pulled tight over bone—time's small skirmishing victories transformed to a lost battlefield at the close of a trying day.

Helen said, "You've been long enough. I should have had my pill half an hour ago. You trying to kill me or something?"

He looked at her with cold disgust. "You could have got it yourself."

"How could I, crippled the way I am?"

"You got to those candies last week, all right."

She said bitterly, "So you're still trying to make me out a liar about that. It was the Helper took them. I told you that."

"God Almighty, you'll put the blame on her rather than admit it! Those kids come and see to you, and maybe a hundred like you, wash and clean your stinking carcass, and don't get a dime in payment, and you'll blame her for taking the lousy candy you stuffed down your fat gullet. You make me sick with your ingratitude."

"They come because that way they don't get put on the draft for Asia. And washing me doesn't stop them liking candy."

"Just because you're rotten with selfishness, you think everyone's the same."

She cackled suddenly with laughter. "Maybe I should study you more. A fine specimen of idealistic manhood. You think I didn't see you when she was out on the veranda yesterday, lying out there pretending to be asleep and looking up her legs? You'd miss those little tits of hers if she stopped coming around, wouldn't you? I've seen the saliva dripping from your mouth, watching them. You get on so well with her, why don't you ask her to let you have a suck? You could give her a bar of candy."

Waring looked down at her, his face working. He said, "You old sow. I wish . . ."

"Wish? Wish what? Wish I was dead? Then you and old Jack could move in together and lead a clean happy life playing checkers together, going for walks along the beach, pretending each of you wasn't looking at the girls, the young flesh you still want and you'll never touch again. His wife's dead. Isn't it a shame yours is still hanging on with her bad heart and all?"

Waring said quietly, "I loathe you. I wouldn't have thought it possible I could go on loathing you more and more, but I do. You'd think there must be a limit to it, but the pit's bottomless. Do I wish you were dead? You bet I do. If I believed in prayers, I'd pray for it. And you're quite right. When you are dead, I'll move in with Jack and I'll know a little peace for the last year or so before it's all over. That's the promise that keeps me going, the promise of a decent companionship. Sure, checkers and walks along the beach, and we'll get a permit to keep a dog, since there will be the two of us. A collie or a spaniel, or just a mutt, maybe. That's what it's going to be like—peace, peace, peace." He bent down toward her. "Why don't you die? Why don't you goddam die?"

She had a gasping, coughing fit, and he watched her. When she had finished, she said, choking, "Get me my pill."

He looked at her with hatred for a moment longer, then turned and went to a high, narrow chest of drawers with painted side panels. He brought back a pill with a glass of water he had filled from a carafe. She took the pill from him, put it in her mouth, and swallowed it in a draft of water with ugly gurgling noises.

Waring said, "They keep you alive, those pills, but they won't go on doing that indefinitely. Not with a heart like yours. And mine's pretty sound. Gottlieb told me that. I've got a few years yet. I look after myself."

She gasped and wheezed. "Like Jack does."

"Sure. I'll outlast you. There'll be some peace before it's over."

It looked and sounded like another coughing fit at first, but it was not that. Hideously, her whole immense body shaking, she was laughing.

"O.K., laugh," Waring said. "Give yourself an attack. It suits me fine."

She brought herself under something like control. She said, "There was another reason I was anxious you should get back. I had a message for you. Two messages, from the hospital. First was that Jack had had a slight coronary—he wanted you to come and see him. Second said not to bother. He had another bigger one on top of it."

Her eyes peered up at him from the folds of flesh, her mouth gaped in a grin. "He died an hour ago." She wheezed with laughter and rocked with the effort of it. "Never mind, honeylamb. You've still got me."

Hanni sat on the bed shivering. It was all so vivid still—the chill gray sky with the wind bitter from the east, the wires and turrets and the long lines of huts, the crowd of faces pinched with cold and hunger, bleak with resignation—and his face, looking down at the black uniform trimmed with silver. The pain of that tore her heart. A nightmare? But so real. Stefan was out of bed, too, staring at her across the room. She wondered if she had

205

cried out and wakened him. She tried to smile and started to get up.

"It's all right . . ." she began, but he stopped her.

His voice shaking, he said, "What are you doing here?"

She did not understand, but started to go forward. "Stefan . . ."

He stopped her with a gesture, his hand raised to ward off, to block a sight, to strike. He said, "They hanged you. I read about it, not then but later. Some of the British protested. It was not their kind of hanging, quick, with a knot in the rope to break the neck as you fell. It was a slow death—strangulation in a noose. Five minutes of agony, perhaps more. But not slow enough. Do you hear? Not slow enough . . ."

He drew breath in a sob that shuddered up from the heart. His hands went to cover his face, and she saw that he was weeping. It racked him like a fever. She tried to move toward him, but he saw the movement and shouted, "Stay! Stay there." He paused, breathing heavily. "That last time, in the cell, when you spoke of Mutti's money. Clean money, you said, and she would wish me to have it. But Grandfather left as much to Aunt Hilde, and what happened to that? She used it, all of it, when Uncle Paul was ill. He would not let her go to you for help, and they had nothing put by—his promotion stopped when he refused to join the party."

He stopped again. His eyes were fixed on her, and there was sweat on his brow. He said, "I don't remember Uncle Paul very well. He did not visit us much after Hitler, did he? But I can remember them coming to us the summer before, and I remember sitting quietly, listening to you and him arguing together. I was late for swimming with the other boys, but I wanted to listen to you. He was a weak man, I saw—weak in body and with a weak cleverness of mind. It was you who had the strength in both. I was ten, and I could understand that. He got angry, but you did not get angry, because you were sure of yourself. And I sat and listened and thanked God that I was your son and not his."

The sweat fell in his eyes, and he blinked and rubbed them with the back of his hand.

"There is no clean or unclean money. Only men. And I am un-

206

clean, because you were. They hanged you, and they should have hanged me at the same time, because everything you were and had is mine. Everything. Everything."

His face showed the despair she had seen through the wires, but here there was no barrier between them. She walked toward him, and he cried, "Stop! Or I will strangle you again."

She went to him with her arms open. "Stefan. It's Hanni. I love you, liebchen."

He did not move but waited, staring, until she was almost on him. Then his hands reached out and took her by the throat. They closed with terrible strength, choking her, shaking her body. She fought for breath and there was a drumming in her ears. Through it, she heard his voice: "Only unclean men! And the uncleanness goes on from generation to generation. But ends here. Do you think I could have had children, sons, after what you were, and I was? But it ends! It ends . . ."

It was not blackness that took her, but a roaring hammering tumult of crimson. Later she was aware of darkness and silence, and then light as her eyelids flickered. She thought at first that his hands were still clamped around her throat, but it was only a soreness. She swallowed, and the soreness stabbed sharply into pain. She opened her eyes fully, and with some difficulty got to her feet.

Stefan was sitting on his bed, his gaze fixed on the wall. It hurt her to speak, but she said, "Stefan . . ." He gave no sign of hearing. She went unsteadily to him and put her hands on his shoulders. He registered nothing. She stroked his face, and there was no response. He sat stiff and unmoving. So she sat by him and rested her head against his shoulder.

They stayed like that for a long time before he spoke. He said her name, and she ignored the pain to answer him. He said, "I killed you, Hanni."

"No," she said, "no! I am alive. See."

"I saw you lying there. I killed you as he killed all the others. Only one death. I am a smaller man than he was. But one is enough."

"Touch me," she said. "Feel me. I am here beside you."

"And now there is nothing. I hear nothing, see nothing. And yet exist. Why do I exist, Hanni? You are wise. Tell me that."

She tried to pull his face around to kiss him, but the rigidity of his body was too much for her strength.

"Forgive me," he said.

"There is nothing to forgive. I love you."

"Forgive me. Without that, I am damned."

She found herself weeping. "I forgive you," she said. "And so do the others, all of them. Sophie and Ruth, Evchen and Esther. And Aunt Miriam and Aunt Sarah and Aunt Eva. They all forgive you. There is no bitterness. And I love you, I love you!"

"No light," he said. "No light, no sound but the sound of my own voice. Nothing. I cannot even see your body any longer. I see nothing, hear nothing, touch nothing. And yet I live still."

Weeping, she said, "I am here, and I love you."

"Forgive me," he said. "Only forgive!"

The lights faded from the sky as they walked hand in hand away from the house, and as they faded, there were the ordinary stars, and in the east a brightness—not dawn, but the rising of the moon. Mat said, "The show seems to be over. Do you want to go back?"

Cherry shook her head. "No. I'd sooner stay, now we're out. What do you think's been happening tonight? Atom bombs? A war somewhere?"

"I don't think so."

Nor care, he thought. There was a terrible selfishness about an alliance like this; one pitied more people, but one pitied them with detachment. A wall around two people instead of one, and the stronger for that. Because one was no longer lonely behind the barricade, no longer moved by the self-treachery which breached the wall in the hope that the one who stormed it would be friend not foe.

She said, "All that shaking, and then the lights, and yet nothing's happened."

He pressed her hand. "Everything."

"I know. But you're not saying it was laid on for us? Like the Ides of March."

He laughed. "No, I'm not saying that."

"Here's a place to sit. Under this tree. We can watch the moon come up."

They settled with their backs to the trunk of the oak. Cherry snuggled up to him, with his arm over her shoulder. She said, "It would be nice to have some champagne."

"I thought you didn't drink."

"Not many things. But I like the taste of champagne. Why do you drink so much?"

He told her: of the drunken years and the sober years, and of what had precipitated the latest bout. She listened, calm, attentive, loving.

She said, "You're an unstable character."

"That's right."

"Like me. Do you think anyone would bet a dime on our future?"

"No one with any sense."

"An alcoholic and a nymphomaniac."

He brought a hand up to stop her mouth. "You can call me names, but not my love."

"I am, aren't I?"

"Yes."

"And you're mine. What chance do you think we have?"

"One worth taking. Nothing else is."

"That's true, anyway. You know what—I think we've got a pretty good chance, really. I think maybe we're the kind of people who need to have something to be strong *for*. And this is it."

"Yes," he said. "This is it."

They talked on while the moon rose. It was an easy, rambling conversation, wandering away into irrelevancies but always coming back to the shining center. Sometimes they lapsed into silences as undemanding as the talk. He thought during one of these of Bridget and tried to recall what it was he had felt for her. All he could think of was the unsureness, the insecurity. It was strange—

to have thought then of Bridget surrendering her body to a man, to any man at any time, would have been to plunge into a fiery sea of jealousy. Whereas, while he accepted what Cherry had told him, and was not trying to forget it, to push it out of sight, it made no difference. He would not have thought he could feel such a wholeness.

He said, "You give me strength."

"And you're going to need it. But me, too. We boost each other. Terrific. We're going to make a great team. Especially with the children."

"Yes." It was a startling idea but, he saw at once, a good one. "How many?"

"We'll see. Lots, I think. They say the world is overpopulated, and I say the hell with them."

He laughed. "You know, at first I thought what a quiet little girl you were, with nothing to say."

"I have been." She smiled up at him. "But I talked to myself a lot. Look, it's still bright over there, and the moon's way up. Sunrise? Oughtn't the birds to have started singing?"

"Irish birds. They sleep late."

There was a single chirp somewhere in the branches overhead. She giggled.

"He heard you."

"That's all right. Comment inside the family doesn't count."

"Like us."

"Like us," he agreed.

They watched the sun come up and heard the birds wake and sing. At last, she said, "It's ordinary day. The magic part's over."

"We might as well go back."

He got up and helped lift her. She said, "Do you mind it being ordinary?"

He shook his head. "Do you?"

She did not answer till they were walking back across the grass to the house. Then, smiling into the sun, she said, "No. I like the day better."

When Bridget broke away from him and ran down the stairs, Daniel started to follow her, but he went cautiously, his hand on the rail, calling to her to stop, not to be a fool and plunge ahead like that. He could not think what had possessed her to do such a thing and was beginning to be angry, when he heard, simultaneously, the sound of her crashing to the floor and the swell of piping laughter from the darkness before him. He stopped then, his hand gripping the banister, and called again.

"Brid? What's happened? Are you all right?"

A renewal of the laughter was the only answer. It seemed louder, as though they were coming up the stairs toward him, and automatically he backed away, climbing two or three steps backwards toward the landing.

It had been a trap of some kind, and Bridget had fallen into it. If he rushed down, the only result would be that two would be trapped instead of one. Which meant that he would have no chance of rescuing her. It was as he had told her in Mrs. Malone's room—one had to think before acting. But he could not think clearly. Thoughts spun inconsequentially through his mind, slipping from him when he tried to force them into logic.

Then he heard her call his name, and heard his own inane reply: "Are you all right?" He was not sure whether she had heard him through the mocking oscillating laughter, but he heard her.

"Help me . . . help me . . ."

He took a step down, and the laughter seemed nearer. He stopped. Bridget is down there, he told himself. She needs help. He tried to will himself into the act of charging forward into the blackness, but the intention was swamped in his mind by a picture of being brought down as she had been, of lying helpless while small merciless figures tortured and tormented him. He had feared spiders from childhood, and all the weight of that fear and horror now transferred to these—but these were larger than spiders, swifter, intelligent, and malign.

She called again, and he knew that the instant of decision was on him. There was no holding back on the excuse of taking thought. If it were Mrs. Malone down there or an unknown stranger, one could not hold back. And it was Bridget, whom he said he loved, and believed the word was true. Whatever the horror, however great his fear, he must go to her. He tensed himself for that, and as he did so, heard the laughter close, so close, just in front of his feet, it seemed. And turned and ran.

He blundered, sobbing, along the landing, found his room, stumbled in and slammed the door behind him. For a time he stood with his forearms pressed against the panel, holding it against any attempt to force it. Later he slumped to the ground, and sat with his back to the door. He felt exhausted, as though he had run a long race, and his mind, too, was drained to a near emptiness. The laughter had stopped and so had the cries. There was absolute stillness all around him. He would have heard her if she had still been crying out. Whatever was happening to her had stopped. Or was finished. He found tears running down his cheeks and wondered whether he was weeping for her or for himself.

Later he slept. When he awoke, light was showing from the window; it was almost sunrise. The world of shadows was passing, yielding to the world of objects; he saw and marveled at the hardness of shape of a bed, a chair, a wardrobe. After a time he got up and rubbed and stretched the cramp from his body.

It was darker on the landing, but still light enough to see his way quite easily, and the stairs were brighter. He came to the top and looked down, steeling his mind to what might be there. What he saw was Bridget's body stretched out in the hall, face down, with one hand under her head, the other limp in front of her. A slipper had come off, showing a white unmoving foot. And around her . . .

They stood roughly in a semicircle about her head, a few feet from her. They were looking at her with their calm and empty eyes. They were very small against her body. He felt anger kindle in him as it had never done before; not just anger, but the need to maim, to kill, to destroy utterly. It was something his body and mind craved for, like lust or hunger. Slowly, not wishing to disturb them too soon, he started to descend the stairs.

They saw him, and their gaze turned to him, but they did not move. They stayed till he was among them, only scattering when the first kick sent one of them spinning to crash against the wall. Then they darted and ran, and he kicked and cursed and sobbed and kicked, half blind with nausea and fury, until a cry stopped him. Not from them; they had been wholly silent. Bridget's voice. He turned and saw her struggling to get up. She said, "I'm cramped."

He helped her to rise. She found it difficult to stand upright; he was ready to support her, but she turned from him and clutched the pillar at the foot of the stairs. She said, "They're going."

He followed the direction of her gaze. The door to the cellar stairs was open, and two of them were half carrying, half dragging a third small body through it. Involuntarily, with no clear motivation, Daniel made a move to follow them, but now she put a hand out and grasped his arm.

"Let them go," she said harshly. "You've done enough."

It was a clear bright morning, after a clear dark night. The weather would break soon, but the clouds heralding the storm were still half an ocean away. Here a blue sky was ruled by the life-giving, light-giving sun, his pallid sister no more than a small wafer of white by comparison. The rulers of the earth went about their business—men to work, children to school, housewives to the care of their homes. All was seen, heard, touched, and understood. Where one sense failed or was insufficient, others filled out the picture. This was a world of fact, and inference from fact. Fancy had no place here. It might for a moment touch the mind, culled from a book, a picture, a vagrant thought, but it could not stay. The sun withered it and dismissed it.

The rulers of the day went about the day's business. The creatures of the night skulked in their holes.

The revels were ended.

213

XVI

THEY SAT, except for Bridget and the Morwitzes, over coffee and talked. Daniel wondered if the others felt as shaken and diminished as he did. They did not show it, but perhaps he did not, either. He hoped he did not. He said, striving for lightness of tone, "It must be something to do with extrasensory perception. Getting into our minds and controlling them."

Waring said, "Well, of course, ESP has been demonstrated intermittently in human beings. And it's been suggested more than once that it's not so much a case of ESP being a plus factor as its absence being a negative one. That there's some kind of barrier or filter in the normal human mind which normally stops it operating. There have been reports of a high incidence of apparent telepathy in psychotics."

"You regard them as psychotics?" Mat asked.

"I don't know. But one of the marks of the psychotic is a divorce between action and emotion—and they show that. It's possible that emotions don't exist for them. Growth is controlled by the pituitary gland, which anatomically is directly connected to the hypothalamus; and the hypothalamus is the part of the brain associated with the emotions. Stunting one could well mean stunting the other."

"They never smiled or laughed," Cherry said. "Does that mean anything?"

Daniel said, "I heard them laugh." The memory of it shivered

214

through his head; he thought it always would. "And doesn't the fact of tormenting people imply some kind of emotion?"

"Not really," Waring said. "It could be imitative—a reflecting back of Seamus' little games. The laughter could be, too—he probably laughed at them. And did you hear the laughter, really hear it? How much was real last night, and how much illusion? Very much more the latter, I would guess."

"There seem to have been so many different illusions going," Mat said. "All that Cherry and I felt was the rocking, and saw the lights in the sky."

They had come in together from outside while Daniel and Bridget were staring at each other in the empty hall. He had been glad to see anyone who could provide an opportunity for him to look away. Only now, seeing the glance that passed between them, did he understand that they had become lovers. So many different illusions, he thought grayly.

Waring said, not very comfortably, "Yes. And we don't know what happened with the Morwitzes, except that it looks like it was pretty bad. She's not talking, and he's a very sick man."

Daniel said, "The rats . . . they could not explain to Stefan how they killed them. Could they have done it this way—getting into their minds, do you think?"

"Most likely," Waring said. "The cats as well."

Cherry said, puzzled, "In that case, why let Seamus do all those things to them? They could have got into his mind, and stopped him. Couldn't they?"

"We don't know how it works," Waring said, "but it must be very largely conditioned by suggestion. It's not so much a question of the power you've got as the power you think you have. I've seen a wolfhound back away from a kitten. Seamus was God to them, as Hofricht had been. That's a pretty inhibiting thing, as far as the exercise of faculties of this sort is concerned. Then the god crawled away, stricken. They went down to the cellars and encountered the rats. They tried using whips on them first, and found that they could reach into their minds and—who knows? Frighten them to death? The cats, as well."

Mat said, "We should have guessed something about the telepathy from the way they came out to Greta's call. The boat must have been ready and manned. That implies either a pretty big coincidence or that she was in touch with them all the time."

"And told them we were harmless," Waring said. "I agree."

Daniel said, "Then why did they wait so long before they attempted to . . . control us?"

Waring shrugged. "I can think of a lot of reasons. One fairly obvious one is that we were made in the image of Seamus the God. They probably didn't imagine they could do anything—at least not until they picked up the smell of fear in Mrs. Malone. And, as I say, suggestion must have a lot to do with it. At night, during sleep particularly, the mind could be fairly easily molded. It's different when the senses are fully operating. They didn't try to do anything to your mind when you were running amok among them, did they? They just picked up their wounded, and crawled away."

Bridget had come to the door while Waring was talking. Daniel was acutely aware of her presence, but could not bring himself to look in her direction. She said, "The influence was very strong while it was operating. Daniel and I were convinced the electricity fuses had blown. Did we only think we tried the switches, or did we actually switch the lights on and still see nothing, even with light all around us?"

Waring shook his head. "God knows."

Cherry asked, "How are they?"

"The Morwitzes? Well, the doctor's coming, but it's fifteen miles. We managed to get him into bed. He's—well, not responding to anything."

Waring said, "It sounds like an acute onset of schizophrenia."

"Caused by them?" Mat asked.

"Precipitated. It's most likely constitutional."

"Poor devils."

Mat spoke, Daniel reflected, with an agreeably detached compassion, his melancholic world transformed to one of elation. Temporarily, anyway.

Bridget said, "Hanni won't say much, but I think theirs was

something to do with the war. Worse than ours, I imagine, though ours was bad enough. The completeness was the terrifying thing, the utter reality, and one only realizes now how complete it was. For instance, why didn't it occur to either Daniel or me to wake someone else up? You, for instance, Waring, or Mat. It would have been an obvious thing to do. And then there was the paralysis. Neither of us able to move a muscle, though God knows we tried hard enough."

Mat said, "It's not surprising that when Daniel found he could move, he went a bit wild."

"Not a bit surprising," Bridget said.

Her voice was brisk. One compulsion overcame another in Daniel's mind, and he looked toward her. She was looking in his direction and smiling, an ordinary smile of sympathy and interest. For the others, though not for him, it effectively disguised the truth: that she knew him now as she had never done before, and despised what she knew.

He said, "There are one or two things I want to do upstairs, if you'll all excuse me."

She made room for him to pass her; just that little more than was necessary.

Bridget left for the kitchen not long after Daniel had gone. The four remained. Waring stared at his empty coffee cup and after a moment shook the vacuum jug. There was a little left. He offered it to the others, who refused it, so he poured some for himself. It was almost cold. They had been sitting here a long time, but he could not think of anything better to do. Anything at all, in fact. The talking, explaining, hypothesizing had not changed or lessened his sense of being drained and empty of purpose. He wondered about Helen. She had been saying very little, almost nothing, her face masklike and unrevealing. She had been with him at the beginning, he was sure of that. But later?

The one question nagged at him. It was the only thing that was important now. What the little people were, how they operated, what would become of them—his own relationship to them, even—

were arid problems whose answers could not move him. That other colored everything. He could not discuss it with Helen, and in any case what could she say that would resolve it?

Cherry said, "Will they come back?"

Mat shrugged. "Who knows? They must be badly wounded, shocked."

Cherry shuddered. "All that blood . . . I know *we* didn't go through anything bad—and I know it must have been pretty bad —but all the same . . ."

"Try to forget it," Mat said. He stretched, tilting his chair back. "We could go for a walk, get some fresh air."

"Sure." She smiled, and he smiled in return. "But how about breaking the news first?"

"Ought I not to ask for an interview with your father, to start with?"

Waring looked up. It took him an appreciable time to work out the implications, and when he did, he presumed it must be a joke. An odd joke, and an odd occasion to choose, but still . . . He saw Helen's face. There was expression in it now, the familiar lines of anger; but surely she could not be taking it seriously?

Cherry said, "No point in that. I'll tell them." She glanced quickly at her parents' faces and back to Mat. "We've decided we're to be married."

He realized with sudden alarm that she meant it. Behind her smile there was a rare seriousness of intent. He started to say something, but Helen cut in ahead of him.

"It adds a nice touch of romance to the story. But have you forgotten how old you are? Or young?"

"Seventeen," Cherry said. "Aren't I lucky?"

Waring remembered his own earlier thoughts about Cherry and the Irishman, but it was impossible to recapture or understand the feelings of approval that had gone with them. Cherry lost to him—married, in Ireland, an ocean away? The idea panicked him so that he felt his throat tighten. What would he do without her? What would they do?

Mat said, "I'm ten years older than that, Mrs. Selkirk. I'll look after her."

"You." The scorn in Helen's look was the sharper for being fleeting. "When you're not on the bottle."

With less ebullience, but in level tones, Cherry said, "This is not doing a lot of good, Mom. I've done pretty much as you wanted before, because there hasn't been anything that mattered. But this matters."

"As I wanted? My God, that's great!" She swung around to Mat. "Listen, I'll tell you something."

She could not, Waring thought—not possibly. He stared at her in nausea and fascination. Her eyes in the fat face were hard and cold. She said, "So you had a lot of fun last night. Pretty lights in the sky. You got yourself laid, I guess, and I doubt if that's happened to you before very much, if at all. An Irish cock-virgin with a dry throat. But Cherry's a different proposition."

Mat broke in: "She's your daughter."

"Don't I know it? And seventeen. And for three years she's been putting out for every male that showed an interest. Do you know she was sent back from summer camp last year for corrupting the other girls? Do you know only a week before we made this trip I came back early and found her with the delivery man from the dry cleaners? How long do you think what you've got is going to keep her interested? I'll tell you. Until the next male with an itch comes along. Marriage. My God, I don't know whether to laugh or vomit."

She had beaten down attempts by Mat to get a word in. He ignored her now and stood up. He said to Cherry, "Come on, my love. We'll go for that walk."

"You can't do it!" Helen shouted. "You can't. I won't let you. I'll get a court order!"

Cherry had got up with him and took the hand he offered her. He turned back to Helen. "You're sick," he said. "That's a good enough reason for taking Cherry away from you, quite apart from anything else."

"You don't believe me, but you'll find out!"

He ignored her. To Cherry he said, "Fresh air. It will do us good."

They went out, and Helen stared at Waring.

"What the hell good are you?" she said. "Why didn't you do something?"

He said, "You did that to her. Even though I said it, I didn't think it was possible. You'd tear her heart out rather than let her get away from you and be happy."

"Happy? A setup like that?"

"You did that to her," he repeated.

She was silent, and he wondered if for once she was going to admit her guilt. Not that admission could detract from it in any way. Then she said softly, "You didn't stop me."

"I couldn't. Nor could Mat."

"At least he tried. You could have hit me and stopped me. There was time enough, and you've hit me before. But you just sat there. And you know why? Because you were glad I was saying it. You talk a lot about how much you love her, but it doesn't mean anything. All that—I was doing it for you, and you know it."

Staring at her, he stared at himself. The question dominated everything, the question that he could not ignore, nor evade. How much had been real and how much illusion? The past they had shown him had been real, but all that had involved had been access to his memory. The events had taken place and were stored in the brain; there was nothing improbable about tapping them. But the future? Could they read that, and show it to him—drape the shadow of that terminus over every day of the thirty pointless years to come? He would not believe it.

And yet, contemplating himself, what he had already become, he knew he could neither deny nor escape what lay ahead.

The ambulance took Stefan away in the early afternoon. Hanni had packed their things and gone with him. He had not spoken for hours, had given no indication that he could hear or see or sense anything. Bridget stood for a while watching the ambulance crawl away along the potholed track and then went back to the house. In the kitchen Mrs. Malone was washing lettuce at the sink, tunelessly humming a popular song. Looking at her, Bridget could hear again those screams of utter anguish, that voice calling for help in agony. Those sounds had been as real as these. And yet it seemed that neither she nor Mary had experienced anything strange. By her own account, Mrs. Malone had spent a peaceful, dreamless night in her bed—that bed which she and Daniel had looked at and seen empty. Was there any reality at all, she thought despairingly? I think, therefore I am. But what if my inmost thoughts deceive me?

She told Mary to tell the guests she would like to see them all in the drawing room. Daniel came in last and stood near the back. Bridget said, "Lunch is going to be a bit scrappy, I'm afraid. Just some cold cuts, with jacket potatoes and a salad. Afterwards . . . there's quite a good hotel in Ballina which can take anyone who wants to stay. Naturally, there will be no bills to pay here."

Waring said, "That's not right. We insist."

Bridget smiled. "Anyone who insists can pay pro rata."

"You are closing the place up?" Mat said.

"Yes."

"For how long?"

"For good."

"And the little people?"

"Can have possession. If any story gets out, I shall deny it. I hope the rest of you will do the same. This will remain my property legally, and I don't propose to issue invitations, either to reporters, cameramen, or"—she glanced at Waring—"eminent scientists."

Waring said, "Yes." He paused. "You're probably doing the right thing."

Bridget was surprised; it was from Waring that she had expected opposition. The situation, it was true, was slightly different —one could understand there being less keenness to conduct studies and experiments on creatures who had shown they could conduct experiments on you—but she would not have thought it enough to bring about this change. Something was obsessing him. The possible loss of a daughter? That seemed unlikely, too, but one could never tell.

The others, she thought, would cause no difficulty. Certainly not Cherry. And Helen and Mat had been in favor of leaving them alone even before last night. Daniel . . . all Daniel wanted was to forget the whole thing, to get back to his familiar world in which he was both safe and respected.

"What will you do, yourself?" Mat asked.

"I'll stay around long enough to find a place for Mrs. Malone and Mary. Then I think I'll go into a catering school." She smiled. "I think I would like to stay in the hotel business. I enjoyed this until it got too complicated."

It was, in fact, as far as she could see, going to be easy. She had enough money to keep herself in Lausanne for a year or two, and she had no doubts about finding herself a place after that. She had a feeling she was going to be quite successful. The abandonment of Cousin Seamus' legacy was no hardship, and what else had she lost? Nothing material. Merely the feeling that one could trust oneself to another human being, at any time, under any circumstances. That was not important, surely. One could get along much better without it. Nor need the loss make one an inferior person. One had responsibilities—toward Mrs. Malone and Mary, for example—and one handled them better where there was no question of love or self-deception.

Cherry said, "What will happen to them?"

"The little people? I should imagine they will be all right. They will have the place to themselves, and there's enough food in to last them for some time."

One could also, she thought, arrange to have more stuff brought in from time to time. Another responsibility? Certainly best viewed unemotionally, if so.

"You don't think they'll sort of—spread out, through the countryside?" Cherry asked.

Waring answered her. "I doubt it. They've been conditioned by one room, remember. I think their horizons are pretty small and will stay that way. And this place is far enough off the track for people with legs of normal length."

"Their descendants, maybe?" Mat suggested.

"I'd be surprised if there were any. Where the pituitary has been taken out in animals, the sex function has always been lost. I would say they're incapable of reproduction."

"So there's no menace to the world waiting to come out of the Killabeg bog," Mat said. "Nor could there be, anyway. Poor little devils. They may cast terror by night, but when the sun rises, a few kicks disperse them. They're best left here on their own."

Cherry, who had been standing beside him, moved closer, and their hands touched and clasped. Helen, Bridget saw, was watching them.

Helen said, "We won't be staying at Ballina. We can hire a car there, though?"

"Of course," Bridget said. "I'll arrange it for you."

She was addressing Waring and Cherry, her voice slightly raised, peremptory. "We'll drive to Dublin and take a plane to France. Then motor on down to Italy, maybe."

Cherry said, "Not me."

Helen bared her teeth in a smile. "You too, baby."

"I don't mind going to Dublin. We're getting married as soon as Mat can get a license."

"Did he tell you that? Then he's a liar as well as a seducer. You're under age and can't marry without consent. He's a lawyer and knows that."

"There's something else he knows," Waring said. "I've told them I'm giving my consent. Which I gather is enough."

Helen stared at him. "I don't get it. What do you think you're doing—running for Father of the Year? If you think . . ."

Waring said, "I think when you can't win, there's no point in going on fighting. And I think you know that, too. Let's do it gracefully, eh, honey? And then settle down to the Darby and Joan life."

Helen said in a surprisingly quiet voice, "You'll regret this."

"I don't think so."

There was a silence before she said, "This sweetness-and-light, mellow-resignation kick—how long do you think it's going to last? What do you think you saw last night: a light on the road to Damascus?"

"No," Waring said. "Not a light. Maybe a vision of judgment." He smiled emptily at her. "We're losing Cherry, but we've got each other, honey. That's really as much as we need."

Helen continued to gaze at him but did not reply. Bridget said, "So we have cause to celebrate? There's a bottle of champagne in the fridge. Can you get it, Daniel—and some glasses?"

"Yes, of course."

He avoided her eye. She had a moment of feeling bereft as he went out, but the loss was not of him, nor even of love, but of something else. Of the pain she should have felt. She told herself how absurd this was. Self-sufficiency was a good and admirable thing and, in any case, nothing really had changed. She was the person she always had been; she merely knew herself better.

Daniel brought the champagne in and opened it. The drink fizzed in the glasses. The desolation would pass; it was passing already. There would be times when it would return, probably, but life was full of a number of things that could be used to keep it at bay. She smiled at Daniel as he gave her a glass, and thanked him.

Bridget thought about the little people hiding in their holes and binding up their wounds. They had brought gifts, she saw. Madness and self-knowledge—or were those two the same? No, she thought, I am sane enough. Just a little unhappy, but it won't last. And perhaps, after all, they had given people what they most wanted, what they were capable of taking.

"A toast, then." She lifted her glass, and the bubbles danced up in a ray of sunshine from the window. "Long life and happiness to the loving couple."